Arnaldur Indriðason was born in 1961. He worked at an Icelandic newspaper, first as a journalist and then for many years as a film reviewer. He won the Glass Key Award for Best Nordic Crime Novel for both *Jar City* and *Silence of the Grave,* and in 2005 *Silence of the Grave* also won the CWA Gold Dagger Award. Indriðason lives in Reykjavík, Iceland.

Also by Arnaldur Indriðason

Jar City

Voices

Additional Praise for *Silence of the Grave*

"One of the finest novels of the year. It is so good, it demands a single sitting. . . . Addictive reading." —*The Tampa Tribune*

"*Silence of the Grave* is a darkly atmospheric novel, a book to be read slowly and savored." —*BookPage*

"Like the long, cold Scandinavian winters, this novel features much darkness, yet as in the Icelandic sagas the author has studied, there is some hope amidst much pain and suffering."

—*Library Journal*

"It may be hard to believe this, but by the end of the book, Erlendur acquires something close to nobility. . . . An intelligent detective." —*The Toronto Star*

"Arnaldur Indriðason has definitely vaulted onto the A-list of Scandinavian crime authors." —*Booklist*

"Indriðason is adept at bringing his often less-than-pleasant characters to life. After the first chapter, you'll have to finish this book." —*Rocky Mountain News*

"Indriðason, a wonderful storyteller, lets the characters lead us. Everything is perfectly paced, and it's impossible to put the book down once you begin reading." —*The Globe and Mail* (Toronto)

"A writer of astonishing gravitas and talent."

—John Lescroart, author of *The Oath*

SILENCE
OF THE GRAVE

Arnaldur Indriðason

Translated from the Icelandic by Bernard Scudder

Picador

Thomas Dunne Books • St. Martin's Minotaur • New York

For information on Picador Reading Group Guides, please contact Picador.
Phone: 646-307-5259
Fax: 212-253-9627
E-mail: readinggroupguides@picadorusa.com

Library of Congress Cataloging-in-Publication Data
Indriðason, Arnaldur, 1961–
    [Grafarþögn. English]
    Silence of the grave / Arnaldur Indriðason ; translated from the Icelandic by Bernard Scudder.
        p. cm.
    "First published under the title *Grafarþögn* in Reykjavík by Edda Publishing"
    ISBN-13: 978-0-312-42732-0
    ISBN-10: 0-312-42732-8
    1. Sveinsson, Erlendur (Fictitious character)—Fiction. 2. Reykjavík (Iceland)—Fiction. I. Title.
    PT7511.A67 G7313 2006
    839'.6934—dc22

                                                    2006045607

Originally published in Iceland by Edda Publishing under the title *Grafarþögn*
First published in the United States by St. Martin's Press

SILENCE OF THE GRAVE

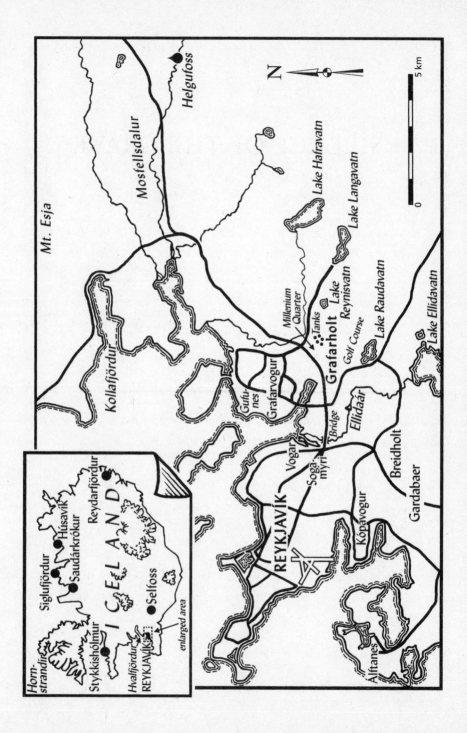

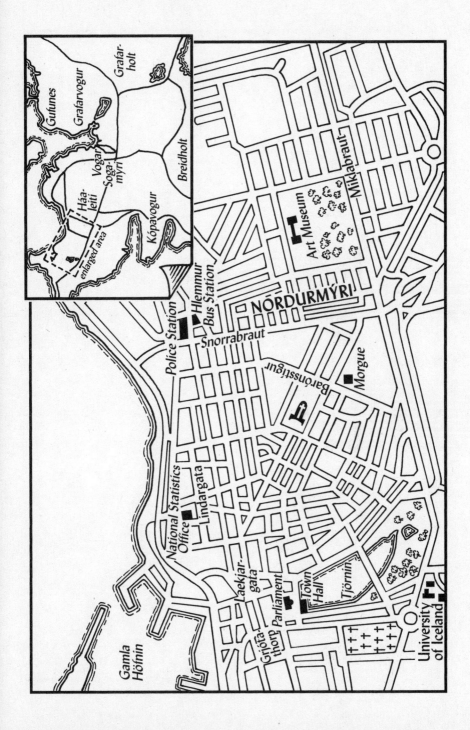

1

He knew at once it was a human bone, when he took it from the baby who was sitting on the floor chewing it.

The birthday party had just reached its climax with a deafening noise. The pizza delivery boy came and went and the children gorged themselves on pizza and swigged Coca-Cola, shouting each other down the whole time. Then they jumped up from the table together, as if a signal had been given, and started running around again, some armed with machine guns and pistols, the younger ones clutching cars or plastic dinosaurs. He couldn't figure out what the game involved. For him it was all one maddening din.

The mother of the birthday boy popped some corn in the microwave. She told the man she would try to calm the children down, switch on the television and play a video. If that failed she would throw them out. This was the third time they had celebrated her son's eighth birthday and her nerves were stretched to breaking point. The third birthday party in a row! First all the family went out for a meal at an extortionate hamburger joint that played ear-splitting rock music. Then she gave a party for relatives and friends of the family, which was as grand an occasion as if he were being confirmed. Today, the boy had invited his classmates and friends from the neighbourhood.

She opened the microwave, took out the swollen bag of popcorn, put another in its place and thought to herself that she would keep it simple next year. One party and have done with it. As when she was a little girl.

It did not help matters that the young man sitting on the sofa was totally withdrawn. She had tried chatting to him, but she gave up and felt stressful with him in her sitting room. Conversation was out of the question: the noise and commotion that the boys were making left her nonplussed. He had not offered to help. Just sat there staring into space, saying nothing. Desperately shy, she thought to herself.

She had never seen the man before. He was probably aged around 25 and was the brother of one of her son's friends at the party. Almost 20 years between them. He was thin as a rake and he shook her hand at the door with long fingers, a clammy palm, reticent. He had come to fetch his brother, who refused point blank to leave while the party was still in full swing. They decided that he should step inside for a while. It would soon be over, she said. He explained to her that their parents, who lived in a town house down the road, were abroad and he was looking after his brother; he actually rented a flat in town. He fidgeted uncomfortably in the hallway. His little brother had escaped back into the fray.

Now he was sitting on the sofa watching the birthday boy's one-year-old sister crawling across the floor in front of one of the children's bedrooms. She wore a white frilly dress and a ribbon in her hair, and squealed to herself. He silently cursed his little brother. Being in an unfamiliar household made him uncomfortable. He wondered whether to offer his assistance. The mother told him that the boy's father was working late into the evening. He nodded and tried to smile. Declined the offer of pizza and Coke.

He noticed that the girl was holding some kind of toy which she gnawed at when she sat down, dribbling profusely. Her gums seemed to be irritating her. Probably teething, he thought.

As the baby girl approached him with her toy in her hand he wondered what it could be. She stopped, wriggled herself onto her backside, then sat on the floor with her mouth open, looking at him. A string of saliva dripped onto her chest. She put the toy in her mouth and bit it, then crawled towards him with it clutched in her jaws. When she stretched forward, pulled a face and giggled, the toy fell out of her mouth. With some difficulty she found it again and went right up to him holding it in her hand, then pulled herself up to the arm of the sofa and stood beside him, wobbly but pleased with her achievement.

He took the object from her and examined it. The baby looked at him in confusion, then started screaming for all she was worth. It did not take long for him to realise that he was holding a human bone – a rib, ten centimetres long. It was off white in colour and worn smooth where it had broken so the edges were no longer sharp, and inside the break were brown blotches, like dirt.

He guessed that it was the front of the rib and saw that it was quite old.

When the mother heard the baby crying, she looked into the sitting room and saw her standing at the sofa beside the stranger. She put down the bowl of popcorn, went over to her daughter, picked her up and looked at the man, who seemed oblivious both to her and to the screaming baby.

"What happened?" the mother asked anxiously as she tried to comfort her child. She raised her voice in an effort to shout over the noisy boys.

The man looked up, got slowly to his feet and handed the mother the bone.

"Where did she get this?" he asked.

"What?" she said.

"This bone," he said. "Where did she get this bone?"

"Bone?" the mother said. When the girl saw the bone again she calmed down and made a grab for it, cross-eyed with concentration, more drool dangling from her gaping mouth. The baby snatched the bone and examined it in her hands.

"I think that's a bone," the man said.

The baby put it in her mouth and calmed down again.

"The thing she's gnawing," he said. "I think it's a human bone." The mother looked at her baby chomping on the bone.

"I've never seen it before. What do you mean, a human bone?"

"I think it's part of a human rib," he said. "I'm a medical student," he added by way of explanation, "in my fifth year."

"Rubbish! Did you bring it with you?"

"Me? No. Do you know where it came from?" he asked.

The mother looked at her baby, then jerked the bone out of its mouth and threw it on the floor. Once again, the baby broke into a wail. The man picked up the bone to examine it more closely.

"Her brother might know..."

He looked at the mother, who looked back awkwardly. She looked at her crying daughter. Then at the bone, and then through the sitting-room window at the half-built houses all around, then back at the bone and the stranger, and finally at her son, who came running in from one of the children's bedrooms.

"Tóti!" she called out. The boy ignored her. She waded into the crowd of children, pulled her son out with considerable difficulty and stood him in front of the medical student.

"Is this yours?" he asked the boy, handing him the bone.

"I found it," Tóti said. He didn't want to miss any of his birthday party.

4

"Where?" his mother asked. She put the baby down on the floor and it stared up at her, uncertain whether to begin howling again.

"Outside," the boy said. "It's a funny stone. I washed it." He was panting for breath. A drop of sweat trickled down his cheek.

"Outside where?" his mother asked. "When? What were you doing?"

The boy looked at his mother. He did not know whether he'd done anything wrong, but the look on her face suggested as much, and he wondered what it could be.

"Yesterday, I think," he said. "In the foundations at the end of the road. What's up?"

His mother and the stranger looked each other in the eye.

"Could you show me exactly where you found it?" she asked.

"Do I have to? It's my birthday party," he said.

"Yes," his mother said. "Show us."

She snatched up her baby from the floor and pushed her son out of the room in the direction of the front door. The man followed close behind. The children fell silent when their host was grounded and they watched his mother push Tóti out of the house with a stern look on her face, holding his little sister on her arm. They looked at each other, then set off after them.

This was in the new estate by the road up to Lake Reynisvatn. The Millennium Quarter. It was built on the slopes of Grafarholt hill, on top of which the monstrous brown-painted geothermal water tanks towered like a citadel over the suburb. Roads had been cleared up the slope on either side of the tanks and a succession of houses was being built along them, the occasional one already sporting a garden, freshly laid turf and saplings that would eventually grow and provide shade for their owners.

The throng set off in hot pursuit behind Tóti along the uppermost street next to the tanks. Newly built town houses stretched out into

5

the grassland, while in the distance to the north and east the old summer chalets owned by people from Reykjavík took over. As in all new estates, the children played in the half-built houses, climbed up the scaffolding, hid in the shadows of solitary walls, or slid down into recently dug foundations to splash in the water that collected there.

Tóti led the stranger, his mother and the whole flock down into one such foundation and pointed out where he had found the strange white stone that was so light and smooth that he put it in his pocket and decided to keep it. The boy remembered the precise location, jumped down into the foundation ahead of them and went straight over to where it had lain in the dry earth. His mother ordered him to keep away, and with the young man's help she clambered down into the foundation. Tóti took the bone from her and placed it in the soil.

"It was lying like this," he said, still imagining the bone to be an interesting stone.

It was a Friday afternoon and no-one was working in the foundation. Timber had been put in place on two sides to prepare for concreting, but the earth was exposed where there were still no walls. The young man went up to the wall of dirt and scrutinised the place above where the boy had found the bone. He scraped at the dirt with his fingers and was horrified to see what looked like the bone of an upper arm buried deep in the ground.

The boy's mother watched the young man staring at the wall of dirt and followed his gaze until she too saw the bone. Moving closer, she thought she could make out a jawbone and one or two teeth.

She gave a start, looked back at the young man and then at her daughter, and instinctively started wiping the baby's mouth.

*

She hardly realised what had happened until she felt the pain in her temple. Out of the blue, he had struck her head with his clenched fist, so fast that she did not see it coming. Or perhaps she did not believe he had hit her. This was the first punch, and in the years that followed she would wonder if her life could have been different had she walked out on him there and then.

If he had allowed her to.

She looked at him in astonishment, at a loss as to why he suddenly struck her. No-one had ever hit her before. It was three months after their wedding.

"Did you punch me?" she said, putting her hand to her temple.

"Do you think I didn't see the way you were looking at him?" he hissed.

"Him? What ...? Do you mean Snorri? Looking at Snorri?"

"Don't you think I didn't notice? How you acted like you were on heat?"

She had never seen this side to him before. Never heard him use that expression. On heat. What was he talking about? She had exchanged a few quick words with Snorri at the basement door, to thank him for returning something she forgot to take from the house where she had been working as a maid; she did not want to invite him in because her husband, who had been peevish all day, said he did not want to see him. Snorri made a joke about the merchant she used to worked for, they laughed and said goodbye.

"It was only Snorri," she said. "Don't act like that. Why have you been in such a foul mood all day?"

"Are you contradicting me?" he asked, approaching her again. "I saw you through the window. Saw you dancing round him. Like a slut!"

"No, you can't ..."

He hit her in the face again with his clenched fist, sending her

7

flying into the crockery cupboard in the kitchen. It happened so quickly that she did not have time to shield her head with her hands.

"Don't go lying to me!" he shouted. "I saw the way you were looking at him. I saw you flirting with him! Saw it with my own eyes! You filthy cunt!"

Another expression she heard him use for the first time.

"My God," she said. Blood trickled into her mouth from her split upper lip. The taste mingled with the salty tears running down her face. "Why did you do that? What have I done?"

He stood over her, poised to attack. His red face burned with wrath. He gnashed his teeth and stamped his foot, then swung round and strode out of the basement. She was left standing there, unable to fathom what had happened.

Later she often thought back to that moment and whether anything would have changed if she had tried to answer his violence immediately by leaving him, walking out on him for good, instead of just finding reasons for self-accusation. She must have done something to produce such a reaction. Something that she might be unaware of, but which he saw, and she could talk to him about it when he came back, promise to make amends and everything would return to normal.

She had never seen him behave like that, neither with her nor anyone else. He was a quiet person with a serious side. A brooder, even. That was one thing she liked about him when they were getting to know each other. He worked in Kjós for the brother of the merchant who employed her, and he delivered goods to him. That was how they met almost a year and a half ago. They were roughly the same age and he talked about giving up labouring and maybe going to sea. There was money to be had from fishing. And he wanted his own house. Be his own master. Labouring was repressive, old-fashioned and ill-paid.

She told him she was bored in service for the merchant. The man was a miser who was always groping at the three girls he employed; his wife was an old hag and a slave-driver. She had no particular plans about what to do. Had never thought about the future. Toil was all she had ever known since her earliest childhood. Her life was not much more than that.

He kept finding excuses for visiting the merchant and frequently called on her in the kitchen. One thing led to another and she soon told him about her child. He said he knew she was a mother. He had asked people about her. This was the first time he revealed an interest in getting to know her better. The girl would soon be three years old, she told him, and fetched her from the backyard where she was playing with the merchant's children.

He asked how many men there were in her life when she came back with her daughter, smiling as if it was an innocent joke. Later he mercilessly used her alleged promiscuity to break her down. He never called the daughter by her name, only nicknames: called her a bastard and a cripple.

She had never had many men in her life. She told him about the father of her child, a fisherman who had drowned in Kollafjördur. He was only 22 when the crew of four perished in a storm at sea. Around the time she found out that she was pregnant. They were not married, so she could hardly be described as a widow. They had planned to marry, but he died and left her with a child born out of wedlock.

While he sat in the kitchen listening, she noticed that the girl did not want to be with him. Normally she was not shy, but she clutched her mother's skirt and did not dare let go when he called her over. He took a boiled sweet out of his pocket and handed it to her, but she just buried her face deeper against her mother's skirt and started to

9

cry, she wanted to go back out with the other children. Boiled sweets were her favourite treat.

Two months later he asked her to marry him. There was none of the romance to it that she had read about. They had met several times in the evening and walked around town or gone to a Chaplin film. Laughing heartily at the little tramp, she looked at her escort. He did not even smile. One evening after they left the cinema and she was waiting with him for the lift he had arranged back to Kjós, he asked her out of the blue whether they shouldn't get married. He pulled her towards him.

"I want us to get married," he said.

In spite of everything, she was so surprised that she did not remember until much later, really when it was all over, that this was not a marriage proposal, not a question about what she wanted.

"I want us to get married."

She had considered the possibility that he would propose. Their relationship had effectively reached that stage. She needed a home for her little girl and wanted a place of her own. Have more children. Few other men had shown an interest in her. Maybe because of her child. Maybe she was not a particularly exciting option, short and quite plump, with angular features, slightly buck teeth, and small but dexterous fingers that never seemed to stop moving. Maybe she would never receive a better proposal.

"What do you say about it?" he asked.

She nodded. He kissed her and they hugged. Soon afterwards they were married in the church at Mosfell. It was a small ceremony, attended by hardly anyone other than the bride and groom, his friends from Kjós and two of her friends from Reykjavík. The minister invited them for coffee after the ceremony. She had asked about his people, his family, but he was taciturn about them. He told her he was an only child, he was still an infant when his father died and his mother, who could not afford to keep him, sent him away to foster parents. Before becoming a farmhand in Kjós he had worked on a number of farms. He did not seem curious about her people. Did not seem to have much interest in the past. She told him their circumstances were quite similar: she did not know who her real parents were. She was adopted and had been brought up in various situations in a succession of homes in Reykjavík, until she ended up in service for the merchant. He nodded.

"We'll make a clean start," he said. "Forget the past."

They rented a small basement flat on Lindargata which was little more than a living room and kitchen. There was an outdoor toilet in the yard. She stopped working for the merchant. He said she no longer needed to earn herself a living. He got a job at the harbour until he could join a fishing boat. Dreamed about going to sea.

She stood by the kitchen table, holding her stomach. Although she had not yet told him, she was certain she was pregnant. It could have been expected. They had discussed having children, but she was not sure how he felt about it, he could be so mysterious. If the baby was a boy, she had already chosen his name. She wanted a boy. He would be called Símon.

She had heard about men who beat their wives. Heard of women who had to put up with violence from their husbands. Heard stories. She could not believe that he was one of them. Did not think him capable of it. It must have been an isolated incident, she told herself. He thought I was flirting with Snorri, she thought. I must be careful not to let that happen again.

She wiped her face and snuffled. What aggression. Although he had walked out he would surely come back home soon and apologise to her. He could not treat her like that. Simply could not. Must not. Perplexed, she went into the bedroom to take a look at her daughter.

The girl's name was Mikkelína. She had woken up with a temperature that morning, then slept for most of the day and was still asleep. The mother picked her up and noticed that she was boiling hot. She sat down holding the girl in her arms and started singing a lullaby, still shocked and distracted from the attack.

> They stand up on the box,
> in their little socks,
> golden are their locks,
> the girls in pretty frocks.

The girl was panting for breath. Her little chest rose and fell and a vague whistle came from her nose. Her face looked ablaze. Mikkelína's mother tried to wake her, but she did not stir.

She screamed.

The girl was seriously ill.

2

Elínborg took the call about the bones found in the Millennium Quarter. She was alone in the office and on her way out when the telephone rang. After hesitating for a moment she looked at the clock, then back at the telephone. She was planning a dinner party that evening and had spent all day imagining chickens smeared with tandoori. She sighed and picked up the phone.

Elínborg was of an indeterminate age, forty-something, well built without being fat, and she loved food. She was divorced and had four children, including a foster child who had now moved away from home. She had remarried, a car mechanic who loved cooking, and she lived with him and their three children in a small town house in Grafarvogur. She had taken a degree in geology long before, but had never worked in that field. She started working for the Reykjavík police as a summer job and ended up joining the force. She was one of the few female detectives.

Sigurdur Óli was in the throes of wild sex with his partner, Bergthóra, when his beeper went off. It was attached to the belt of his trousers, which were lying on the kitchen floor and beeping intolerably. He knew that it would not stop until he got out of bed. He had left work early. Bergthóra had already been home and had greeted him with a deep, passionate kiss. Things took their natural

13

cause and he left his trousers in the kitchen, unplugged the telephone and switched off his mobile. He forgot his beeper.

With a deep sigh Sigurdur Óli looked up at Bergthóra straddling him. He was sweating and red in the face. From her expression he could tell that she was not prepared to let him go just yet. She squeezed her eyes shut, lay down upon him and pumped her hips gently and rhythmically until her orgasm ebbed away and every muscle in her body could relax again.

Himself, he would have to wait for a more suitable occasion. In his life the beeper took priority.

He slipped out from beneath Bergthóra, who lay with her head on the pillow as if knocked out cold.

Erlendur was sitting in Skúlakaffi eating salted meat. He sometimes ate there because it was the only restaurant in Reykjavík that offered Icelandic home cooking the way he would prepare it himself if he could be bothered to cook. The interior design appealed to him as well: brown and shabby veneer, old kitchen chairs, some with the sponge poking up through the plastic upholstery, and the linoleum on the floor worn thin from the trampling boots of lorry drivers, taxi drivers and crane operators, tradesmen and navvies. Erlendur sat alone at a table in one corner, his head bowed over meat, boiled potatoes, peas and turnips drenched with a sugary flour sauce.

The lunchtime rush was long over but he persuaded the cook to serve him some salted meat. He carved himself a large lump, piled potato and turnip on top of it and plastered creamy sauce over the whole trophy with his knife before it all vanished into his gaping mouth.

Erlendur arranged another such banquet on his fork and had just opened his mouth when his mobile phone started to ring where he had left it on the table beside his plate. He stopped the fork in mid-air, glanced at the phone for an instant, looked at the crammed fork and back at the phone, then finally put the fork down with an air of regret.

"Why don't I ever get any peace?" he said before Sigurdur Óli could say a word.

"Some bones found in the Millennium Quarter," Sigurdur Óli said. "I'm heading out there and so is Elínborg."

"What kind of bones?"

"I don't know. Elínborg phoned and I'm on my way over there. I've alerted forensics."

"I'm eating," Erlendur said slowly.

Sigurdur Óli almost blurted out what he had been doing, but managed to stop himself in time.

"See you up there," he said. "It's on the way to Lake Reynisvatn, on the north side beneath the hot water tanks. Not far from the road out of town."

"What's a Millennium Quarter?" Erlendur asked.

"Eh?" Sigurdur Óli said, still irritated about being interrupted with Bergthóra.

"Is it a quarter of a millennium? Two-hundred and fifty years? What does it mean?"

"Christ," Sigurdur Óli groaned and rang off.

Shortly afterwards Erlendur pulled up in his battered old car and stopped in the street in Grafarholt beside the foundation of the house. The police had arrived on the scene and sealed off the area with yellow tape, which Erlendur slipped underneath. Elínborg and Sigurdur Óli were down in the foundation, standing by a wall of earth. The medical student who had reported the bones was with them. The mother who was hosting the birthday party had rounded up the boys and sent them back indoors. The Reykjavík district medical officer, a chubby man aged about 50, clambered down one of the three ladders that had been propped up in the foundation. Erlendur followed him.

The media took quite an interest in the bones. Reporters gathered at the scene and the neighbours lined up around it. Some had already moved into the estate while others, who were working on their roofless houses, stood with hammers and crowbars in their hands, puzzled by all the fuss. This was at the end of April in mild and beautiful spring weather.

The forensic team was at work, carefully scraping samples from the wall of earth. They let the soil drop onto little trowels which they emptied into plastic bags. Part of the upper skeleton could be seen inside the wall. An arm was visible, a section of the ribcage and the lower jawbone.

"Is that the Millennium Man?" Erlendur asked, walking up to the wall of earth.

Elínborg cast a questioning glance at Sigurdur Óli, who stood behind Erlendur, pointing his index finger at his head and twirling it around.

"I phoned the National Museum," Sigurdur Óli said, and started scratching his head when Erlendur turned suddenly to look at him. "There's an archaeologist on his way here. Maybe he can tell us what it is."

"Don't we need a geologist too then?" Elínborg asked. "To find out about the soil. The position of the bones relative to it. To date the strata."

"Can't you help us with that?" Sigurdur Óli asked. "Didn't you study that?"

"I can't remember a word of it," Elínborg said. "I know that the brown stuff is called dirt, though."

"He's not six feet under," Erlendur said. "He's a metre down, one and a half at the most. Bundled away there in a hurry. As far as I can see this is the remains of a body. He hasn't been here long. This is no Viking."

"Why do you think it's a him?" the district medical officer asked.

"Him?" Erlendur said.

"I mean," the doctor said, "it could just as easily be a her. Why do you feel sure it's a man?"

"Or a woman then," Erlendur said. "I don't care." He shrugged. "Can you tell us anything about these bones?"

"I can't really see anything of them," the doctor said. "Best to say as little as possible until they pick them out of the ground."

"Male or female? Age?"

"Impossible to tell."

A man wearing jeans and a traditional Icelandic woollen sweater, tall, with a scruffy, greying beard and two yellow dogteeth fangs that protruded out of it through his big mouth, came over to them and introduced himself as the archaeologist. He watched the forensic team at work and asked them for pity's sake to stop that nonsense. The two men with trowels hesitated. They wore white overalls, rubber gloves and protective glasses. To Erlendur they could have been straight out of a nuclear power station. They looked at him, awaiting instructions.

"We need to dig down to him, for God's sake," said Fang, waving his arms. "Are you going to pick him out with those trowels? Who's in charge here anyway?"

Erlendur owned up.

"This isn't an archaeological find," Fang said, shaking his hand. "The name's Skarphédinn, hello, but it's best to treat it as such. You understand?"

"I don't have a clue what you're talking about," said Erlendur.

"The bones haven't been in the ground for any great length of time. No more than 60 or 70 years, I'd say. Maybe even less. The clothes are still on them."

"Clothes?"

"Yes, here," Skarphédinn said, pointing with a fat finger. "And in more places, I'm certain."

"I though that was flesh," Erlendur said sheepishly.

"The most sensible thing to do in this situation, to keep the evidence intact, would be to let my team excavate it using our methods. The forensic squad can help us. We need to rope off the area up here and dig down to the skeleton, and stop chipping away at the soil here. We don't make a habit of losing evidence. Just the way the bones lie could tell us a hell of a lot. What we find around them could provide clues."

"What do you think happened?" Erlendur asked.

"I don't know," Skarphédinn said. "Far too early to speculate. We need to excavate it, hopefully something useful will emerge then."

"Is it someone who's frozen to death and been covered by the earth?"

"No-one sinks this deep into the ground."

"So it's a grave."

"It would appear so," Skarphédinn said pompously. "Everything points to that. Shall we say that we'll dig down to it?"

Erlendur nodded.

Skarphédinn strode over to the ladder and climbed up out of the foundation. Erlendur followed close behind. As they stood above the skeleton the archaeologist explained the best way to organise the excavation. Erlendur was impressed by him and everything he said, and soon Skarphédinn was on his mobile phone, calling out his team. He had taken part in several of the main archaeological discoveries in recent decades and knew what he was talking about. Erlendur put his faith in him.

The head of the forensic squad disagreed. He ranted about transferring the excavation to an archaeologist who didn't have the faintest idea about criminal investigations. The quickest way was to chip the skeleton free from the wall to give them scope to examine both its position and the clues – if there were any – about whether an act of violence had been committed. Erlendur listened to this speech for a while and then declared that Skarphédinn and his team would be allowed to dig their way down to the skeleton even if it took much longer than anticipated.

"The bones have been lying here for half a century, a couple of days either way won't make any difference," he said, and the matter was settled.

Erlendur looked around at the new houses under construction. He looked up at the brown geothermal water tanks and to where he knew Lake Reynisvatn lay, then turned and looked east over the grassland that took over where the new quarter ended.

Four bushes caught his attention, standing up out of the brush about 30 metres away. He walked over to them and thought he could tell that they were redcurrant bushes. They were bunched together in a straight line to the east of the foundation and he wondered, stroking his hands over the knobbly, bare branches, who would have planted them there in this no man's land.

3

The archaeologists arrived in their fleece jackets and thermal suits, armed with spoons and shovels, and roped off a fairly large area around the skeleton, and by dinner time they had started cautiously digging up the grassy ground. It was still broad daylight, the sun would not set until after 9 p.m. The team comprised four men and two women who worked calmly and methodically, carefully examining each trowelful they took. There was no sign of the soil having been disturbed by the gravedigger. Time and the work on the house foundation had seen to that.

Elínborg located a geologist at the university who was more than willing to assist the police, dropped everything and turned up at the foundation just half an hour after they had spoken. He was middle-aged, black-haired and slim with an exceptionally deep voice, and had a doctorate from Paris. Elínborg led him over to the wall of earth. The police had put a tent over the wall to obscure it from passers-by, and she gestured to the geologist to go in under the flap.

The tent was illuminated by a large fluorescent light, which cast gloomy shadows over to where the skeleton lay. The geologist did not rush anything. He examined the soil, took a handful from the wall and clenched his fist to crumble it. He compared the strata beside the skeleton with those above and below it, and examined the density of the soil around the bones. Proudly he told her how he had once been called in to help with an investigation, to analyse a clump of earth found at the scene of a crime, which made a useful contribution. Then he went on to discuss academic works on criminology and the earth sciences, a kind of forensic geology, if Elínborg understood him correctly.

She listened to him rambling away until she lost her patience.

"How long has he been in there?" she asked.

"Difficult to say," the geologist said in his deep voice, assuming an academic pose. "It needn't be long."

"How long is that, geologically speaking?" Elínborg asked. "A thousand years? Ten?"

The geologist looked at her.

"Difficult to say," he repeated.

"How accurate an answer can you give?" Elínborg asked. "Measured in years."

"Difficult to say."

"In other words, it's difficult to say anything?"

The geologist looked at Elínborg and smiled.

"Sorry, I was thinking. What do you want to know?"

"How long?"

"What?"

"He's been lying here," Elínborg groaned.

"I'd guess somewhere between 50 and 70 years. I still have to do some more detailed tests, but that's what I'd imagine. From the density of the soil, it's out of the question that it's a Viking or a heathen burial mound."

"We know that," Elínborg said, "there are shreds of clothing . . . "

"This green line here," the geologist said and pointed to a stratum in the lowest part of the wall. "This is ice-age clay. These lines at regular intervals here," he continued, pointing further up, "these are volcanic tuff. The uppermost one is from the end of the fifteenth century. It's the thickest layer of tuff in the Reykjavík area since the country was settled. These are older layers from eruptions in Hekla and Katla. Now we're thousands of years back in time. It's not far down to the bedrock as you can see here," he pointed to a large layer in the foundation. "This is the Reykjavík dolerite that covers the whole area around the city."

He looked at Elínborg.

"Relative to all that history, the grave was only dug a millionth of a second ago."

The archaeologists stopped work around 9.30 and Skarphédinn told Erlendur they would be back early the next morning. They had not found anything of note in the soil and had barely started stripping the vegetation above it. Erlendur asked whether they could not speed up the work a little, but Skarphédinn looked at him disdainfully and asked him if he wanted to destroy the evidence. They agreed that there was still no rush to dig down to the skeleton.

The fluorescent light in the tent was switched off. All the reporters had left. The discovery of the skeleton was the main story on the evening news. There were pictures of Erlendur and his team down in the foundation and one station showed its reporter trying to interview Erlendur, who waved his hands in his face and walked away.

Calm had descended upon the estate once more. The banging hammers had fallen silent. Everyone who had been working on their half-built houses had left. Those who had already moved in were going to bed. No children could be heard shouting any more. Two policeman in a patrol car were appointed to watch over the area during the night. Elínborg and Sigurdur Óli had gone home. The forensic squad, who had been helping the archaeologist, had gone home as well by now. Erlendur had spoken to Tóti and his mother about the bone that the boy found. Tóti was elated by all the attention he received. "What a turn up for the books," his mother sighed. Her son finding a human skeleton just lying around. "This is the best birthday I've had," Tóti told Erlendur. "Ever."

The medical student had gone back home, taking his little brother with him. Erlendur and Sigurdur Óli had spoken briefly to him. He described how he had been watching the baby without noticing at first the bone it was gnawing. When he examined it more closely it turned out to be a human rib.

"How could you tell at once that it was a human rib?" Erlendur asked. "It could have been from a sheep, for instance."

"Yes, wasn't it more likely to have been from a sheep?" asked Sigurdur Óli, a city boy who knew nothing about Icelandic farm animals.

"There was no mistaking it," the student said. "I've done autopsy work and there was no question."

"Can you tell us how long you'd estimate that the bones have been buried there?" Erlendur asked. He knew he would eventually be given the findings of the geologist Elínborg had called out, the archaeologist and the forensic pathologist, but he did not mind hearing the student's opinion.

"I took a look at the soil and, based on the rate of decay, we're maybe talking about 70 years. Not much more than that. But I'm no expert."

"No, quite," Erlendur said. "The archaeologist thought the same and he's no expert either."

He turned to Sigurdur Óli.

"We need to check out the records of people who went missing from that time, around 1930 or 1940. Maybe even earlier. See what we can find."

Erlendur stood beside the foundation, in the evening sun, and

looked north towards the town of Mosfellsbaer, to Kollafjördur and
Mount Esja, and he could see the houses across the bay on Kjalarnes.
He could see the cars on the West Road skirt the foot of Úlfarsfell on
their way to Reykjavík. He heard a car drive up to the foundation and
a man stepped out of it, about the same age as Erlendur, fat, wearing
a blue windcheater and a peaked cap. He slammed the door and
looked at Erlendur and the police car, the disturbed ground by the
foundation and the tent covering the skeleton.

"Are you from the taxman?" he asked brashly, walking over to
Erlendur.

"Taxman?" Erlendur said.

"Never a bloody moment's peace from you," the man said. "Have
you got a writ or . . . ?"

"Is this your land?" Erlendur asked.

"Who are you? What's this tent? What's going on here?"

Erlendur explained to the man, who said his name was Jón, what
had happened. It turned out that he was a building contractor and
owned the building plot; he was on the verge of bankruptcy and
plagued by debt collectors. No work had been done on the
foundation for some time, but he said he came regularly to check
whether the formwork had been vandalised; those bloody kids in
these new suburbs who play silly buggers in the houses. He had not
heard about the discovery of the skeleton and looked down into the
foundation in disbelief while Erlendur explained to him what the
police and archaeologists were doing.

"I didn't know about it, and the carpenters certainly wouldn't have
seen those bones. Is it an ancient grave then?" Jón asked.

"We don't know yet," Erlendur said, unwilling to give any further
information. "Do you know anything about that land over there to
the east?" he asked, pointing towards the redcurrant bushes.

"All I know is that it's good building land," Jón said. "I didn't think I'd live to see the day that Reykjavík would spread all the way out here."

"Maybe the city's grown out of all proportion," Erlendur said. "Do redcurrants grow wild in Iceland, would you happen to know?"

"Redcurrants? No idea. Never heard of it."

They talked briefly before Jón drove away again. Erlendur gained the impression that his creditors were about to expropriate the land, but that there was a glimpse of hope if he could manage to squeeze out yet another loan.

Erlendur intended to go home himself. The evening sun shed a beautiful red glow on the western sky, spreading in from the sea and across the land. It was beginning to cool down.

He scrutinised the dark swath. He kicked at the soil and strolled around, unsure why he was dithering. There was nothing waiting for him at home, he thought, swinging his foot at the dirt. No family to welcome him, no wife to tell him what her day had been like. No children to tell him how they were doing at school. Only his clapped out television, an armchair, a worn carpet, wrappers from takeaway meals in the kitchen and whole walls of books that he read in his solitude. Many of them were about missing persons in Iceland, the tribulations of travellers in the wilds in days of old, and deaths on mountain roads.

Suddenly he felt something hard against his foot. It was like a little pebble standing up out of the dirt. He nudged at it a few times with his toe, but it stood firm. He bent down and began carefully to claw the soil away from it. Skarphédinn had told him not to move anything while the archaeologists were away. Erlendur pulled at the pebble half-heartedly but could not manage to free it.

He dug deeper, and his hands were filthy by the time he finally reached a similar pebble, then a third and fourth and fifth. Erlendur got down on his knees, scooping up dirt around him in all directions.

The object came gradually into view and soon Erlendur stared at what, as far as he could make out, was a hand. Five bony fingers and the bone of a palm, standing up out of the earth. He rose slowly to his feet.

The five fingers were spread apart as if the person down there had stretched out a hand to clutch at something or defend himself, or perhaps to beg for mercy. Erlendur stood there, thunderstruck. The bones stretched up towards him out of the ground like a plea for clemency, and a shiver passed through him in the evening breeze.

Alive, Erlendur thought. He looked in the direction of the redcurrant bushes.

"Were you alive?" he said to himself.

At that very moment his mobile rang. Standing in the calm of evening, engrossed in his thoughts, he took a while to realise the phone was ringing. He took it out of his coat pocket and answered it. At first all he could hear was rumbling.

"Help me," said a voice that he recognised immediately. "Please." Then the call was cut off.

4

He could not tell where the call came from. His mobile's screen display said "Unknown". It was the voice of his daughter, Eva Lind. He winced as he stared at the phone, like a splinter that had pierced his hand, but it did not ring again. He could not call back. Eva Lind had his number and he remembered that the last time they spoke was when she called him to say she never wanted to see him again. He stood transfixed, dumbfounded, waiting for a second call that never came.

Then he leaped into his car.

He had not been in touch with Eva Lind for two months. In itself there was nothing unusual about that. His daughter had been living her life without giving him much chance to interfere in it. She was in her twenties. A drug addict. Their last meeting had ended with yet another furious argument. It was in the block of flats where he lived and she stormed out, saying that he was repulsive.

Erlendur also had a son, Sindri Snaer, who had little contact with his father. He and Eva Lind were infants when Erlendur walked out and left them with their mother. Erlendur's wife never forgave him after their divorce and did not allow him to see the children. He increasingly regretted having let her decide. They sought him out themselves when they were old enough.

The calm spring dusk was descending over Reykjavík when Erlendur sped out of the Millennium Quarter, onto the main road and into the city. He checked that his mobile was switched on and put it on the front seat. Erlendur did not know much about his daughter's personal life and had no idea where to start looking for her until he remembered a basement flat in the Vogar district where Eva Lind had been living about a year before.

First he checked whether she had gone to his flat, but Eva Lind was nowhere to be seen. He ran around the block where he lived and up the other staircases. Eva had a key to his flat. He called out to her inside the flat, but she wasn't there. He wondered about telephoning her mother, but couldn't bring himself to do so. They had hardly spoken for 20 years. He picked up the phone and called his son. He knew that his children kept in contact with each other, albeit intermittently. He found out Sindri's mobile number from directory enquiries. It turned out that Sindri was working out of town and had no idea of his sister's whereabouts.

Erlendur hesitated.

"Bugger it," he groaned.

He picked up the phone again and asked for his ex-wife's number.

"Erlendur here," he said when she answered. "I think Eva Lind's in trouble. Do you know where she could be?"

Silence.

"She called me asking for help but was cut off and I don't know where she is. I think something's wrong."

Still no reply.

"Halldóra?"

"Are you calling me after 20 years?"

He felt the cold hatred still in her voice after all that time and realised that he'd made a mistake.

"Eva Lind needs help, but I don't know where she is."

"Help?"

"I think there's something wrong."

"Is that my fault?"

"Your fault? No. It's not . . ."

"Don't you think I didn't need help? Alone with two kids. You weren't helping me."

"Hall . . ."

"And now your kids have gone off the rails. Both of them! Are you beginning to realise what you've done? What you've done to us? What you've done to me and to your children?"

"You refused to let me see . . ."

"Don't you suppose I haven't needed to sort her out a million times? Don't you think I've never needed to be there for her? Where were you then?"

"Halldóra, I . . ."

"You bastard," she snarled.

She slammed down the phone on him. Erlendur cursed himself for having called. He got into his car, drove to the Vogar district and stopped outside a dilapidated building with basement flats half-submerged in the ground. At one of them he pressed the bell which hung loose from the doorframe, but couldn't hear it ring inside, so he knocked on the door. He waited impatiently for the sound of someone coming to answer it, but nothing happened. He took hold of the handle. The door was not locked and Erlendur stepped cautiously inside. As he entered the cramped hallway he could hear a child's faint crying from somewhere within. A stench of urine and faeces confronted him as he approached the living room.

A baby girl, about a year old, sat on the living-room floor, exhausted from crying. She shivered with heavy sobs, naked apart from a vest. The floor was covered with empty beer cans, vodka bottles, fast-food wrappers and dairy products that had gone mouldy, and the acrid stench mingled with the stink from the baby. There was little else in the living room apart from a battered sofa on which a woman was lying, naked, with her back to Erlendur. The baby paid no attention to him as he moved towards the sofa. He took the woman by the wrist and felt her pulse. There were needle marks on her arm.

A kitchen went off the living room and in a small room beside that Erlendur found a blanket, which he draped over the woman on the sofa. Inside the room was another door, leading to a little bathroom with a shower. Erlendur picked up the baby from the floor, carried her into the bathroom, carefully washed her with warm water and wrapped her in a towel. The baby stopped crying. Between her legs her skin was raw with a rash from urine. He presumed that the baby must be starving, but could not find anything edible to give her apart from a little bar of chocolate which he happened to have in his pocket. He broke off a lump and gave it to the baby while talking to her in a soothing voice. When he noticed the marks on her arms and back, he grimaced.

He found a cot, tossed away the beer can and hamburger wrapper that were inside it, and gently laid the baby down. Seething with rage, he went back into the living room. He didn't know whether the heap on the sofa was the baby girl's mother. Nor did he care. He snatched the woman up and carried her into the bathroom, laid her on the floor of the shower and sprayed ice-cold water over her. She twitched, gasped for breath and screamed as she tried to protect herself from it.

Erlendur kept spraying the woman for a good while before he turned off the water, threw the blanket in to her, led her back into the living room and made her sit down on the sofa. She was awake but dazed and looked at Erlendur with slothful eyes. Looked all around as if something was missing. Suddenly she remembered what it was.

"Where's Perla?" she asked, shivering beneath the blanket.

"Perla?" Erlendur said angrily. "That's the kind of name you give to a puppy!"

"Where's my girl?" the woman repeated. She looked 30 or so, with hair cut short, wearing make-up that had run under the shower and was now smeared all over her face. Her upper lip was swollen, she had a bump on her forehead and her right eye was bruised and blue.

"You've no right even to ask about her," Erlendur said.

"What?"

"Stubbing out cigarettes on your baby?"

"What? No! Who ...? Who are you?"

"Or is it the brute who beats you up who does that too?"

"Beats me up? What? Who are you?"

"I'm going to take Perla away from you," Erlendur said. "I'm going to catch the man who does that to her. So you need to tell me two things."

"Take her away from me?"

"A girl used to live here a few months back, maybe a year ago, do you know anything about her? Her name's Eva Lind. Slim, black hair ..."

"Perla's a pest. Cries. All the time."

"Poor you ..."

"It drives him crazy."

"Let's start with Eva Lind. Do you know her?"

"Don't take her away from me. Please."

"Do you know where Eva Lind is?"

"Eva moved out months ago."

"Do you know where to?"

"No. She was with Baddi."

31

"Baddi?"

"He's a bouncer. I'll tell the papers if you take her away. What about that? I'll tell the papers."

"Where is he a bouncer?"

She told him. Erlendur stood up and called an ambulance and the emergency shift at the Child Welfare Council, giving a brief account of the circumstances.

"Then there's the second thing," Erlendur said as he waited for the ambulance. "Where's that bastard who beats you up?"

"Leave him out of this," she said.

"So he can keep doing it? Is that what you want?"

"No."

"So where is he?"

"It's just ..."

"Yes, what? What's just ..."

"If you're going to take him ..."

"Yes."

"If you're going to take him, make sure you kill him. If you don't, he'll kill me," she said with a cold smile at Erlendur.

Baddi was muscular with an unusually small head, and he worked as a bouncer at a strip club called Count Rosso in the centre of Reykjavík. He hadn't been on the door when Erlendur arrived, but another bouncer of a similar build had told Erlendur where he could find him.

"He's taking care of the privates," the bouncer had said, and Erlendur didn't understand him immediately.

"The private dancing," the bouncer explained. "Private shows." Then he rolled his eyes in resignation.

Erlendur walked inside the club which was lit up with dull red lights. There was one bar in the room, a few tables and chairs and a couple of men watching a young girl sliding up against a metal pole on a raised dance floor to the monotonous beat of a pop tune. She looked at Erlendur, started dancing in front of him as if he were a likely customer, and slipped off her tiny bra. Erlendur gave her a look of such profound pity that she became flustered and lost her footing, then regained her balance and wriggled away from him before dropping her bra casually to the floor in an attempt to preserve some dignity.

Trying to work out where the private shows might be held, he saw a long corridor directly opposite the dance floor and walked over to it. The corridor was painted black with stairs at the end leading down to the basement. Erlendur could not see very well, but he inched his way down the stairs until he reached another black corridor. A lonely red light bulb hung down from the ceiling and at the end of the corridor stood a huge beefy bouncer with his stout arms crossed over his chest, and he glared at Erlendur. In the corridor between them were six doors, three on either side. He could hear the sound of a violin playing melancholy music in one of the rooms.

The muscular bouncer walked up to Erlendur.

"Are you Baddi?" Erlendur asked him.

"Where's your girl?" the bouncer demanded, his little head protruding like a wart on top of his fat neck.

"I was about to ask *you* that," Erlendur said in surprise.

"Me? No, I don't set up the girls. You have to go upstairs and get one and then bring her down here."

"Oh, I see," Erlendur said, realising the misunderstanding. "I'm looking for Eva Lind."

"Eva? She quit ages ago. Were you with her?"

Erlendur stared at him.

"Quit ages ago? What do you mean?"

"She was here sometimes. How do you know her?"

33

A door opened along the corridor and a young man walked out, zipping up his flies. Erlendur could see a naked girl bending down to pick up some clothes from the floor in the room. The young man squeezed past them, patted Baddi on the shoulder and disappeared up the stairs. The girl in the room looked Erlendur in the face, then slammed the door.

"Do you mean down here?" Erlendur said in astonishment. "Eva Lind was down here?"

"Long time ago. There's one who looks just like her in this room," Baddi said with all the enthusiasm of a used-car salesman, and pointed to a door. "She's a medical student from Lithuania. And that girl playing the violin. Did you hear her? She's in some famous school in Poland. They come over here. Make some money. Then go on studying."

"Do you know where I can find Eva Lind?"

"We never say where the girls live," Baddi said with a peculiarly beatific expression.

"I don't want to know where the girls live," Erlendur said wearily. He took care not to lose his temper, knew he had to be cautious, had to obtain the information diplomatically, even though he felt most of all like wringing the man's neck. "I think Eva Lind's in trouble and she asked me to help her," he said as calmly as he could possibly manage.

"And who are you, her dad?" Baddi said sarcastically, with a giggle.

Erlendur looked at him, wondering how he could get a hold on that little bald head. The grin froze on Baddi's face when he realised that he had scored a bull's-eye. By accident as usual. He slowly took one step backwards.

"Are you the cop?" he asked.

Erlendur nodded.

"This is a completely legitimate establishment."

"That's none of my business. Do you know about Eva Lind?"

"Is she lost?"

"I don't know," Erlendur said. "She's lost to me. She spoke to me earlier and asked me to help her, but I don't know where she is. I was told you knew her."

"I was with her for a while, did she tell you that?"

Erlendur shook his head.

"She's hopeless to be with. A real nutter."

"Can you tell me where she is?"

"It's a long time since I've seen her. She hates you. Did you know that?"

"When you were going out with her, who got her stuff for her?"

"You mean her dealer?"

"Her dealer, yes."

"Are you going to lock him up?"

"I'm not going to lock anyone up. I've got to find Eva Lind. Can you help me or not?"

Baddi weighed up his options. He didn't need to help this man at all, or Eva Lind. She could go to hell for all he cared. But there was an expression on the detective's face that told him it would be better to have him on his side rather than against him.

"I don't know anything about Eva," he said. "Talk to Alli."

"Alli?"

"And don't tell him I sent you."

5

Erlendur drove into the oldest part of town, down by the harbour, thinking about Eva Lind and thinking about Reykjavík. He had been born elsewhere and considered himself an outsider even though he had lived in the city for most of his life and had seen it spread across the bays and hills as the rural communities depopulated. A modern city swollen with people who did not want to live in the countryside or fishing villages any more, or could not live there, and came to the city to build new lives for themselves, but lost their roots and were left with no past and an uncertain future. He had never felt comfortable in the city.

Felt like a stranger.

Alli was about 20, scrawny, gingery and freckled; his front teeth were missing, his face was drawn and wan and he had a nasty cough. He was where Baddi had said he would be, sitting inside Kaffi Austurstraeti, alone at a table with an empty beer glass in front of him. He looked asleep, his head drooping and his arms folded over his chest. He wore a dirty green parka with a fur collar. Baddi had given a good description of him. Erlendur sat down at his table.

"Are you Alli?" he asked, but received no reply. He looked around the bar. It was dark inside and only a handful of people sat at the occasional table. A miserable country singer performed a melancholy song about lost love over a loudspeaker above them. A middle-aged barman sat on a stool behind the bar, reading a dog-eared paperback.

Erlendur repeated the question and at length prodded the man's shoulder. He woke up and looked at Erlendur with gormless eyes.

"Another beer?" Erlendur asked, trying his best to smile. A grimace moved across his face.

"Who are you?" Alli asked, his eyes glazed. He made no attempt to conceal his idiotic expression.

"I'm looking for Eva Lind. I'm her father and I'm in a hurry. She phoned me and asked for help."

"Are you the cop?" Alli asked.

"Yes, I'm the cop," Erlendur said.

Alli sat up in his seat and looked around furtively.

"Why are you asking me?"

"I know that you know Eva Lind.".

"How?"

"Do you know where she is?"

"You gonna buy me a beer?"

Erlendur looked at him and wondered for an instant whether he was using the right approach, but carried on anyway, he was running out of time. He stood up and walked quickly to the bar. The barman looked up reluctantly from his paperback, put it down with an air of regret and got up from his stool. Erlendur asked for a large beer. He was fumbling for his wallet when he noticed that Alli was gone. He took a quick look around and saw the door closing. Leaving the barman holding the glass of beer, he ran out and saw Alli making for the old houses in Grjótathorp.

Alli did not run very fast and did not last long either. He looked round, saw Erlendur in pursuit and tried to speed up, but had no stamina. Erlendur soon caught up with him and sent him moaning to the ground with a shove. Two bottles of pills rolled out of his pockets and Erlendur picked them up. They looked like Ecstasy. He tore Alli's coat off and heard more bottles rattling. When he had emptied the coat pockets Erlendur was left holding enough to fill an sizeable medicine cabinet.

"They'll . . . kill . . . me," Alli panted as he clambered to his feet. There were few people around. An elderly couple on the other side of the street, who had watched the action, hurried away when they saw Erlendur picking up one bottle of pills after another.

"I don't care," Erlendur said.

"Don't take that from me. You don't know how they . . ."

"Who?"

Alli huddled up against the wall of a house and started to cry.

"It's my last chance," he said, snot running from his nose.

"I don't give a shit what chance it is. When was the last time you saw Eva Lind?"

Alli snuffled, suddenly glared at Erlendur, as if eying a way out.

"Okay."

"What?"

"If I tell you about Eva, will you give those back to me?" he asked. Erlendur thought it over.

"If you know about Eva I'll let you have it. If you're lying I'll come back and use you as a trampoline."

"Okay, okay. Eva came to see me today. If you see her, she owes me a bunch of money. I refused to give her any more. I don't deal to pregnant chicks."

"No," Erlendur said. "A man of principle, I suppose."

"She came round with her belly stuck out in the air and whined at me and started getting heavy when I wouldn't give her anything, then she left."

"Do you know where she went?"

"No idea."

"Where does she live?"

"A chick with no money. I need money, see. Or they'll kill me."

"Do you know where she lives?"

"Lives? Nowhere. She just crashes where she can. Scrounges. Reckons she can get it for nothing." Alli snorted disdainfully. "Like you could just give it away. Like it's just for free."

The gap where his teeth were missing gave his speech a soft lisp and he suddenly looked like a big child in his dirty parka, trying to put on a brave act.

Snot started dripping from his nose again.

"Where could she have gone?" Erlendur asked.

Alli looked at him and sniffed.

"Will you let me have that back?"

"Where is she?"

"Do I get it back if I tell you?"

"If you're not lying. Where is she?"

"There was a girl with her."

"Who? What's her name?"

"I know where she lives."

Erlendur took a step closer.

"You'll get it all back," he said. "Who was this girl?"

"Ragga. She lives just round the corner. On Tryggvagata. At the top of the big building overlooking the dock." Alli hesitantly stretched out his hand. "Okay? You promised. Give it back to me. You promised."

"There's no way I could give it back to you, you idiot," Erlendur said. "If I had the time I'd take you down to the station and throw you in a cell. So you've come off the better for it."

"No, they'll kill me! Don't! Let me have it, please. Let me have it!"

Ignoring him, Erlendur left Alli snivelling up against the building, where he cursed himself and banged his head against the wall in feeble rage. Erlendur could hear the curses a long way off, but to his surprise Alli directed them not at him, but at himself.

"Fucking jerk, you're a fucking jerk . . ."

He looked round and saw Alli slapping himself in the face.

A little boy, possibly four years old, wearing pyjama bottoms, barefoot, his hair filthy, opened the door and looked up at Erlendur, who stooped down to him. When Erlendur put out his hand to stroke the boy's cheek he jerked his head back. Erlendur asked if his mother was home, but the boy just gave him a questioning look and made no reply.

"Is Eva Lind with you, sonny?" he asked.

Erlendur had the feeling time was running out. It was two hours since Eva Lind had phoned. He tried to dispel the thought that he was already too late to help her. Tried to imagine what kind of quandary she was in, but soon stopped torturing himself that way and concentrated on finding her. Now he knew who she was with when she left Alli that evening. He could sense he was getting closer to her.

Without answering, the boy darted back into the flat and disappeared. Erlendur followed, but could not see where he went. The flat was pitch dark and Erlendur fumbled to find a light switch on the walls. After trying several that did not work, he groped his way into a small room. At last a solitary light bulb, hanging from the ceiling, flickered on. There was nothing on the floor, only cold concrete. Dirty mattresses were spread all around the flat and on one of them lay a girl, slightly younger than Eva Lind, in tattered jeans and a red T-shirt. A metal box containing two hypodermic needles was open beside her. A thin plastic tube lay curled on the floor. Two men were sleeping on mattresses on either side of her.

Erlendur knelt down by the girl and prodded her, but got no

response. He lifted her head, sat her up and patted her cheek. She mumbled. He stood up, lifted her to her feet and tried to make her walk around, and soon she seemed to come to her senses. She opened her eyes. Erlendur noticed a kitchen chair in the darkness and made her sit down. She looked at him and her head slumped to her chest. He slapped her face lightly and she came to again.

"Where's Eva Lind?" Erlendur asked.

"Eva," the girl mumbled.

"You were with her today. Where did she go?"

"Eva . . ."

Her head slumped again. Erlendur saw the little boy standing in the doorway. He was holding a doll in one hand and in the other he had an empty feeding bottle which he held out towards Erlendur. Then he put the bottle in his mouth and Erlendur heard him sucking in the air. He watched the boy and gnashed his teeth before taking out his mobile to call for help.

A doctor arrived with the ambulance, as Erlendur had insisted.

"I have to ask you to give her a shot," Erlendur said.

"A shot?" said the doctor.

"I think it's heroin. Have you got any naloxone or narcanti? In your bag?"

"Yes, I . . ."

"I have to talk to her. Immediately. My daughter's in danger. This girl knows where she is."

The doctor looked at the girl, then back at Erlendur. He nodded.

Erlendur had laid the girl back on the mattress and it took her a while to come round. The paramedics stood over her, holding the stretcher between them. The little boy was hiding in the room. The two men lay knocked out on their mattresses.

Erlendur crouched by the girl, who was slowly regaining consciousness. She looked at Erlendur and up to the doctor and the paramedics.

"What's going on?" she asked in a low voice, as if talking to herself.

"Do you know about Eva Lind?" Erlendur asked.

"Eva?"

"She was with you tonight. I think she might be in danger. Do you know where she went?"

"Isn't Eva okay?" she asked, then looked around. "Where's Kiddi?"

"There's a little boy in the room over there," Erlendur said. "He's waiting for you. Tell me where I can find Eva Lind."

"Who are you?"

"Her father."

"The cop?"

"Yes."

"She can't stand you."

"I know. Do you know where she is?"

"She started getting pains. I told her to go to the hospital. She was going to walk there."

"Pains?"

"Her gut was killing her."

"Where did she set off from? From here?"

"We were at the bus station."

"The bus station?"

"She was going to the National Hospital. Isn't she there?"

Erlendur stood up and the doctor told him the hospital switchboard number. He phoned, only to hear that no-one by the name of Eva Lind had been admitted in the past few hours. No woman of her age had been there. He was put through to the maternity ward and tried to describe his daughter as well as he could, but the duty midwife didn't think she'd seen her.

He ran out of the flat, got into his car and raced to the bus station. There was not a soul around. The bus station closed at midnight. He left his car and hurried along Snorrabraut, broke into a run up the street past the houses in Nordurmýri and scanned the gardens for his daughter. He started calling her name as he drew closer to the hospital, but no-one answered.

At last he found her lying in a pool of blood on a lawn sheltered by trees, about 50 metres from the old maternity home. But he was too late. The grass beneath her was stained with blood and so were her jeans.

Erlendur knelt beside his daughter, looked up at the maternity home and saw himself going through the door with Halldóra all those years ago when Eva Lind herself was born. Was she going to die at the very same place?

Erlendur stroked Eva's forehead, unsure about whether he dared moved her.

He thought she was seven months pregnant.

*

She had tried running away from him, but had given up long ago.

She had left him twice. Both times while they were still living in the basement flat on Lindargata. A whole year elapsed from the first time he beat her up until he lost control of himself again. That was what he called it. When he still talked about the violence he had inflicted on her. She never regarded it as losing control of himself. To her it seemed he never had more self-control than when he was beating the living daylights out of her and showering her with abuse. Even at the height of his frenzy he was cold and collected and sure of what he was doing. Always.

Over time she realised that she too would need to cultivate that quality to be able to triumph over him.

Her first attempt to flee was doomed to failure. She did not prepare herself, did not know the options available, had no idea where to turn and was suddenly standing outside in the chill breeze one February evening with her two children, holding Símon by the hand and carrying Mikkelína on her back, but she had no idea where to go. All she knew was that she had to get away from the basement.

She had seen the vicar who told her that a good wife does not leave her husband. Marriage was sacred in the eyes of God and people had to put up with much in order to keep it together.

"Think about your children," the vicar said.

"I am thinking about the children," she replied, and the vicar gave a kindly smile.

She did not try to approach the police. Her neighbours had twice called them when he attacked her, and the officers had gone to the basement to break up a domestic quarrel and then left. When she stood in front of the policemen with a swollen eye and split lip, they told the couple to take things easy. Said they were disturbing the peace. The second time, two years later, the policemen took him outside for a talk. She had screamed about him attacking her and threatening to kill her, and that this was not the first time. They asked if she had been drinking. The question did not register with her. Drinking, they repeated. No, she said. She never drank. They said something to him outside, by the front door. Shook his hand and left.

When they were gone he stroked her cheek with his razor.

That same evening, when he was fast asleep, she put Mikkelína on her back and quietly pushed Símon out of the flat in front of her and up the basement steps. She had made a pushchair for Mikkelína from the carriage of an old pram she found on the rubbish dump, but he had smashed it up in a fit of rage, as if sensing that she was going to leave him and thinking this would restrain her.

Her escape was completely unplanned. In the end she went to the Salvation Army and was given a place to sleep for the night. She had

44

no relatives, neither in Reykjavík nor anywhere else, and the moment that he woke up the next morning and saw that they were gone he ran out to search for them. Roaming the city in his shirt sleeves in the cold, he saw them leaving the Salvation Army. The first she knew of him was when he snatched the boy away from her, picked up her daughter and set off for home without saying a word. The children were too terrified to put up a struggle, but she saw Mikkelína stretch out her arms towards her and break into silent tears.

What was she thinking?

Then she hurried after them.

After the second attempt he threatened to kill her children, and she did not try to run away after that. That time she was better prepared. She imagined that she could start a new life. Move north with the children to a fishing town, rent a room or small flat, work in a fish factory and make sure that they wanted for nothing. On the second attempt she took time to plan everything. She decided to move to Siglufjördur to begin with. There were plenty of jobs to be had now that the worst years of the depression were over, outsiders flocked there to work and she could keep a low profile alone with two children. She could spend a while in the workers' dormitory before finding a room of her own.

The bus journey for her and the children did not come cheap and her husband kept a tight hold on every penny he earned at the harbour. Over a long time she had managed to scrape together a few coins until she had enough for the fare. She took all the children's clothes that she could fit into a small suitcase, a handful of personal belongings and the pushchair, which could still carry Mikkelína after she mended it. She hurried down to the bus station, looking everywhere in terror as if she expected to meet him on the next street corner.

He went home at lunchtime as usual and immediately realised that she had left him. She knew she was supposed to have lunch ready when he came home and had never allowed herself not to. He saw that the pushchair was missing. The wardrobe was open. Remembering her previous attempt, he marched straight to the Salvation Army and made a scene when he was told she was not there. He didn't believe them, and ran all over the building, into the rooms and the basement, and when he could not find them he attacked the Salvation Army captain who ran the shelter, knocked him to the ground and threatened to kill him if he did not say where they were.

When eventually he realised that she had not gone to the Salvation Army after all, he prowled the town without catching sight of her. He stormed into shops and restaurants, but she was nowhere to be seen. His rage and desperation intensified as the day wore on and he went home out of his mind with fury. He turned the basement flat upside down in search of hints as to where she might have gone, then ran to two of her old friends from the time she worked for the merchant, barged his way in and called out to her and the children, then ran back out without a word and disappeared.

She arrived in Siglufjördur at two o'clock in the morning after travelling almost non-stop all day. The coach had made three stops to allow the passengers to stretch their legs, eat their packed lunches or buy a meal. She had taken sandwiches and bottles of milk, but they were hungry again when the bus drew into Haganesvík in Fljót, where a boat was waiting to ferry the passengers to Siglufjördur, in the cold of night. After she found the workers' dormitory, the foreman showed her into a little room with a single bed and lent her a mattress to spread on the floor, with two blankets, and they spent their first night of freedom there. The children fell asleep the moment they touched the mattress, but she lay in bed staring out into the darkness and, unable to control the trembling that passed through her whole body, she broke down and wept.

He found her a few days later. One possibility that occurred to him was that she had left the city, perhaps by bus, so he went down to the station, asked around and found out that his wife and children had taken the northbound bus to Siglufjördur. He spoke to the driver who remembered the woman and children clearly, especially the disabled girl. He caught the next coach north and was in Siglufjördur just after midnight. Threading his way from one dormitory to the next, he eventually found her asleep in her little room, shown the way by a foreman he had woken up. He explained matters to the foreman. She had gone to the village ahead of him, he said, but they probably would not be staying very long.

He crept into the room. A dull glow entered from the street through a small window and he stepped over the children on the mattress, bent over her until their faces almost touched, and shook her. She was fast asleep and he shook her again, more roughly, until she opened her eyes, and he smiled when he saw the genuine terror in her eyes. She was about to scream for help, but he put his hand over her mouth.

"Did you seriously think you'd manage it?" he whispered threateningly.

She stared up at him.

"Did you seriously think it'd be that easy?"

She shook her head slowly.

"Do you know what I really want to do now?" he hissed between his clenched teeth. "I want to take that girl up the mountainside and kill her, and bury her where no-one will ever find her, and say the poor bugger must have crawled into the sea. And you know what? That's what I'm going to do. I'll do it this minute. If there's as much as a squeak from the boy I'll kill him too. Say he crawled into the sea after her."

She gave a low whimper when she darted a look at the children, and he smiled. He took his hand from her mouth.

"I'll never do it again," she groaned. "Never. I'll never do it again. Sorry. Sorry. I don't know what I was thinking. Sorry. I'm crazy. I know. I'm crazy. Don't let the children pay for it. Hit me. Hit me. As hard as you can. Hit me as hard as you can. We can leave if you want."

Her desperation repulsed him.

"No, no," he said. "This is what you want. So let's just have it your way."

He made as if to reach out for Mikkelína who was sleeping by Símon's side, but the girl's mother grabbed his hand, frightened out of her wits.

"Look," she said, hitting herself in the face. "Look." She tugged at her hair. "Look." She sat up and threw herself back against the cast-iron head of the bed, and whether she meant to or not she knocked herself out cold and slumped before him, unconscious.

They started back early the next morning. She had been working at the fish factory for a few days and he went with her to collect her wages. By working in the salting yard she could keep an eye on her children, who played nearby or stayed in the room. He explained to the foreman that they were going back to Reykjavík. They had received news that altered their plans and she had some pay owing to her. The foreman scribbled on a piece of paper and pointed to the office. He looked at her as he handed her the paper. She seemed poised to say something. He mistook her fear for shyness.

"Are you all right?" the foreman asked.

"She's fine," her husband said and strutted away with her.

When they returned to their basement flat in Reykjavík he did not touch her. She stood in the living room wearing her shabby coat and holding the suitcase in her hand, expecting the thrashing of a lifetime, but nothing happened. The blow she had dealt herself had caught him unawares. Instead of going to fetch help he tried to nurse her and bring her round, the first act of care he had shown her since

48

they were married. When she came round he said she had to understand that she could never leave him. He would sooner kill her and the children. She was his wife and always would be.

Always.

She never tried to run away after that.

The years went by. His plans to become a fisherman came to nothing after only three trips. He suffered from severe sea sickness that he could not shake off. On top of that, he found he was afraid of the sea, and never overcame that either. He was scared that the boat would sink. Scared of falling overboard. Scared of bad weather. On his last trip a storm struck and, convinced that the boat would capsize, he sat crying in the mess, thinking his days were numbered. After that, he never went to sea again.

He seemed incapable of showing tenderness towards her. At best he treated her with total indifference. For the first two years of their marriage he seemed to regret having hit her or having cursed her so foully that she burst into tears. But as time went by he stopped showing any sign of guilt, as if what he did to her had ceased to be unnatural or a disfiguration of their relationship, and had become something necessary and right. It sometimes occurred to her, which perhaps he too knew deep down inside, that the violence he inflicted on her was above all a manifestation of his own weakness. That the more he hit her, the more wretched he himself became. He blamed her for it. Screamed that it was her fault that he treated her as he did. She was the one who made him do it.

They had few friends, and shared none, and after they started living together she soon became isolated. On the rare occasions when she met her old friends from work she never talked about the violence she had to put up with from her husband, and over time she lost touch with them. She felt ashamed. Ashamed of being beaten and thrashed when she least expected it. Ashamed of her black eyes, split lips and bruises all over her body. Ashamed of the life she lived, which was surely incomprehensible to others, abominable. She wanted to hide it. Wanted to hide herself in the prison he made for her. Wanted to lock herself inside, throw away the key and hope that no-one would find it. She had to accept his maltreatment. Somehow it was her destiny, absolute and immutable.

The children meant everything to her. In effect they became the friends and soul mates she lived for, especially Mikkelína, but also Símon when he grew older and the younger boy, who was given the name Tómas. She chose the names for the children herself. The only attention he paid to them was when he complained about them. How much food they ate. The noise they made at night. The children suffered for the violence he inflicted on her and brought her precious comfort in times of need.

He knocked out of her what little self-respect she had. Reticent and unassuming by nature, she was eager to please everyone, kind, helpful, even submissive. Smiled awkwardly when spoken to and had to steel herself not to look shy. Such feebleness filled him with an energy that drove him to abuse her until she had nothing left of her own self. Her entire existence revolved around him. His whims. Serving him. She stopped taking care of herself the way she once had. She stopped washing regularly. Stopped thinking about her appearance. Rings appeared under her eyes, her face went flabby and a greyness descended upon her, she developed a stoop, her head down on her chest as if she did not dare to look up properly. Her thick, pretty hair grew lifeless and dull and stuck to her head, filthy. She cut it herself using kitchen scissors when she felt it was too long.

Or when he felt it was too long.

Ugly old bag.

6

The archaeologists continued excavating in the morning after the bones were found. The policemen who had patrolled the area that night showed them where Erlendur had exposed the hand and Skarphédinn was furious when he saw how Erlendur had picked away at the soil. Bloody amateurs, he was heard muttering into his beard well past noon. To him, an excavation was a sacred ritual in which the soil was peeled back, one stratum after another, until the history of all that lay beneath came to light and the secrets were revealed. Every detail mattered, every handful of dirt might contain vital evidence and charlatans could destroy important data.

He preached all this to Elínborg and Sigurdur Óli, who had done nothing wrong, in between giving orders to his team. Work progressed very slowly by these painstaking archaeological methods. Ropes were stretched across the length and breadth of the area, marking out zones according to a specific system. The crucial consideration was to leave the position of the skeleton unmoved during the excavation; they made sure that the hand did not budge even when they brushed the dirt away from it, and scrutinised every grain of soil.

"Why is the hand sticking up out of the ground?" Elínborg asked Skarphédinn, stopping him as he hurried busily past.

"Impossible to say," Skarphédinn said. "In a worst-case scenario the person lying there could have been alive when he was covered with the earth and tried to put up some resistance. Tried to dig his way out."

"Alive!" Elínborg groaned. "Digging his way out?"

"That's not necessarily the case. We can't rule out that the hand ended up in that position when the body was put in the ground. It's too soon to say anything about that."

Sigurdur Óli and Elínborg were surprised that Erlendur had not turned up for the excavation. Eccentric and unpredictable as he was, they also knew of his great fascination with missing persons, past and present, and the buried skeleton could well be the key to an old disappearance that Erlendur would delight in unearthing from parched documents. When it was past midday Elínborg tried to phone him at home and on his mobile, but to no avail.

Around two o'clock, Elínborg's mobile rang.

"Are you up there?" a deep voice said over the phone, and she recognised it at once.

"Where are you?"

"I got delayed. Are you at the excavation?"

"Yes."

"Can you see the bushes? I think they're redcurrant. About 30 metres east of the foundations, standing almost in a straight line, going south."

"Redcurrant bushes?" Elínborg squinted and scoured around for some bushes. "Yes," she said, "I can see them."

"They were planted a long time ago."

"Yes."

"Check why. Whether anyone lived there. Whether there was a house there in the old days. Go down to the City Planning Office and get some maps of the area, even aerial photos if they have any. You might need to look up documents from the beginning of the century until 1960 at least. Maybe even later."

"Do you think there was a house on the hill here?" Elínborg said, looking all around. She made no attempt to conceal her disbelief.

"I think we ought to check it out. What's Sigurdur Óli doing?"

"He's browsing through the files of missing persons since World War II, to start with. He was waiting for you. Said you enjoyed that sort of thing."

"I spoke to Skarphédinn just now and he said he remembered a camp there, on the other side, the south slope of Grafarholt, in wartime. Where the golf course is now."

"A camp?"

"A British or American camp. Military. Barracks. He couldn't remember the name. You ought to check that too. Check whether the British reported anyone missing from the camp. Or the Americans who took it over from them."

"British? Americans? In the war? Wait a minute, where do I find that out?" Elínborg asked in surprise. "When did the Americans take over from them?"

"1941. Could have been a supply depot. Anyway that's what Skarphédinn thought. Then there's the question of the chalets on the hill and around it. Whether there could be a missing person connected with them. Even just stories or suspicions. We need to talk to the local chalet owners."

"That's a lot of work for some old bones," Elínborg said peevishly, kicking at the gravel around the foundation where she stood. "What are you doing?" she then asked, almost accusingly.

"Never you mind," Erlendur said and rang off.

He walked back into intensive care wearing a thin green paper smock with a gauze over his mouth. Eva Lind lay in a big bed in a single room on the ward. She was connected to all kinds of equipment and devices that Erlendur had never even seen before and an oxygen mask covered her mouth and nose. He stood by the bed head, looking down at his daughter. She was in a coma. Had not yet regained consciousness. Over what he could see of her face, an air of peace reigned which Erlendur had not seen before. A calmness unfamiliar to him. When she lay like that her features became stronger, her brows sharper, her cheeks stretching the skin and her eyes sunk into their sockets.

He had called emergency services when he could not manage to bring Eva Lind back to consciousness where she lay in front of the old maternity home. He felt a weak pulse and laid his coat over her, trying to tend to her as best he could, but not daring to move her. The next thing he knew, the same ambulance turned up that had come to Tryggvagata, with the same doctor in it. Eva Lind was gently lifted onto a stretcher and slid inside the ambulance, which sped off the short distance remaining to Accident and Emergency.

She was sent straight into surgery that lasted almost the rest of the night. Erlendur paced the little waiting room by the operating theatre, wondering whether he ought to let Halldóra know. He baulked at phoning her. In the end he found some kind of solution. He woke up Sindri Snaer, told him about his sister and asked him to contact Halldóra so that she could visit the hospital. They exchanged a few words. Sindri was not planning to come to the city anytime soon. Saw no reason to make a journey just for Eva Lind's sake. Their conversation faded out.

Erlendur chain smoked beneath a sign that said smoking was strictly prohibited – until a surgeon wearing a gauze mask walked past and gave him a dressing-down for infringing the ban. Erlendur's mobile rang when the doctor had gone. It was Sindri with a message from Halldóra: "It would do Erlendur good to take on some of the responsibility for once."

The surgeon who had led the operating team spoke to Erlendur towards the morning. The prognosis wasn't good. They hadn't been able to save the baby and it was uncertain whether Eva Lind herself would pull through.

"She's in a very bad state," said the surgeon, a tall but delicate man aged around 40.

"I understand that," Erlendur said.

"Persistent malnutrition and drug abuse. There's not much chance the baby would have been born healthy so . . . although it's a nasty thing to say of course . . ."

"I understand," Erlendur said.

"Did she ever contemplate an abortion? In cases like this it's . . ."

"She wanted to have the baby," Erlendur said. "She thought it could help her, and I encouraged her too. She wanted to stop. There's some tiny part of Eva that wants to escape from this hell. A tiny part that sometimes comes out and wants to give it all up. But normally it's a completely different Eva who's in charge. More ferocious and merciless. Some Eva who eludes me. Some Eva who seeks this destruction. This hell."

Realising that he was talking to a man he did not know in the slightest, Erlendur fell silent.

"I can imagine it's difficult for parents to have to go through this," the surgeon said.

"What happened?"

"*Placenta abruptio.* A massive internal haemorrhage that occurred when the placenta was torn, combined with toxic effects that we are still awaiting the results on. She lost a lot of blood and we haven't managed to bring her back to consciousness. That need not mean anything in particular. She's extremely weak."

After a pause the surgeon said, "Have you contacted your people? So they can be with you or . . ."

"There aren't any 'my people'," Erlendur said. "We're divorced. Her mother and I. I've let her know. And Eva's brother. He's working in the countryside. I don't know whether her mother will come here. It's like she's had enough. It's been very tough for her. All the time."

"I understand."

"I doubt that," Erlendur said. "I don't understand it myself."

He took out a couple of small plastic bags and a box of pills from his coat pocket and showed them to the doctor.

"She might have taken some of this," he said.

The surgeon took the drugs from him and looked at them.

"Ecstasy?"

"Looks like it."

"That's one explanation. We identified a number of substances in her blood."

Erlendur hesitated. He and the surgeon said nothing for a while.

"Do you know who the father is?" the surgeon asked.

"No."

"Do you think she knows?"

Erlendur looked at him and shrugged in resignation. Then they fell silent again.

"Is she going to die?" Erlendur asked after some time.

"I don't know," the surgeon said. "We can only hope for the best."

Erlendur hesitated about asking his question. He'd been grappling with it, horrific as it was, without reaching any conclusion. He was not certain that he wanted to insist. In the end he went ahead.

"Can I see it?"

"It? You mean . . . ?"

"Can I see the foetus? Can I have a look at the baby?"

The surgeon looked at Erlendur without the slightest hint of surprise on his face, only understanding. He nodded and told Erlendur to follow. They walked along the corridor and into an empty room. The surgeon pressed a button and the fluorescent lights on the ceiling flickered before shedding a bluish white light around the room. He went over to a cold steel table and lifted up a little blanket to reveal the dead baby.

Erlendur looked down and stroked his finger across its cheek.

It was a girl.

"Will my daughter come out of this coma, can you tell me that?"

"I don't know," the doctor said. "It's impossible to tell. She'll have to want to herself. It depends a lot on her."

"The poor girl," Erlendur said.

"They say that time heals all wounds," the surgeon said when he felt Erlendur was about to lose his grip. "That's just as true of the body as of the mind."

"Time," Erlendur said, putting the blanket back over the baby. "It doesn't heal any wounds."

7

He sat by his daughter's bedside until about six in the evening. Halldóra did not turn up. Sindri Snaer kept his word and did not come to the city. There was no-one else. Eva Lind's condition was unchanged. Erlendur had neither eaten nor slept since the previous day, and was exhausted. He was in touch with Elínborg by telephone during the day and decided to meet her and Sigurdur Óli at the office. He stroked his daughter's cheek and kissed her on the forehead when he left.

He didn't talk about the night's events when he sat down with Sigurdur Óli and Elínborg at their meeting that evening. The two of them had heard through the station grapevine about what had happened to his daughter, but didn't dare ask about it.

"They're still scratching their way down to the skeleton," Elínborg said. "It's going terribly slowly. I think they're using toothpicks now. The hand you found is sticking up out of the ground, they're down to the wrist. The medical officer examined it, but the only definite thing he can say is that it's a human with fairly small hands. Not much joy there. The archaeologists haven't found anything in the soil to suggest what happened or who is buried there. They think they'll have dug down to the torso late tomorrow afternoon or evening, but that doesn't mean we'll get any neat answers about who it is. Naturally, we'll have to search elsewhere for those."

"I've been looking up statistics on missing persons in the Reykjavík area," Sigurdur Óli said. "There are more than 40 disappearances from the '30s and '40s which remain unsolved to this day, and it's probably one of those. I've sorted the files by sex and age and I'm just waiting for the pathologist's report on the bones."

"Do you mean someone from the hill disappeared?" Erlendur asked.

"Not according to the addresses on the police reports," Sigurdur Óli said, "though I haven't been through them all. Some place names I don't recognise. When we've excavated the skeleton and got an accurate age, size and sex from the pathologist we can surely narrow the group down quite a bit. I expect it's someone from Reykjavík. Isn't that a reasonable assumption?"

"Where's the pathologist?" Erlendur asked. "The one pathologist we have."

"He's on holiday," Elínborg said. "In Spain."

"Did you check whether there was ever a house by those bushes?" Erlendur asked her.

"What house?" Sigurdur Óli asked.

"No, I haven't got round to it," Elínborg said. She looked at Sigurdur Óli. "Erlendur reckons there were houses on the north side of the hill and the British or American military had a base on the south side. He wants us to talk to everyone who owns a chalet in the area down from Reynisvatn and their grandmothers too and then I'm supposed to go to a seance and have a word with Churchill."

"And that's just for starters," Erlendur said. "What are your theories about the skeleton?"

"Isn't it obviously a murder?" Sigurdur Óli said. "Committed half

59

a century ago or more. Hidden in the ground all that time and no-one knows a thing."

"He, or rather, this person," Elínborg corrected herself, "was clearly buried to conceal a crime. I think we can take that as read."

"It's not true that no-one knows a thing," Erlendur said. "There's always someone who knows something."

"We know the ribs are broken," Elínborg said. "That has to be a sign of a struggle."

"Does it?" Sigurdur Óli said.

"Well, doesn't it?"

"Can't being in the ground cause that?" Sigurdur Óli said. "The weight of the soil. Even temperature change. The freeze-thaw effect. I talked to that geologist you called in and he said something about that."

"There must have been a struggle because someone's been buried. That's obvious, isn't it?" Elínborg looked at Erlendur and saw that his thoughts were miles away. "Erlendur?" she said. "Don't you agree?"

"If it is a murder," said Erlendur, coming back to earth.

"*If* it's a murder?" Elínborg asked.

"We know nothing about that," Erlendur said. "Maybe it's an old family burial plot. Maybe they couldn't afford a funeral. Maybe it's the bones of some old bloke who popped off and was buried there with everyone's knowledge. Maybe the body was put there a hundred years ago. Maybe 50. What we still need is a decent lead. Then we can waffle as much as we like."

"Isn't it the law that you have to bury people in hallowed ground?" Sigurdur Óli said.

"I think you can have yourself buried where you please," Erlendur said, "if someone's prepared to have you in their garden."

"What about the hand sticking up out of the ground?" Elínborg said. "Isn't that a sign of a struggle?"

"It seems to be," Erlendur said, "I think something's been kept secret all these years. Someone was hustled away and never supposed to be found. But then Reykjavík caught up with him and now it's up to us to find out what happened."

"If he . . . let's just say him, the Millennium Man . . ." Sigurdur Óli said, "if he was murdered all those years ago, isn't it a pretty safe bet that the murderer has died of old age by now? And if he's not dead already he'll have one foot in the grave, so it's ridiculous to track him down and punish him. Everyone connected with the case is probably dead already so we won't have witnesses even if we ever find out what happened. So . . ."

"What are you driving at?"

"Shouldn't we ask whether we ought to be continuing this investigation in the first place? I mean, is it worth it?"

"You mean just forget it?" Erlendur asked. Sigurdur Óli shrugged indifferently. "A murder's a murder," Erlendur said. "It doesn't matter how many years ago it was committed. If this is a murder, we need to find out what happened, who was killed and why and who the murderer was. I think we ought to approach this like any other investigation. Get information. Talk to people. With luck we'll stumble onto a solution."

Erlendur stood up.

"We're bound to pick up something. Talk to the chalet owners and their grandmothers." He looked at Elínborg. "Find out whether there was a house by those bushes. Take an interest in it."

He bade them an absent-minded farewell and went out into the corridor. Elínborg and Sigurdur Óli looked each other in the eye and Sigurdur Óli nodded towards the door. Elínborg stood up and went after Erlendur.

"Erlendur," she said, stopping him.

"Yes, what?"

"How's Eva Lind doing?" she asked hesitantly.

Erlendur looked at her and said nothing.

"We heard about it here at the station. How she was found. It was a terrible thing to hear. If there's anything Sigurdur Óli or I can do for you, don't hesitate to ask."

"There's nothing to be done," Erlendur said wearily. "She's just lying in the ward and no-one can do a thing." He hesitated. "I went through that world of hers when I was looking for her. I knew some of it because I've had to find her in those places before, those streets, those houses, but I never cease to be surprised at the life she leads, the way she treats herself, abuses herself. I've seen the crowd she hangs around with, the people she turns to in desperation, people she even does indescribable things for." He paused. "But that's not the worst thing. Not the hovels or the small-time crooks or the dope dealers. It's right, what her mother said."

Erlendur looked at Elínborg.

"I'm the worst part of all this," he said, "because I was the one who let them down."

When Erlendur got home he sat in an armchair, exhausted. He called the hospital to ask about Eva Lind and was told that her condition was unchanged. They would contact him as soon as any change occurred. He thanked them and rang off. Then sat staring into space, deep in thought. He thought about Eva Lind lying in intensive care, about his ex-wife and the hatred that still coloured her life, about the son he only spoke to when something was wrong.

Through his thoughts he felt the deep silence that reigned in his life. Felt the solitude all around him. The burden of monotonous days piling up in an unbreakable chain that enveloped him, tightened around him and smothered him.

Just as he was about to fall asleep his thoughts turned to his childhood, when the days grew brighter again after the dark winter and life was innocent and free from care and concern. Although it was rare, he could sometimes escape into the peacefulness of the past and then, for a brief time, he felt good.

If he could block out the loss.

He woke with a start when someone had already been ringing him for a good while, first the mobile in his pocket and then the home telephone on the old desk which was one of the few pieces of furniture in the sitting room.

"You were right," Elínborg said when he finally answered. "Oh, sorry, did I wake you?" she asked. "It's only ten," she added apologetically.

"What was I right about?" Erlendur said, not fully awake.

"There *was* a building on that spot. By the bushes."

"Bushes?"

"The redcurrant bushes. In Grafarholt. It was built in the 1930s and demolished around 1980. I asked the City Planning Office to contact me as soon as they found out and they've just been on the phone, they worked all evening looking for it."

"What sort of building was it?" Erlendur asked, tired. "A house, a stable, kennel, chalet?"

"A house. A kind of chalet or that sort of thing."

"From what time?"

"Before 1940."

"And who was the owner?"

"His name was Benjamín. Benjamín Knudsen. A merchant."

"Was?"

"He died. Years ago."

8

Many of the chalet owners on the north side of Grafarholt were occupied with their spring chores when Sigurdur Óli cruised around the hill looking for a good enough road to drive up. Elínborg was with him. Some of the people were pruning their hedges, others were weather-coating their chalets or mending fences, or had saddled horses and were setting off for a ride.

It was high noon and the weather was calm and beautiful. After talking to several chalet owners without making any headway, Sigurdur Óli and Elínborg slowly worked their way towards the houses nearest to the hill. In such fine weather they were in no hurry. Enjoyed a jaunt away from the city, strolling in the sunshine and talking to the chalet owners who were surprised to be visited by the police so early in the day. Some had heard on the news about the skeleton being found on the hill. Others had absolutely no idea.

"Will she survive, or . . . ?" Sigurdur Óli asked when they got into the car for the umpteenth time and drove on to the next chalet. They had been talking about Eva Lind on their way out of town and returned to the topic at regular intervals.

"I don't know," Elínborg said. "I don't think anyone knows. The poor girl," she said, heaving a deep sigh. "And him," she added. "Poor Erlendur."

"She's a junkie," Sigurdur Óli said seriously. "Gets pregnant and gets stoned without a care in the world and ends up killing the baby. I can't feel sorry for people like that. I don't understand them and never will."

"No-one's asking you to feel sorry for them," Elínborg said.

"Oh, really? When people talk about that crowd all I ever hear is what a hard time they have. From what I've seen of them . . . " He paused. "I can't feel sorry for them," he repeated. "They're losers. Nothing else. Wankers."

Elínborg sighed.

"What's it like being so perfect? Always smartly dressed, clean-shaven and neatly groomed, with that degree from America, unbitten nails, not a care in the world other than being able to afford those flashy clothes? Don't you ever get tired of it? Don't you ever get tired of yourself?"

"Nope," Sigurdur Óli said.

"What's wrong with showing those people a bit of understanding?"

"They're losers and you know it. Just because she's the old man's daughter doesn't make her any better than the rest of them. She's like all the other bums who are on the streets getting stoned and then sleep it off in the shelters and rehab. centres before they get wasted again, because that's the only thing those creeps want. To laze around and get stoned."

"How are you and Bergthóra getting along?" Elínborg asked, having given up all hope of changing his opinions about anything whatsoever.

"Fine," Sigurdur Óli said wearily as he pulled up outside yet another chalet. Bergthóra simply wouldn't leave him alone. She was insatiable, in the evenings and the mornings and in the middle of the day, in every possible position and place in their flat, in the kitchen and sitting room, even the laundry room, lying down and standing up. And although he had enjoyed it to begin with, he was starting to

65

notice himself growing tired of it, and had begun to suspect her motives. Not that their sex life had ever been dull, far from it. But she had never before had such a strong urge or so much zeal. They had not discussed in any seriousness the matter of having children, although they had been together long enough. He knew that Bergthóra was on the pill, but he couldn't help feeling that she wanted to tie him down by having children. There was no need, because he was particularly fond of her and had no desire to live with anyone else. But women are unpredictable, he thought. You never know what they are up to.

"Strange that the National Statistics Office hasn't got the names of any people who lived in that house, if anyone ever did," Elínborg said, getting out of the car.

"The records for that period are all in a mess. Reykjavík was swamped with people during and after the war, registration was a bit hit and miss while they were moving in. And I think they've lost part of the population records. A bit of a mix-up. Said he wouldn't be able to find it immediately, the man I spoke to."

"Maybe no-one actually lived there."

"They needn't have been there long. Might have been listed somewhere else and didn't register the new address. Maybe lived on the hill for a couple of years, months even, during the housing crisis, then moved into one of the converted barracks after the war. What do you think of that theory?"

"Fits like a Burberry."

The chalet owner met them at the door, a very old man, spindly and stiff in his movements, with thin white hair, and wearing a light blue shirt with a string vest clearly visible underneath it, grey corduroy trousers and new trainers. When Elínborg saw all the rubbish inside, she wondered whether he might live there all year round. She asked him.

"I suppose you could say that," the man answered, sitting down in an armchair and gesturing to them to sit on some chairs in the middle of the room. I started building this place 40 years ago and moved everything here in my old Lada about five years ago. Or was it six years? It all becomes a blur. I couldn't be bothered to live in Reykjavík any more. An awful place, that city, so . . ."

"Was there a house up here on the hill then, maybe a summer chalet like this but not necessarily used for that purpose?" Sigurdur Óli hurried to ask, not wanting to listen to a lecture. "I mean, 40 years ago, when you started building yours?"

"A summer chalet but not a summer chalet . . . ?"

"Standing by itself on this side of Grafarholt," Elínborg said. "Built some time before the war." She looked out of the sitting-room window. "You would have seen it from this window."

"I remember a house there, not painted, not properly finished. It disappeared ages ago. It was definitely quite a sizeable chalet, or should have been, quite big, bigger than mine, but a total shambles. Almost falling down. The doors were gone and the windows were broken. I used to walk up there sometimes when I could still be bothered to fish in the lake. Gave that up years ago."

"So no-one lived in the house?" Sigurdur Óli asked.

"No, there was no-one in the house then. No-one could have lived in it. It was on the verge of collapse."

"And it was never occupied, as far as you know?" Elínborg said. "You don't remember anyone from the house?"

"Why do you want to know about that house anyway?"

"We found a human skeleton on the hill," Sigurdur Óli said. "Didn't you see it on the news?"

"A skeleton? No. From the people in that house?"

"We don't know. We still don't know the history of the house and the people who lived there," Elínborg said. "We know who the owner was but he died a long time ago and we still haven't found anyone registered as living in it. Do you remember the wartime barracks on the other side of the hill? On the south side. A depot or something like that?"

"There were barracks all over the countryside," the old man said. "British and American too. I don't recall any on the hill here in particular, that was before my time anyway. Quite a way before my time. You ought to talk to Róbert."

"Róbert?" Elínborg said.

"If he isn't dead. He was one of the first people to build a chalet on this hill. I know he was in an old people's home. Róbert Sigurdsson. You'll find him, if he's still alive."

Since there was no bell at the entrance, Erlendur banged on the thick oak door with the palm of his hand in the hope of being heard inside. The house was once owned by Benjamín Knudsen, a businessman from Reykjavík, who died in the early 1960s. His brother and sister inherited it, moved in when he died and lived there for the rest of their lives. They were both unmarried, as far as Erlendur knew, but the sister had a daughter. She was a doctor, and now lived on the middle floor and rented out the flats above and below. Erlendur had spoken to her on the telephone. They were to meet at midday.

Eva Lind's condition was unchanged. He had dropped in to see her before going to work and sat by her bedside for a good while, looking at the instruments monitoring her vital signs, the tubes in her mouth and nose and veins. She could not breathe unaided and the pump gave out a suction noise as it rose and fell. The cardiac monitor line was steady. On his way out of intensive care he talked to a doctor who said that no change had been noted in her condition. Erlendur asked whether there was anything he could do and the doctor replied that even though his daughter was in a coma, he should talk to her as often as he could. Let her hear his voice. It often did the family as much good to talk to the patient under such circumstances. Helped them to deal with the shock. Eva Lind was certainly not lost to him and he ought to treat her as such.

The heavy oak door finally opened and a woman aged around 60 held out her hand and introduced herself as Elsa. She was slender with a friendly face, wearing a little make-up, her hair dyed dark, cut short and parted on one side; she was dressed in jeans and a white shirt, no rings or bracelets or necklaces. She showed him in to the sitting room and offered him a seat. She was firm and self-confident.

"And what do you think these bones are?" she asked once he had told her his business.

"We don't know yet, but one theory is that they are connected with the chalet which used to stand next to them, and which was owned by your uncle Benjamín. Did he spend a lot of time up there?"

"I don't think he ever went to the chalet," she said in a quiet voice. "It was a tragedy. Mother always told us how handsome and intelligent he was and how he earned a fortune, but then he lost his fiancée. One day she just disappeared. She was pregnant."

Erlendur's thoughts turned to his own daughter.

"He went into a depression, lost all interest in his shop and his properties and everything went to ruin, I think, until all he had left was this house here. He died in the prime of life, so to speak."

"How did she disappear, his fiancée?"

"It was rumoured she threw herself into the sea," Elsa said. "At least, that's what I heard."

"Was she a depressive?"

"No-one ever mentioned that."

"And she was never found?"

"No. She . . ."

Elsa stopped mid-sentence. Suddenly she seem to follow his train of thought and she stared at him, disbelieving at first, then hurt and shocked and angry, all at once. She blushed.

"I don't believe you."

"What?" Erlendur said, watching her suddenly turn hostile.

"You think it's her. Her skeleton!"

"I don't think anything. This is the first time I've heard about this woman. We don't have the faintest idea who's in the ground up there. It's far too early to say who it may or may not be."

"So why are you so interested in her? What do you know that I don't?"

"Nothing," Erlendur said, confounded. "Didn't it occur to you when I told you about the skeleton there? Your uncle had a chalet nearby. His fiancée went missing. We find a skeleton. It's not a difficult equation."

"Are you mad? Are you suggesting . . ."

"I'm not suggesting anything."

". . . that he killed her? That Uncle Benjamín murdered his fiancée and buried her without telling anyone all those years until he died, a broken man?"

Elsa had stood up and was pacing the floor.

"Hang on a minute, I haven't said any such thing," Erlendur said, wondering whether he could have been more diplomatic. "Nothing of the sort," he said.

"Do you think it's her? The skeleton you found? Is it her?"

"Definitely not," Erlendur said, with no basis for doing so. He wanted to calm her down at any price. He had been tactless. Suggested something not based on any evidence, and regretted it. It was all too sudden for her.

"Do you know anything about the chalet?" he said in an effort to change the subject. "Whether anyone lived in it 50, 60 years ago?

During the war or just afterwards? They can't find the details in the system at the moment."

"My God, what a thought!" Elsa groaned, her mind elsewhere. "Sorry. What were you saying?"

"He might have rented out the chalet," Erlendur said quickly. "Your uncle. There was a great housing shortage in Reykjavík from the war onwards, rents soared and it occurred to me that he might have rented it out on the cheap. Or even sold it. Do you know anything about that?"

"Yes, I think there was some talk of him renting the place out, but I don't know to whom, if that's what you're getting at. Excuse me for acting this way. It's just so ... What sort of bones are they? A whole skeleton, male, female, a child?"

Calmer. Back on track. She sat down again and looked him inquisitively in the eye.

"It looks like an intact skeleton, but we haven't exposed all of it yet," Erlendur said. "Did your uncle keep any records of his business or properties? Anything that hasn't been thrown away?"

"The cellar is full of his stuff. All kinds of papers and boxes that I've never got round to throwing away and never been bothered to sort through. His desk and some cabinets are downstairs. I'll soon have the time to go through it."

She said this with an air of regret and Erlendur wondered if she might not be satisfied with her lot in life, living alone in a large house that was a legacy from times gone by. He looked around the room and had the feeling that somehow her entire life was a legacy.

"Do you think we ... ?"

"Be my guest. Look as much as you want," she said with a vacant smile.

"I was wondering about one thing," Erlendur said, standing up. "Do you know why Benjamín would have rented out the chalet? Was he short of money? He didn't seem to have needed money that much. With this house here. His business. You said he lost it in the end, but during the war he must have earned a decent living and more besides."

"No, I don't think he needed the money."

"So what was the reason?"

"I think someone asked him to. When people started moving to Reykjavík from the countryside during the war. I think he must have taken pity on someone."

"Then he wouldn't necessarily even have charged any rent?"

"I don't know anything about that. I can't believe that you think Benjamín . . ."

She stopped mid-sentence as if reluctant to articulate what she was thinking.

"I don't think anything," Erlendur tried to smile. "It's far too early to start thinking anything."

"I just don't believe it."

"Tell me another thing."

"Yes?"

"Does she have any relatives who are still alive?"

"Who?"

"Benjamín's fiancée. Is there anyone I could talk to?"

"Why? What do you want to look into that for? He would never have done a thing to her."

"I understand that. All the same, we have these bones and they belong to someone and they won't go away. I have to investigate all the avenues."

"She had a sister who I know is still alive. Her name's Bára."

"When did she go missing, this girl?"

"It was 1940," Elsa said. "They told me it was on a beautiful spring day."

9

Róbert Sigurdsson was still alive, but just barely, Sigurdur Óli thought. He sat with Elínborg in the old man's room, thinking to himself as he looked at Róbert's pallid face that he would not want to be 90 years old. He shuddered. The old man was toothless, with anaemic lips, his cheeks sunken, tufts of hair standing up from his ghoulish head in all directions. He was connected to an oxygen cylinder which stood on a trolley beside him. Every time he needed to say something he took off his oxygen mask with a trembling hand and let out a couple of words before he had to put it back on.

Róbert had sold his chalet long ago and it had changed hands twice more before eventually it was demolished and a new one built nearby. Sigurdur Óli and Elínborg woke up the owner of the new chalet shortly before noon to hear this rather vague and disjointed story.

They had the office staff locate the old man while they were driving back from the hill. It turned out that he was in the National Hospital, just turned 90.

Elínborg did the talking at the hospital and explained the case to Róbert while he sat shrivelled up in a wheelchair, gulping down pure oxygen from the cylinder. A lifelong smoker. He seemed in full command of his faculties, despite his miserable physical state, and nodded to show that he understood every word and was well aware of the detectives' business. The nurse who showed them in to him and stood behind his wheelchair told them that they ought not to tire him by spending too long with him.

"I remember . . ." he said in a low, hoarse voice. His hand shook as he put the mask back on and inhaled the oxygen. Then he took the mask off again.

". . . that house, but . . ."

Mask up.

Sigurdur Óli looked at Elínborg and then at his watch, making no attempt to conceal his impatience.

"Don't you want . . ." she began, but the mask came off again.

". . . I only remember . . ." Róbert interjected, wracked with breathlessness.

Mask up.

"Why don't you go to the canteen and get something to eat?" Elínborg said to Sigurdur Óli, who looked again at his watch, at the old man and then at her, sighed, stood up and disappeared from the room.

Mask down.

". . . one family who lived there."

Mask up. Elínborg waited a moment to see whether he would continue, but Róbert said nothing and she pondered how to phrase the questions so that he only needed to answer with a yes or a no, and could use his head without having to speak. She told him she wanted to try that and he nodded. Clear as a bell, she thought.

"Did you own a chalet there during the war?"

Róbert nodded.

"Did this family live there during the war?"

Róbert nodded.

"Do you remember the names of the people who lived in the house at that time?"

74

Róbert shook his head. No.

"Was it a big family?"

Róbert shook his head again. No.

"A couple with two, three children, more?"

Róbert nodded and held out three anaemic fingers.

"A couple with three children. Did you ever meet these people? Did you have any contact with them or not know them at all?" Elínborg had forgotten her rule about yes and no and Róbert took off his mask.

"Didn't know them." Mask up again. The nurse was growing restless as she stood behind the wheelchair glaring at Elínborg as if she ought to stop immediately and looking ready to intervene at any second. Róbert took off his mask.

". . . die."

"Who? Those people? Who died?" Elínborg leaned over closer to him, waiting for him to take the mask off again. Yet again he put a trembling hand to the oxygen mask and took it off.

"Useless . . ."

Elínborg could tell that he was having trouble speaking and she strained with all her might to urge him on. She stared at him and waited for him to say more.

Mask down.

". . . vegetable."

Róbert dropped his mask, his eyes closed and his head sank onto his chest.

"Ah," the nurse said curtly, "So now you've finished him off for good." She picked up the mask and stuck it over Róbert's nose and mouth with unnecessary force as he sat with his head on his chest and his old eyes closed as if he had fallen asleep. Maybe he really was dying for all Elínborg knew. She stood up and watched the nurse push Róbert over to his bed, lift him like a feather out of the wheelchair and lay him down there.

"Are you trying to kill the poor man with this nonsense?" the nurse said, a strapping woman aged about 50 with her hair in a bun, wearing a white coat, white trousers and white clogs. She glared ferociously at Elínborg. "I should never have allowed this," she muttered in self-reproach. "He'll hardly live until the morning," she said in a loud voice directed back at Elínborg, with an obvious tone of accusation.

"Sorry," Elínborg said, without being completely aware why she was apologising. "We thought he could help us about some old bones. I hope he's not feeling too bad."

Lying flat out now, Róbert suddenly opened his eyes. He looked around as if gradually realising where he was, and took off his oxygen mask despite the nurse's protests.

"Often came," he panted, ". . . later. Green . . . lady . . . bushes . . ."

"Bushes?" Elínborg said. She thought for a moment. "Do you mean the redcurrants?"

The nurse put the mask back on Róbert, but Elínborg thought she detected a nod towards her.

"Who was it? Do you mean yourself? Do you remember the redcurrant bushes? Did you go there? Did you go to the bushes?"

Róbert slowly shook his head.

"Get out and leave him alone," the nurse ordered Elínborg, who had stood up to lean over to Róbert, but not too closely so as not to provoke her more than she already had.

"Can you tell me about it?" Elínborg went on. "Did you know who it was? Who used to go to the redcurrant bushes?"

Róbert had closed his eyes.

"Later?" Elínborg continued. "What do you mean later?"

Róbert opened his eyes and lifted up his old, bony hands to

indicate that he wanted a pencil and piece of paper. The nurse shook her head and told him to rest, he had been through enough. He clutched her hand and looked imploringly at her.

"Out of the question," the nurse said. ".Would you please get out of here," she said to Elínborg.

"Shouldn't we let him decide? If he dies tonight . . ."

"We?" the nurse said. "Who's we? Have you been looking after these patients for 30 years?" she snorted. "Will you get out before I have you removed."

Elínborg glanced down at Róbert who had closed his eyes again and seemed to be asleep. She looked at the nurse and reluctantly started moving towards the door. The nurse followed her and shut the door behind her the moment Elínborg was out in the corridor. Elínborg thought of calling in Sigurdur Óli to argue with the nurse and inform her how important it was for Róbert to tell them what he wanted to say. She dropped the idea. Sigurdur Óli was certain to enrage her even more.

Elínborg walked down the corridor and could see Sigurdur Óli in the canteen devouring a banana with an apish look on his face. On her way to join him, she stopped. There was an alcove or TV den at the end of the corridor and she retreated into it and hid behind a tree that was planted in a huge pot and stretched all the way up to the ceiling. She waited there, watching the door, like a lioness hiding in the grass.

Before long the nurse came out of Róbert's room, breezed down the corridor and through the canteen for the next ward. She did not notice Sigurdur Óli, nor he her as he chomped on his banana.

Elínborg sneaked out of her hiding place behind the tree and tiptoed back to Róbert's room. He was lying asleep in the bed with the mask over his face just as when she had left him. The curtain was closed, but the dim glow of a lamp shed light into the gloom. She went over to him, hesitated for a moment and looked around furtively before bracing herself to prod the old man.

Róbert did not budge. She tried again but he was sleeping like a log. Elínborg assumed he must be in a very deep sleep, if not simply dead, and she bit her nails while she wondered whether to prod him harder or disappear and forget the whole business. He had not said much. Only that someone had been hanging around the bushes on the hill. A green lady.

She was turning to leave when Róbert suddenly opened his eyes and stared at her. Elínborg was unsure whether he recognised her, but he nodded and she felt sure she detected a grin behind his oxygen mask. He made the same sign as before to ask for a paper and pencil and she searched in her coat for her notebook and pen. She put them in his hands and he started writing in big capitals with a shaky hand. It took him a long time and Elínborg cast a terrified look towards the door, expecting the nurse to enter at any moment and start shouting curses. She wanted to tell Róbert to hurry, but did not dare to pressure him.

When he had finished writing, his pallid hands slumped onto the quilt, and the book and pen with them, and he closed his eyes. Elínborg picked up the book and was about to read what the old man had written when the cardiac monitor that he was connected to suddenly started to beep. The noise was ear-piercing when it broke out in the silent room and Elínborg was so startled that she jumped back. She looked down at Róbert for a moment, unsure of what to do, then rushed straight out of the room, down the corridor and into the canteen where Sigurdur Óli was still sitting, his banana finished. An alarm rang somewhere.

"Did you get anything out of the old sod?" Sigurdur Óli asked Elínborg when she sat down beside him, gasping for breath. "Hey, are you okay?" he added when he noticed her puffing and panting.

"Yes, I'm fine," Elínborg said.

A team of doctors, nurses and paramedics came running through the canteen and into the corridor in the direction of Róbert's room. Soon afterwards a man in a white gown appeared, pushing in front of him a piece of equipment that Elínborg thought was a cardiac massage device, and went down the corridor as well. Sigurdur Óli watched the crowd disappear around the corner.

"What the hell have you been up to now?" Sigurdur Óli said, turning to Elínborg.

"Me?" Elínborg muttered. "Nothing. Me! What do you mean?"

"What are you sweating like that for?" Sigurdur Óli asked.

"I'm not sweating."

"What happened? Why is everyone running?"

"No idea."

"Did you get anything out of him? Is he the one who's dying?"

"Come on, try to show a bit of respect," Elínborg said, looking all around.

"What did you get out of him?"

"I haven't checked yet," Elínborg said. "Shouldn't we get away from here?"

They stood up and walked out of the canteen, left the hospital and sat down in Sigurdur Óli's car. He drove off.

"So, what did you get out of him?" Sigurdur Óli asked impatiently.

"He wrote me a note," Elínborg sighed. "Poor man."

"Wrote you a note?"

She took the book out of her pocket and flicked through it until she found the place Róbert had written in it. A single word was jotted there, in the trembling hand of a dying man, an almost incomprehensible scribble. It took her a while to puzzle out what he had written in the notebook, then she became convinced, although she did not understand the meaning. She stared at Robert's last word in this mortal life: CROOKED.

*

That evening it was the potatoes. He did not think they were boiled well enough. They could equally have been over-boiled, boiled to a pulp, raw, unpeeled, badly peeled, over-peeled, not cut into halves, not in gravy, in gravy, fried, unfried, mashed, sliced too thick, sliced too thin, too sweet, not sweet enough . . .

She could never figure him out.

That was one of his strongest weapons. The attacks always occurred without warning and when she was least expecting them, just as often when everything seemed rosy as when she could sense that something was upsetting him. He was a genius at keeping her on tenterhooks and she could never feel safe. She was always tense in his presence, ready to be at his beck and call. Have the food ready at the right time. Have his clothes ready in the morning. Keep the boys under control. Keep Mikkelína out of his sight. Serve him in every way, even though she knew it was pointless.

She had long ago given up all hope that things would get better. His home was her prison.

After finishing dinner he picked up his plate, surly as ever, and put it in the sink. Then went back to the table as if on his way out of the kitchen, but stopped where she still sat at the table. Not daring to look up, she watched the two boys who were sitting with her and went on eating her meal. Every muscle in her body was on the alert. Perhaps he would leave without touching her. The boys looked at her and slowly put down their forks.

Deathly silence fell in the kitchen.

Suddenly he grabbed her by the head and slammed it down on her plate, which broke, then he snatched her up by the hair and threw

80

her backwards, off her chair and onto the floor. He swept the crockery from the table and kicked her chair into the wall. She was dazed by the fall. The whole kitchen seemed to be spinning. She tried to get back to her feet although she knew from experience that it was better to lie motionless, but some perverse spirit within her wanted to provoke him.

"Keep still, you cow," he shouted at her, and when she had struggled to her knees he bowed over her and screamed:

"So you want to stand up, then?" He pulled her by the hair and slammed her face-first into the wall, kicking her thighs until she lost all the strength in her legs, shrieked and dropped back to the floor. Blood spurted from her nose and she could barely hear him shouting for the ringing in her ears.

"Try standing up now, you filthy cunt!" he screeched.

This time she lay still, huddled up with her hands protecting her head, waiting for the kicks to rain down upon her. He raised his foot and slammed it with all his might into her side, and she gasped with the scorching pain in her chest. Bending down, he grabbed her hair, lifted her face up and spat in it before slamming her head back against the floor.

"Dirty cunt," he hissed. Then he stood up and looked at the shambles after his assault. "Look what a mess you always make, you fucker," he blared down at her. "Clear it up this minute or I'll kill you!"

He backed slowly away from her and tried to spit at her again, but his mouth was dry.

"Fucking creep," he said. "You're useless. Can't you ever do anything right, you fucking useless whore? Aren't you going to realise that some day? Aren't you going to realise that?"

He didn't care if she was left marked. He knew there was no-one who would interfere. Visitors were rare. Occasional chalets lay scattered around the lowlands, but few people ever went to the hill, even though the main road between Grafarvogur and Grafarholt ran nearby, and no-one who had any business calling on that family.

The house they lived in was a large chalet that he rented from a man in Reykjavík; it was half built when the owner lost interest in it and agreed to rent it to him cheaply if he would finish it. At first he was enthusiastic about working on the house and had almost completed it, until it turned out that the owner did not care either way, and afterwards it began to fall into disrepair. It was made of timber and consisted of an adjacent sitting room and kitchen with a coal stove for cooking, two rooms with coal stoves for heating and a passage between the rooms. In the mornings they fetched water from a well near the house, two buckets every day that were put up on a table in the kitchen.

They had moved there about a year before. After the British occupation of Iceland people flocked to Reykjavík from the countryside in search of work. The family lost their basement flat. Could not afford it any more. The influx meant housing became expensive and rents soared. When he took charge of the half-built chalet in Grafarholt and the family moved out there he started looking for work that suited his new situation and found a job delivering coal to the farms around Reykjavík. Every morning he walked down to the turning to Grafarholt where the coal lorry would pick him up and drop him off again in the evening. Sometimes she thought his sole reason for moving out of Reykjavík was that no-one would hear her screams for help when he attacked her.

One of the first things she did after they moved to the hill was to get the redcurrant bushes. Finding it a barren place, she planted the bushes on the south side of the house. They were supposed to mark one end of the garden that she planned to cultivate. She wanted to plant more bushes, but he thought it was a waste of time and forbade her to do it.

She lay motionless on the floor, waiting for him to calm down or go into town to meet his friends. Sometimes he went to Reykjavík and did not come back until the next morning. Her face was ablaze with pain and she felt the same burning in her chest as when he had broken her ribs two years before. She knew that it was not the potatoes. Any more than the stain he noticed on his freshly washed shirt. Any more than the dress she sewed for herself, but that he thought was tarty and ripped to shreds. Any more than the children crying at night, for which he blamed her. "A hopeless mother! Make them shut up or I'll kill them!" She knew he was capable of that. Knew that he could go that far.

The boys darted out of the kitchen when they saw him attack their mother, but Mikkelína stayed put as usual. She could hardly move unassisted. There was a divan in the kitchen where she slept and spent all the day as well because that was the easiest place to keep an eye on her. Generally she kept still after he came in, and when he started thrashing her mother she would pull the blanket over her head with her good hand, as if trying to make herself disappear.

She did not see what happened. Did not want to see. Through the blanket she heard him shouting and her mother shrieking in pain, and she shuddered when she heard her smash into the wall and slump to the floor. Huddled up under her blanket, she started to recite silently to herself:

> They stand up on the box,
> in their little socks,
> golden are their locks,
> the girls in pretty frocks.

When she stopped, it was quiet again in the kitchen. For a long while the girl did not dare to pull the blanket away. She peeped out from beneath it, warily, but could not see him. Down the passage she saw the front door open. He must have gone out. The girl sat up and saw her mother lying on the floor. She threw off her blanket, crawled down from her sleeping place and pulled her way across the floor and under the table to her mother, who was still lying hunched up and motionless.

Mikkelína snuggled up to her mother. The girl was thin as a rake and weak, and found the hard floor difficult to crawl across. Normally, if she needed to move, her brothers or mother carried her. He never did. He had repeatedly threatened to "kill that moron". "Strangle that monster on that disgusting bed! That cripple!"

Her mother did not move. She felt Mikkelína touch her back and then stroke her head. The pain in her ribcage did not let up and her nose was still bleeding. She didn't know whether she had fainted. She had thought he was still in the kitchen, but since Mikkelína was up and about that was out of the question. Mikkelína feared her stepfather more than anything else in her life.

Gingerly her mother straightened herself, moaning with pain and clutching the side he had kicked. He must have broken her ribs. She rolled over onto her back and looked at Mikkelína. The girl had been crying and she wore a terrified expression. Shocked at the sight of her mother's bloody face, she burst into tears again.

"It's all right, Mikkelína," her mother sighed. "We'll be all right."

Slowly and with great difficulty she got to her feet, supporting herself against the table.

"We'll survive."

She stroked her side and felt the pain piercing her like a sword.

"Where are the boys?" she asked, looking down at Mikkelína on the floor. Mikkelína pointed to the door and made a noise that conveyed agitation and terror. Her mother had always treated her like a normal child. Her stepfather never called her anything but "the moron", or worse. Mikkelína had contracted meningitis at the age of three and wasn't expected to live. For days the girl had been at death's door at Landakot hospital, which was run by nuns, and her mother was not allowed to be with her no matter how she pleaded and cried outside the ward. When Mikkelína's fever died down she had lost all power of movement in her right arm and her legs, and also in her facial muscles, which gave her a crooked expression, one eye half-closed and her mouth so twisted that she could not help dribbling.

The boys knew they were incapable of defending their mother: the younger one was seven and the older one twelve. By now they knew their father's state of mind when he attacked her, all the invective he used to work himself up to it and then the rage that seized him when he screamed curses at her. Then they would flee the scene. Símon, the older one, went first. He would grab his brother and snatch him away too, pulling him along like a frightened lamb, petrified that their father would turn his wrath upon them.

One day he would be able to take Mikkelína with them.

And one day he would be able to defend his mother.

The terrified brothers ran out of the house and headed for the redcurrant bushes. It was autumn and the bushes were in bloom, with thick foliage and little red berries swollen with juice that burst in their hands when they picked them to fill tins and jars that their mother had given them.

They threw themselves to the ground on the other side of the bushes, listening to their father's curses and oaths and the sound of breaking plates and their mother's screams. The younger boy covered his ears, but Símon looked in through the kitchen window that cast its yellowish glow out into the twilight, and he forced himself to listen to her howls.

He had stopped covering his ears. He had to listen if he was to do what he needed to do.

10

Elsa was not exaggerating about the cellar in Benjamín's house. It was packed with junk and for a moment Erlendur found the prospect too daunting. He wondered about calling in Elínborg and Sigurdur Óli, but decided to keep that on hold. The cellar measured about 90 square metres and was partitioned off into a number of different-sized rooms, with no doors or windows, full of boxes and more boxes, some labelled, but most not. There were cardboard boxes that once contained wine bottles and cigarettes, and wooden crates, in all conceivable sizes and filled with an endless assortment of rubbish. In the cellar were also old cupboards, chests, suitcases and sundry items that had accumulated over a long time: dusty bicycles, lawn mowers, an old barbecue grill.

"You can rummage through that as you please," Elsa said when she followed him down. "If there's anything I can help you with, just call me." She half pitied this frowning detective who seemed somewhat absent-minded, shabbily dressed in his tatty cardigan under an old jacket with worn patches on the elbows. She sensed a certain sorrow about him when she talked to him and looked him in the eye.

Erlendur gave a vague smile and thanked her. Two hours later he found the first documents from Benjamín Knudsen the merchant. He had an awful time working through the cellar. Everything was disorganised. Old and more recent junk was mixed up in huge piles that he had to examine and move in order to make progress into the heap. However, the further he slowly made his way across the floor, the older the rubbish seemed to be that he was sorting through. He felt like having a coffee and a cigarette and he wondered whether to pester Elsa or go out for a break and find a café.

Eva Lind never left his thoughts. He had his mobile on him and was expecting a call from the hospital at any moment. His conscience plagued him for not being with her. Maybe he should take a few days off, sit beside his daughter and talk to her as the doctor had urged him to. Be with her instead of leaving her in intensive care, unconscious, with no family or comforting words, all by herself. But he knew he could never sit idly waiting by her bedside. Work was a form of salvation. He needed it to occupy his mind. Prevent himself from thinking the worst. The unthinkable.

He tried to concentrate as he worked his way through the cellar. In an old desk he found some invoices from wholesalers addressed to Knudsen's shop. They were handwritten and difficult to decipher, but they seemed to involve deliveries of goods. Similar bills were in the desk cupboard and Erlendur's first impression was that Knudsen had run a grocery. Coffee and sugar were mentioned on the invoices, with figures beside them.

Nothing about work on a chalet far outside Reykjavík where the city's Millennium Quarter was now being built.

Eventually the urge for a cigarette got the better of Erlendur and he found a door in the cellar that opened onto a beautifully kept garden. The flowers were just beginning to bud after the winter, although Erlendur paid no particular attention to that as he stood hungrily smoking. He quickly finished two cigarettes. The mobile rang in his

jacket pocket when he was about to go back to the cellar. It was
Elínborg.

"How's Eva Lind doing?" she asked.

"Still unconscious," Erlendur said curtly. Did not want any small
talk. "Any developments?" he asked.

"I talked to that old chap, Róbert. He owned a chalet up by the
hill. I'm not quite sure what he was going on about, but he
remembered someone roaming around in your bushes."

"Bushes?"

"By the bones."

"The redcurrant bushes? Who was it?"

"And then I think he died."

Erlendur heard Sigurdur Óli giggle in the background.

"The person in the bushes?"

"No, Róbert," Elínborg said. "So we won't be getting anything
more out of him."

"And who was it? In the bushes?"

"It's all very unclear," Elínborg said. "There was someone who
often used to go there later. That was really all I got out of him. Then
he started to say something. Said 'green lady' and then it was all
over."

"Green lady?"

"Yes. Green."

"Often and later and green," Erlendur repeated. "Later than what?
What did he mean?"

"As I said, it was very disjointed. I think it might have been . . . I
think she was . . ." Elínborg hesitated.

"Was what?" Erlendur asked.

"Crooked."

"Crooked?"

"That was the only description he gave of the person. He'd lost the

88

power of speech and he wrote down that one word, 'crooked'. Then he fell asleep and I think something happened to him because the medical team rushed in to him and . . ."

Elínborg's voice faded out. Erlendur mulled over her words for a while.

"So it looks like a lady often used to go to the redcurrant bushes some time later."

"Perhaps after the war," Elínborg said.

"Did he remember anyone living in the house?"

"A family," Elínborg said. "A couple with three children. I couldn't get any more out of him about that."

"So people did live around there, by the bushes?"

"It looks that way."

"And she was crooked. What's being crooked? How old is Róbert?"

"He's . . . or was . . . I don't know . . . past 90."

"Impossible to tell what he means by that word," Erlendur said as if to himself. "A crooked woman in the redcurrant bushes. Does anyone live in Róbert's chalet? Is it still standing?"

Elínborg told him that she and Sigurdur Óli had talked to the present owners earlier that day, but there had been no mention of any woman. Erlendur told them to go back and ask the owners directly whether any people, specifically a woman, had ever been seen around the area of the redcurrant bushes. Also to try to locate any relatives that Róbert may have had to find out whether he'd ever talked about the family on the hill. Erlendur said he would spend a little more time rummaging around in the cellar before going to the hospital to visit his daughter.

He returned to browsing through Benjamín's things, wondering as he looked around the cellar if it would not take several days to plough through all the junk in there. He squeezed his way back to Benjamín's desk which as far as he could tell contained only documents and invoices connected with his shop. Erlendur did not remember it, but it was apparently on Hverfisgata.

Two hours later, after drinking coffee with Elsa and smoking a further two cigarettes in the back garden, he reached the grey painted chest on the floor. It was locked but had the key in it. Erlendur had to strain to turn it and open the chest. Inside were more documents and envelopes tied up with an elastic band, but no invoices. A few photographs were mixed in with the letters, some framed and others loose. Erlendur looked at them. He had no idea who the people in the photographs were, but assumed that Benjamín himself was in some. One was of a tall, handsome man who was starting to develop a paunch and was standing outside a shop. The occasion was obvious. A sign was being mounted over the door: KNUDSEN'S SHOP.

Examining more photographs, Erlendur saw the same man. On some of them he was with a younger woman and they smiled at the camera. All the photographs were taken outdoors and always in sunshine.

He put them down, picked up the bundle of envelopes, and discovered they contained love letters from Benjamín to his bride-to-be. Her name was Sólveig. Some were merely very brief messages and confessions of love, others more detailed with accounts of everyday incidents. They were all written with great affection for his sweetheart. The letters appeared to be arranged in chronological order and Erlendur read one of them, though somewhat reluctantly. He felt as if he were prying into something sacrosanct, and felt almost ashamed. Like standing up against a window and peeping in.

My sweetheart,

How terribly I miss you, my beloved. I have been thinking of you all day and count the minutes until you come back. Life without you is like a cold winter, so drab and empty. Imagine, you

being away for two whole weeks. I honestly do not know how I can
stand it.

Yours lovingly
Benjamín K.

Erlendur put the letter back in its envelope and took out another from further down the pile, which was a detailed account of the prospective merchant's intention to open a shop on Hverfisgata. He had big plans for the future. Had read that in big cities in America there were huge stores selling all kinds of merchandise, clothes as well as food, where people chose off the shelves what they wanted to buy. Then put it in trolleys that they pushed around the shop floor.

He went to the hospital towards evening, intending to sit by Eva Lind's side. First he phoned Skarphédinn, who said that the excavation was making good progress, but refused to predict when they would get down to the bones. They had still not found anything in the soil to indicate the cause of the Millennium Man's death.

Erlendur also phoned Eva Lind's doctor before setting off, and was told that her condition was unchanged. When he arrived at intensive care he saw a woman wearing a brown coat, sitting by his daughter's bedside, and he was almost inside the room when he realised who it was. He tensed up, stopped in his tracks and slowly backed through the door until he was out in the corridor, looking at his ex-wife from a distance.

She had her back to him, but he knew it was her. A woman of his age, sitting and stooping, plump in a bright purple jogging suit under her brown coat, putting a handkerchief to her nose and talking to Eva Lind in a low voice. What she was saying, he couldn't hear. He noticed she had dyed her hair, but apparently quite some time ago because a white strip was visible at the roots where she parted it. He worked out how old she must be now. Three years older than he was.

He had not seen her close up for two decades. Not since he walked out and left her with the two children. She, like Erlendur, had not remarried, but she had lived with several men, some better than others. Eva Lind told him about them when she was older and started seeking his company.

Although the girl was suspicious of him at first, they had nonetheless reached a certain understanding and he tried to help her whenever he could. The same applied to the boy, who was much more distant from him. Erlendur had virtually no contact with his son.

Erlendur watched his ex-wife and backed further down the corridor. He wondered whether to join her, but could not bring himself to. He expected trouble and did not want a scene in this place. Did not want that kind of scene anywhere. Did not want it in his life if he could avoid it. They had never properly come to terms with their failed relationship which, Eva Lind told him, was what hurt her the most.

How he had left.

He turned round and walked slowly down the corridor, thinking about the love letters in Benjamín K.'s cellar. Erlendur could not remember properly, and the question remained unanswered when he got home, slumped in the armchair and allowed sleep to push it out of his mind.

Had Halldóra ever been his sweetheart?

11

It was decided that Erlendur, Sigurdur Óli and Elínborg would handle the Bones Mystery, as the media was calling it, by themselves. The CID couldn't afford to put more detectives onto what was not a priority case. An extensive narcotics investigation was in full swing, using up a great deal of time and manpower, and the department could not deploy any more people on historical research, as their boss Hrólfur put it. No-one was sure yet that it was even a criminal case at all.

Erlendur dropped in at the hospital early the next morning on his way to work, and sat by his daughter's bedside for two hours. Her condition was stable. There was no sign of her mother. For a long while he sat in silence, watching his daughter's thin, bony face, and thought back. Tried to recall the time he'd spent with his daughter when she was small. Eva Lind had just turned two when her parents separated, and he remembered her sleeping between them in their bed. Refusing to sleep in her cot, even though, because they only had a small flat with that single bedroom, a sitting room and kitchen, it was in their bedroom. She climbed out of hers, flopped into the double bed and snuggled up between them.

He remembered her standing by the door of his flat, well into her teens by then, after she had tracked down her father. Halldóra flatly refused to allow him to see the children. Whenever he tried to arrange to meet them she would hurl abuse at him and he felt that every word she said was the absolute truth. Gradually he stopped calling them. He had not seen Eva Lind for all that time and then suddenly there she was, standing in his doorway. Her expression looked familiar. Her facial features were from his side of the family.

"Aren't you going to invite me in?" she said after he had taken a long stare at her. She was wearing a black leather jacket, tattered jeans and black lipstick. Her nails were painted black. She was smoking, exhaling through her nose.

There was still a teenage look about her face, almost pristine.

He dithered. Caught unawares. Then invited her inside.

"Mum threw a wobbler when I said I was coming to see you," she said as she walked past him, trailing smoke, and slammed herself down in his armchair. "Called you a loser. Always says that. To me and Sindri. 'A fucking loser, that father of yours.' And then: 'You're just like him, fucking losers.'"

Eva Lind laughed. She searched for an ashtray to put out her cigarette, but he took the butt and stubbed it out for her.

"Why . . ." he began, but did not manage to finish the sentence.

"I just wanted to see you," she said. "Just wanted to see what the hell you look like."

"And what do I look like?" he asked.

She looked at him.

"Like a loser," she said.

"So we're not that different," he said.

She stared at him for a long time and he thought he detected a smile.

When Erlendur arrived at the office, Elínborg and Sigurdur Óli sat down with him and told him how they had learned nothing more from the present owners of Róbert's chalet. As the new owners put it, they had never noticed any crooked woman anywhere on the hill. Róbert's wife had died ten years before. They had two children. One of them, the son, died around the same time at the age of 60, and the other, a woman of 70, was waiting for Elínborg to call on her.

"And what about Róbert, will we get anything more out of him?" Erlendur asked.

"Róbert passed away last night," Elínborg said with a trace of guilt in her voice. "He'd had enough of life. Seriously. I think he wanted to call it a day. A miserable old vegetable. That's what he said. God, I'd hate to waste away in hospital like that."

"He wrote a few words in a notebook just before he died," Sigurdur Óli said. "She killed me."

"Aiee, that sense of humour," groaned Elínborg.

"You don't need to see any more of him today," Erlendur said, nodding in Sigurdur Óli's direction. "I'm going to send him to Benjamín's cellar to dig out some clues."

"What do you expect to find there anyway?" Sigurdur Óli said, the grin on his face turning sour.

"He must have written something down if he rented out his chalet. No question of it. We need the names of the people who lived there. The National Statistics Office doesn't seem likely to find them for us. Once we have the names we can check the missing persons register and whether any of these people are alive. And we need an analysis to determine the sex and age as soon as the skeleton is fully uncovered."

"Róbert mentioned three children," Elínborg said. "At least one of them must still be alive."

"Well, this is what we've got to go on," Erlendur said. "And it's not much: a family of five lived in a chalet in Grafarholt, a couple with three children, at some time before, during or after the war. They are the only people we know to have lived in the house, but others could

95

have been there too. It doesn't look as though they were registered as living there. So for now we can assume that one of them is buried there, or someone connected with them. And someone connected with them, the lady Róbert remembered, used to go up there..."

"Often and later and was crooked," Elínborg finished the sentence for him. "Could crooked mean she was lame?"

"Wouldn't he have written 'lame' then?" Sigurdur Óli asked.

"What happened to that house?" Elínborg asked. "There's no sign of it on the hill."

"Maybe you'll find that out for us in Benjamín's cellar or from his niece," Erlendur said to Sigurdur Óli. "I clean forgot to ask."

"All we need is the names of the residents and then to check them against the list of missing persons from that time, and it's all sewn up. Isn't that obvious?" Sigurdur Óli said.

"Not necessarily," Erlendur said.

"Why not?"

"You're only talking about the people who were reported missing."

"Who else that went missing should I be talking about?"

"The disappearances that go unreported. You can't be sure that everyone tells the police when someone disappears from their lives. Someone moves to the countryside and is never seen again. Someone moves abroad and is never seen again. Someone flees the country and is slowly forgotten. And then there are travellers who freeze to death. If we have a list of people who were reported to have got lost and died in the area at that time, we ought to examine that too."

"I think we can all agree that it's not that sort of case," Sigurdur Óli said in an authoritative tone that was beginning to get on Erlendur's nerves. "It's out of the question that this man, or whoever it is lying there, froze to death. It was a wilful act. Someone buried him."

"That's precisely what I mean," said Erlendur, who was a walking

96

encyclopaedia about ordeals in the wilderness. "Someone sets off from a farm, say. It's the middle of winter and the weather forecast is bad. Everyone tries to dissuade him. He ignores their advice, convinced he'll make it. The strangest thing about stories of people who freeze to death is that they never listen to advice. It's as if death lures them. They seem to be doomed. As if they want to challenge their fate. Anyway. This man thinks he'll succeed. Except when the storm breaks, it's much worse than he could have imagined. He loses his bearings. Gets lost. In the end he gets covered over in a snowdrift and freezes to death. By then he's miles off the beaten track. That's why the body's never found. He's given up for lost."

Elínborg and Sigurdur Óli exchanged glances, uncertain of what Erlendur was driving at.

"That's a typical Icelandic missing person scenario and we can explain it and understand it because we live in this country and know how the weather suddenly turns bad and how the story of that man repeats itself at regular intervals without anyone questioning it. That's Iceland, people think, and shake their heads. Of course, it was a lot more common in the old days when almost everyone travelled on foot. Whole series of books have been written about it; I'm not the only one who's interested in the subject. Modes of travel have only really changed over the past 60 to 70 years. People used to go missing and although you could never reconcile yourself to it, you understood their fate. There were rarely grounds for treating such disappearances as police or criminal matters."

"What do you mean?" Sigurdur Óli said.

"What was that lecture all about?" Elínborg said.

"What if some of these men or women never set off from the farm in the first place?"

"What are you getting at?" Elínborg asked.

"What if people said so-and-so had set off for the moors or for another farm or went to lay a fishing net in the lake and was never heard of again? A search is mounted, but he's never found and is given up for lost."

"So the whole household conspires to kill this person?" Sigurdur Óli said, sceptical about Erlendur's hypothesis.

"Why not?"

"Then he is stabbed or beaten or shot and buried in the garden?" Elínborg added.

"Until one day Reykjavík has grown so big that he can't rest in peace any longer," Erlendur said.

Sigurdur Óli and Elínborg looked at each other and then back at Erlendur.

"Benjamín Knudsen had a fiancée who disappeared under mysterious circumstances," Erlendur said. "Around the time that the chalet was being built. It was said that she threw herself into the sea and Benjamín was never the same afterwards. Seems to have had plans to revolutionise the Reykjavík retail trade, but he went to pieces when the girl disappeared and his burgeoning ambition evaporated."

"Only she didn't disappear at all, according to your new theory?" Sigurdur Óli said.

"Oh yes, she disappeared."

"But he murdered her."

"Actually I find it difficult to imagine that," Erlendur said. "I've read some of the letters he wrote to her and judging from them he wouldn't have touched a hair on her head."

"It was jealousy then," said Elínborg, an avid reader of romances. "He killed her out of jealousy. His love for her seems to have been genuine. Buried her up there and never went back. Finito."

"What I'm thinking is this," Erlendur said. "Isn't a young man overreacting a bit if he turns senile when his sweetheart dies on him?

Even if she commits suicide. I gather that Benjamín was a broken man after she went missing. Could there be something more to it?"

"Could he have kept a lock of her hair?" Elínborg pondered, and Erlendur thought she still had her mind on pulp fiction. "Maybe inside a picture frame or a locket," she added. "If he loved her that much."

"A lock of hair?" Sigurdur Óli repeated.

"He's so slow on the uptake," said Erlendur, who had grasped Elínborg's train of thought.

"What do you mean, a lock of hair?" Sigurdur Óli said.

"That would rule her out if nothing else."

"Who?" Sigurdur Óli looked at them in turn. "Are you talking about DNA?"

"Then there's the lady on the hill," Elínborg said. "It would be good to track her down."

"The green lady," Erlendur said thoughtfully, apparently to himself.

"Erlendur," Sigurdur Óli said.

"Yes?"

"Obviously she can't be green."

"Sigurdur Óli."

"Yes?"

"Do you think I'm a total idiot?"

The telephone on Erlendur's desk rang. It was Skarphédinn, the archaeologist.

"We're getting there," Skarphédinn said. "We could uncover the rest of the skeleton in two days or so."

"Two days!" Erlendur roared.

"Or thereabouts. We haven't found anything yet that looks like a weapon. You might think we're being a little meticulous about it, but

I think it's better to do the job properly. Do you want to come and take a look?"

"Yes, I was on my way," Erlendur said.

"Maybe you could buy some pastries on the way," Skarphédinn said, and in his mind's eye Erlendur could see his yellow fangs.

"Pastries?"

"Danish pastries," Skarphédinn said.

Erlendur slammed down the phone, asked Elínborg to join him in Grafarholt and told Sigurdur Óli to go to Benjamín's cellar to try to find something about the chalet that the merchant built but apparently lost all interest in after his life turned to misery.

On the way to Grafarholt, Erlendur, still thinking about people who went missing and were lost in snowstorms, remembered the story about Jón Austmann. He froze to death, probably in Blöndugil in 1780. His horse was discovered with its throat slit, but all that was found of Jón was one of his hands.

It was inside a blue knitted mitten.

*

Símon's father was the monster in all his nightmares.

It had been that way for as long as he could remember. He feared the monster more than anything else in his life, and when it attacked his mother all that Símon could think of was coming to her defence. He imagined the inevitable battle like an adventure story in which the knight vanquishes the fire-breathing dragon, but in his dreams Símon never won.

The monster in Símon's dreams was called Grímur. It was never his father or Dad, just Grímur.

Símon was awake when Grímur tracked them down in the fish factory dormitory in Siglufjördur, and heard when he whispered to their mother how he was going to take Mikkelína up to the mountain and kill her. He saw his mother's terror, and he saw when she suddenly seemed to lose all control, slammed herself against the bed head and knocked herself out. Grímur slowed down then. He saw when Grímur brought her round by repeatedly slapping her face. The boy could smell Grímur's acrid stench and he buried his face in the mattress, so afraid that he asked Jesus to take him up to heaven, there and then.

He did not hear any more of what Grímur whispered to her. Just her whimpering. Repressed, like the sound of a wounded animal, and mingling with Grímur's curses. Through a crack in his eyes he saw Mikkelína staring through the darkness in indescribable terror.

Símon had stopped praying to his God and stopped talking to his "good brother Jesus", even though his mother said never to lose faith in him. Although convinced otherwise, Símon had stopped talking to his mother about it because he could tell from her expression that what he said displeased her. He knew that no-one, least of all God, would help his mother to overcome Grímur. For all he had been told, God was the omnipotent and omniscient creator of heaven and earth, God had created Grímur like everyone else, God kept the monster alive and God made it attack his mother, drag her across the kitchen floor by the hair and spit on her. And sometimes Grímur attacked Mikkelína, "that fucking moron", as he called her, beating her and mocking her, and sometimes he attacked Símon and kicked him or punched him, one time with such force that the boy lost one of his upper teeth and spat blood.

"My good brother Jesus, the friend of every child . . ."

Grímur was wrong about Mikkelína being retarded. Símon had a feeling that she was more intelligent than the rest of them put together. But she never said a word. He was certain she could talk but did not want to. Certain she had chosen silence, from the way she was just as scared of Grímur as the others were, perhaps more so because Grímur sometimes talked about how they ought to throw her on the rubbish dump with that pushchair contraption of hers, she was useless anyway and he was fed up with watching her eat his food without doing anything around the house except be a burden. He said she made them a laughing stock, the whole family and him too, because she was a moron.

Grímur made sure that Mikkelína could hear when he talked like this, and he laughed at her mother's feeble attempts to curtail the abuse. Mikkelína didn't mind him ranting at her and calling her names, but she didn't want her mother to suffer for her sake. Símon could tell that when he looked at her. Mikkelína's relationship with him had always been close, much closer than with little Tómas, who was more of a puzzle, more of a loner.

Their mother knew that Mikkelína was not retarded. She did regular exercises with her, but only when Grímur was not there to see it. Helped her to limber up her legs. Lifted her withered arm, which was twisted inwards and stiff, and rubbed her paralysed side with an ointment that she made from wild herbs from the hill. She even thought that Mikkelína would be able to walk one day. She put her arm around her and tottered with her back and forth across the floor, urging her on and encouraging her.

She always spoke to Mikkelína like any other normal, healthy child, and told Símon and Tómas to do the same. She included her in everything they did together when Grímur was not at home. The mother and daughter understood each other. And her brothers understood her too. Every movement, every expression on her face. Words were superfluous, even if Mikkelína knew the words but never used them. Her mother had taught her to read and the one thing she enjoyed more than being carried out to lie in the sun was reading, or being read to.

And then one day the words started to come out, the summer after

102

the world went to war and the British army set up camp on the hill. When Símon was carrying Mikkelína back indoors out of the sun. She had been exceptionally lively during the day, wiggling her ears and opening her mouth and poking out her tongue. Símon was about to put her back on the divan in the kitchen, because evening was falling and the weather was cooling, when Mikkelína suddenly made a noise that startled her mother into dropping a plate into the washing-up bowl, where it broke. Forgetting for an instant the terror that would usually fill her after such clumsiness, she spun round and stared at Mikkelína.

"EMAAEMAAA," Mikkelína repeated.

"Mikkelína!" their mother gasped.

"EMAAEMAAA," Mikkelína shouted, rolling her head around in wild rejoicing at her achievement.

Their mother walked slowly towards her as if unable to believe her own ears, then looked, open mouthed, at her daughter, and Símon thought he could see tears filling her eyes.

"Maammmmaa," Mikkelína said, and her mother took her out of Símon's arms and laid her slowly and gently onto her bed, stroking her head. Símon had never seen their mother cry before. No matter what Grímur did to her, she never cried. She shrieked in pain, called for help, pleaded with him to stop or otherwise suffered his blows in silence, but Símon had never seen her cry. Thinking that she must be upset, he put his arm around her, but she told him not to worry. This was the best thing that could ever have happened in her life. He could tell that she was crying not only about Mikkelína's condition, but about her achievement as well, which had made her happier than she had ever before allowed herself to feel.

That was two years ago, and Mikkelína had steadily added to her vocabulary since then and could now say whole sentences, her face like a beetroot from the strain, poking out her tongue and dangling her head back and forth in such furious spasms from the effort that they thought it would drop off her withered body. Grímur did not know that she could talk. Mikkelína refused to say anything within his hearing and their mother concealed it from him, because she never tried to draw his attention to the girl, not even such triumphs. They pretended that nothing had happened or changed. A few times Símon heard his mother very guardedly mention to Grímur whether they ought to try to find help for Mikkelína. That she could become more mobile and stronger with age, and seemed to be able to learn. She could read and was learning to write with her good hand.

"She's a moron," Grímur said. "Don't ever think she's anything more than a moron. And stop talking to me about her."

So she stopped, because she obeyed Grímur's every word; the only help that Mikkelína ever received was from their mother, and what Símon and Tómas did for her by carrying her out into the sunshine and playing with her.

Símon avoided his father as far as possible, but from time to time he was forced to go out with him. When Símon grew up he proved more useful to Grímur, who took him to Reykjavík and made him carry provisions back to the hill. The trip to town took two hours, down to Grafarvogur, crossing the bridge over Ellidaár and skirting the Sund and Laugarnes districts. Sometimes they took the route up the slope to Háaleiti and across Sogamýri. Símon kept four or five of his little steps behind Grímur, who never spoke to him or paid him any attention until he loaded him with supplies and ordered him to carry them home. The return journey could take three or four hours, depending upon how much Símon had to carry. Sometimes Grímur would stay in town and not return to the hill for days.

When that happened, a certain joy reigned in the household.

On his trips to Reykjavík, Símon discovered an aspect of Grímur that he took a while to assimilate and never wholly understood. At home, Grímur was surly and violent. Hated being spoken to. Foul-mouthed if he did speak, and coarse in the way he belittled his children and their mother; he made them serve his every need and woe betide any shirker. But in dealing with everyone else, the monster seemed to shed its skin and become almost human. On Símon's first trips to town he expected Grímur to act the way he always behaved at home, snarling abuse or swinging punches. He feared this, but it never happened. On the contrary. All of a sudden Grímur wanted to please everyone. He chattered away merrily to the merchant and bowed and scraped to people who entered the shop. He addressed them formally, even smiled. Shook their hands. Sometimes when Grímur bumped into people he knew he would break into guffaws – not the strange, dry and raucous laugh that he occasionally let out when he was vilifying his wife. When people pointed to Símon, Grímur put his hand on the boy's head and said yes, he was his son, grown so big. Símon ducked at first as if expecting a blow, and Grímur joked about it.

It took Símon a long time to grasp this incomprehensible duplicity on Grímur's part. His father's new countenance was unrecognisable. He could not understand how Grímur could be one person at home and a completely different man the moment he left the house. Símon could not fathom how he could be sycophantic and subservient and bow politely, when at home he ruled as the ultimate dispenser of life and death. When Símon discussed this with his mother she shook her head wearily and told him, as always, to be wary of Grímur. Be wary of provoking him. No matter whether it was Símon, Tómas or Mikkelína who sparked him off, or whether it was something that had happened when Grímur was away and which threw him into a rage, he almost invariably attacked their mother.

Months would sometimes pass between assaults, even a whole year, but they never stopped altogether and were sometimes quite frequent. A matter of weeks. The intensity of his fury varied. Sometimes a single punch out of the blue, sometimes he would fly into an uncontrollable rage, knock their mother to the ground and kick her mercilessly.

And it was not only physical violence that weighed down upon the family and home. The language he used was like a lash across the face. Denigrating remarks about Mikkelína, that crippled moron. The sarcastic tirade that Tómas suffered for not being able to stop wetting the bed at night. When Símon acted like a lazy bastard. And all that their mother was forced to hear and they tried to close their ears to.

Grímur didn't care if his children saw him beating up their mother or humiliating her with words that stabbed like stilettos.

The rest of the time, he paid them virtually no attention. Normally acted as though they did not exist. Very occasionally he played cards with the boys and even allowed Tómas to win. Sometimes, on Sundays, they all walked to Reykjavík and he would buy sweets for the boys. Very seldom Mikkelína was allowed to go with them and Grímur arranged a ride in the coal lorry so they did not need to carry her down from the hill. On these trips – which were few and far between – Símon felt his father was almost human. Almost like a father.

On the rare occasions when Símon saw his father as something other than a tyrant, he was mysterious and unfathomable. He sat at the kitchen table once, drinking coffee and watching Tómas playing on the floor, and he stroked the surface of the table with the flat of his hand and asked Símon, who was about to sneak out through the kitchen, to bring him another cup. And while Símon poured the coffee for him, he said:

"It makes me furious thinking about it."

Símon stopped, holding the coffee jug in both hands, and stood still beside him.

"Makes me furious," he said, still stroking the surface of the table.

Símon backed slowly away and put the jug down on the stove plate.

Looking at Tómas playing on the floor, Grímur said: "It makes me furious to think I couldn't have been much older than him."

Símon had never imagined his father as ever being any younger than he was then, or that he had ever been different. Now, suddenly, he became a child like Tómas, and a completely new side to his father's character was revealed.

"You and Tómas are friends, aren't you?"

Símon nodded.

"Aren't you?" he repeated, and Símon said yes.

His father went on stroking the table.

"We were friends too."

Then he fell silent.

"That woman," Grímur said eventually. "I was sent there. The same age as Tómas. Spent years there."

He fell silent again.

"And her husband."

He stopped rubbing the table with his hand and clenched his fist.

"That fucking bastard. That bloody fucking bastard."

Símon slowly retreated. Then his father seemed to regain his calm.

"I don't understand it myself," he said. "And I can't control it."

He finished his coffee, stood up, went into the bedroom and closed the door behind him. On his way, he picked up Tómas from the floor and took him with him.

Símon sensed a change in his mother as the years went by and as he grew up, matured and acquired a sense of responsibility. It was not as fast a change as when Grímur was suddenly transformed and became almost human; on the contrary, his mother changed gradually and subtly, over a long period, many years, and he realised the meaning behind it, with a sensitivity denied to most. He had a growing sense that this change in her was dangerous, no less dangerous than Grímur, and that inexplicably it would be his responsibility to intervene before it was too late. Mikkelína was too weak and Tómas was too small. He alone could help her.

Símon had trouble understanding this change or what it meant, but he became more intensely aware of it than ever around the time that Mikkelína shouted out her first word. Mikkelína's progress pleased her mother immeasurably. For a moment it was as if her gloom had been swept away, she smiled and hugged the girl and the two boys, and for the next weeks and months she helped Mikkelína to learn to talk, delighting in her slightest advances.

But it was not long before their mother was back in her old routine, as if the gloom that had lifted from her returned with greater intensity than ever. Sometimes she sat on the side of the bed, staring into space for hours, after cleaning every speck of dust from the little house. Glared in silent misery with half-closed eyes, her expression so infinitely sad, alone in the world. Once, when Grímur had punched her in the face and stormed out, Símon found her holding the carving knife, with the palm of her hand turned up, stroking the blade slowly across her wrist. When she noticed him she gave a wry smile and put the knife back in the drawer.

"What are you doing with that knife?" Símon asked.

"Checking that it's sharp. He likes the knives to be kept sharp."

"He's completely different in town," Símon said. "He's not nasty then."

"I know."

"He's happy then, and he smiles."

"Yes."

"Why isn't he like that at home? To us?"

"I don't know. He doesn't feel well."

"I wish he was different. I wish he was dead."

His mother looked at him.

"None of that. Don't talk like him. You mustn't think like that. You're not like him and you never will be. Neither you nor Tómas. Never. Do you hear? I forbid you to think like that. You mustn't."

Símon looked at his mother.

"Tell me about Mikkelína's dad," he said. Símon had sometimes heard her talking about him to Mikkelína and tried to imagine what her world would have been like had he not died and left her. Imagined himself as that man's son in a family where his father was not a monster but a friend and companion who loved his children.

"He died," his mother said with a hint of accusation in her voice. "And that's that."

"But he was different," Símon said. "You would be different."

"If he hadn't died? If Mikkelína hadn't fallen ill? If I hadn't met your father? What's the point of thinking like that?"

"Why is he so nasty?"

He asked her this repeatedly and sometimes she answered, sometimes she just said nothing as if she herself had searched for the answer to that question for years without getting any closer to it. She just stared past Símon, alone in the world, and talked to herself sadly and remotely, as if nothing she said or did mattered any more.

"I don't know. I only know that we're not to blame. It's not our fault. It's something inside him. I blamed myself at first. Tried to find something I was doing wrong that made him angry, and I tried to change it. But I never knew what it was and nothing I did made any difference. I stopped blaming myself long ago and I don't want you or Tómas or Mikkelína to think the way he acts is your fault. Even when he curses and abuses you. It's not your fault."

She looked at Símon.

"The little power that he has in this world, he has over us, and he doesn't intend to let go of it. He'll never let go of it."

Símon looked at the drawer where the carving knives were kept.

"Is there nothing we can do?"

"No."

"What were you going to do with the knife?"

"I told you. I was checking how sharp it was. He likes the knives kept sharp."

Símon forgave his mother for lying because he knew she was trying, as always, to protect him, safeguard him, ensure that their terrible life as a family would have the least effect on his.

When Grímur got home that evening, filthy black from shovelling coal, he was in exceptionally good spirits and started talking to their mother about something he had heard in Reykjavík. He sat down on a kitchen stool, told her to bring him some coffee and said her name had cropped up at work. He didn't know why, but the coalmen had been talking about her and claimed she was one of them. One of the doomsday kids who were conceived in the Gasworks.

She kept her back turned to Grímur and didn't say a word. Símon sat at the table. Tómas and Mikkelína were outside.

"At the Gasworks!?"

Then Grímur laughed an ugly, gurgling laugh. Sometimes he coughed black phlegm from the coal dust and was black around the eyes, mouth and ears.

"In the doomsday orgy in the fucking gas tank!" he shouted.

"That's not true," she said softly, and Símon was surprised because he had seldom heard her contest anything Grímur said. He stared at his mother and a shiver ran down his spine.

"They fucked and boozed all night because they thought the end of the world was nigh and that's where you came from, you twat."

"It's a lie," she said, more firmly than before, but still without looking up from what she was doing at the sink. Her back remained turned to Grímur and her head dropped lower onto her chest and her petite shoulders arched up as if she wanted to hide between them.

Grímur had stopped laughing.

"Are you calling me a liar?"

"No," she said, "but it's not true. It's a misunderstanding."

Grímur got to his feet.

"Is it a misunderstanding," he mimicked her voice.

"I know when the gas tank was built. I was born before then."

"That's not what I heard. I heard your mother was a whore and your father was a tramp and they threw you in the dustbin when you were born."

The drawer was open and she stared down into it and Símon saw her glaring at the big carving knife. She looked at Símon then back down at the knife and for the first time he believed that she was capable of using it.

12

Skarphédinn had arranged for a big white tent to be put up over the excavation site and when Erlendur went inside it out of the spring sunshine he saw the incredibly slow progress they had made. By the foundation they had cut an area of ten square metres and the skeleton was embedded in one edge of it. The arm still pointed up, as before, and two men were kneeling with brushes and spoons in their hands, picking away at the dirt and sweeping it into pans.

"Isn't that a bit too painstaking?" Erlendur asked when Skarphédinn walked up to greet him. "You'll never get it finished like that."

"You just can't be too careful in an excavation," Skarphédinn said as pompously as ever, proud that his methods were producing results. "And you, of all people, ought to be aware of that," he added.

"Aren't you just using this for field training?"

"Field training?"

"For archaeologists? Isn't this the class you teach at the university?"

"Listen, Erlendur. We're working methodically. There's no other way to do it. Believe me."

"Yes, maybe there's no rush," Erlendur said.

"We'll get there in the end," Skarphédinn said, running his tongue over his fangs.

"They tell me the pathologist is in Spain," Erlendur said. "He's not expected back for a few days. So we do have plenty of time, I suppose."

"Who could it be, lying there?" Elínborg asked.

"We can't determine whether it's a male or a female, a young body or an old one," Skarphédinn said. "And maybe it's not our job to do so either. But I don't think there's the slightest doubt any more that it was a murder."

"Could it be a young, pregnant woman?" Erlendur asked.

"We'll have that settled soon," Skarphédinn said.

"Soon?" Erlendur said. "Not if we go on at this rate."

"Patience is a virtue," Skarphédinn said. "Remember that."

Erlendur would have told him where to stick his virtue if Elínborg had not interrupted.

"The murder doesn't have to be connected with this place," she said out of the blue. She had agreed with most of what Sigurdur Óli had said the day before, when he started criticising Erlendur for being too preoccupied with his first hunch about the bones: that the person buried there had lived on the hill, even in one of the chalets. In Sigurdur Óli's opinion it was stupid to concentrate on a house that used to be there and people who may or may not have lived in it. Erlendur was at the hospital when Sigurdur Óli delivered this sermon, and Elínborg decided to hear Erlendur's views on it.

"He could have been murdered in, say, the west of town, and brought over here," she said. "We can't be sure that the murder was actually committed on the hill. I was discussing this with Sigurdur Óli yesterday."

Erlendur rummaged deep in his coat pockets until he found his lighter and cigarette packet. Skarphédinn gave him a disdainful look.

"You don't smoke inside the tent," he snarled.

"Let's go outside," Erlendur said to Elínborg, "We don't want to make virtue lose its patience."

They left the tent and Erlendur lit up.

"Of course you're right," he said. "It's by no means certain that the murder, if indeed it was a murder, was committed here. As far as I can see," he continued, exhaling a thick cloud of smoke, "we have three equally plausible theories. First, it's Benjamín Knudsen's fiancée, who got pregnant, disappeared, and who everyone thought had thrown herself into the sea. For some reason, possibly jealousy, as you say, he killed the girl and hid the body here by his chalet; and was never the same man afterwards. Second, someone was murdered in Reykjavík, even in Keflavík or Akranes for that matter; anywhere around the city. Brought here, buried and forgotten. Third, there's a possibility that people lived on this hill, committed a murder and buried the body on their doorstep because they had nowhere else to go. It might have been a traveller, a visitor, maybe one of the British who came here in the war and built the barracks on the other side of the hill, or the Americans who took over from them, or maybe a member of the household."

Erlendur dropped the cigarette butt by his feet and stamped it out.

"Personally, and I can't explain why, I favour the last theory. The one about Benjamín's fiancée would be easiest, if we can link her DNA to the skeleton. The third one could prove toughest for us, because we're talking about someone who went missing, assuming it was ever reported, in a large, populated area, donkey's years ago. That option is wide open."

"If we find the remains of an embryo with the skeleton, haven't we more or less got the answer?" Elínborg said.

"That would be a very neat solution, as I say. Was the pregnancy documented?" Erlendur asked.

"What do you mean?"

"Do we know it for a fact?"

"Are you saying that Benjamín might have been lying? And she wasn't pregnant?"

"I don't know. She could have been pregnant, but not necessarily by him."

"She cheated on him?"

"We can speculate until the cows come home before those archaeologists present us with something."

"What could have happened to that person?" Elínborg sighed, wondering about the bones in the dirt.

"Maybe they deserved it," Erlendur said.

"What?"

"That person. Let's hope so, anyway. Let's hope it wasn't an innocent victim."

His thoughts turned to Eva Lind. Did she deserve to be lying in intensive care, more dead than alive? Was it his fault? Was anyone to blame except her? Wasn't the state she was in of her own doing? Wasn't her drug addiction her private business? Or did he have some part in it? She was convinced he did, and had told him so when she felt he was being unfair to her.

"You never should have left us," she shouted at him once. "Okay, you look down on me. But you're no better yourself. You're just as much a goddam loser!"

"I don't look down on you," he said, but she didn't even listen to him.

"You look down on me like a piece of shit," she shouted. "Like you're more important than me. Like you're smarter and better. Like you're better than me and Mum and Sindri! Walking out on us like some bigshot, then ignoring us. Like you're, like you're God fucking Almighty."

"I tried ..."

"You didn't try shit! What did you try? Nothing. Fuck all. Ran out like the creep you are."

"I've never looked down on you," he said. "That's wrong. I can't understand why you say that."

"Oh yes you do. That's why you left. Because we're so ordinary. So bloody ordinary that you couldn't stand us. Ask Mum! She knows. She says it's all your fault. The whole lot. Your fault. The state I'm in too. What do you reckon to that, mister God fucking Almighty?"

"Not everything your mother says is true. She's angry and bitter and ..."

"Angry and bitter! If you only knew how angry and bitter she really is and hates your guts and hates her kids because it wasn't her fault you left because she's the Virgin fucking Mary. It was OUR fault. Sindri and me. Don't you get it, you fucking jerk. Don't you get it, you fucking jerk ..."

"Erlendur?"

"What?"

"Are you all right?"

"Fine. Perfectly all right."

"I'm going to drop in on Róbert's daughter." Elínborg waved her hand in front of his face as if he had slipped into a trance. "Are you going to the British embassy?"

"Eh?" Erlendur snapped back to his senses. "Yes, let's do it that way," he said remotely. "Let's do it that way. And one thing, Elínborg."

"Yes?"

"Get the district medical officer back here to take a look at the bones when they're exposed. Skarphédinn doesn't know his arse from his elbow. He increasingly reminds me of some monstrosity out of the Brothers Grimm."

13

Before Erlendur went to the British embassy he drove to the Vogar district and parked a short distance from the basement flat where Eva Lind had once lived and where he had begun the search for her. He thought back to the child he found in the flat with the cigarette burns on its body. He knew the girl had been taken away from her mother and was in care, and he knew that the man she lived with was the father. A quick enquiry revealed that the mother had twice been to Accident and Emergency in the past year, once with a broken arm and the other time with multiple injuries which she claimed were the result of a road accident.

Another simple check showed that the mother's partner had a police record, although never for violence. He was awaiting sentence on charges of burglary and drug trafficking. Once he had been to prison, for an accumulation of minor crimes. One was an unsuccessful shop robbery.

Erlendur sat in his car for a good while, watching the door to the flat. He refrained from smoking and was about to drive away when the door opened. A man came out, wreathed in smoke from a cigarette, which he flicked into the front garden. He was of average height, powerfully built with long, black hair, dressed in black from top to toe. His appearance fitted the description in the police reports.

When the man disappeared around the corner, Erlendur quietly drove away.

Róbert's daughter welcomed Elínborg at the door. Elínborg had phoned beforehand. The woman, whose name was Harpa, was confined to a wheelchair, her legs withered and lifeless, but her torso and arms strong. Elínborg was somewhat taken aback but said nothing. Harpa smiled and invited her in. She left the door open, Elínborg entered and closed it behind her. The flat was small but cosy, custom built for its owner.

"I'm sorry about your father," Elínborg said, following Harpa into the sitting room.

"Thank you," the woman in the wheelchair said. "He was extremely old. I hope I don't live that long. There's nothing I'd hate more than to end up as a patient in an institution, waiting to die. Fading away."

"We're enquiring about people who might have lived in a chalet in Grafarholt, on the north side," Elínborg said. "Not so far from yours. Wartime or thereabouts. We spoke to your father shortly before he died and he told us he knew about a family living there, but unfortunately couldn't tell us much more."

Elínborg thought about the mask over Róbert's face. His breathlessness and anaemic hands.

"You mentioned finding some bones," Harpa said, sweeping back the hair which had fallen over her forehead. "The ones on the news."

"Yes, we found a skeleton there and we're trying to discover who it might be. Do you remember this family that your father spoke of?"

"I was seven when the war reached Iceland," Harpa said. "I remember the soldiers in Reykjavík. We lived downtown, but I didn't have a clue what it was all about. They were on the hill too. On the south side. They built barracks and a bunker. There was a long slit in it with the barrel of a cannon sticking out. All very dramatic. Our parents told us to keep away from it, my brother and me. I have a vague memory of fences all around it. Barbed wire. We didn't go over that way much. We spent a lot of time in the chalet that Dad built, mostly in the summer, and naturally we got to know the neighbours a little."

"Your father said that there were three children in that house. They could have been about your age." Elínborg glanced down at Harpa's wheelchair. "Maybe you didn't get about."

"Oh, sure," Harpa said, rapping her knuckles on the wheelchair. "This happened later. A car accident. I was 30. I don't remember any children on the hill. I remember children in other chalets, but not up there."

"Some redcurrant bushes are growing near the site of the old house, where we found the bones. Your father mentioned a lady who went there, later, I believe. She went there a lot . . . I think he said that anyway . . . probably dressed in green and she was crooked."

"Crooked?"

"That's what he said, or I should say, wrote."

Elínborg took out the note Róbert had written and handed it to her.

"This was apparently when you still owned your chalet," Elínborg went on. "I understand you sold it some time after 1970."

"1972," Harpa said.

"Did you notice this lady?"

"No, and I never heard Dad talk about her. I'm sorry I can't help you, but I never saw that lady and don't know anything about her, though I do remember people at the place you mean."

"Can you imagine what your father meant by this word? Crooked?"

"What it says. He always said what he meant, nothing more. He was a very precise man. A good man. Good to me. After my accident. And when my husband left me – he stuck it out for three years after the crash, then he was gone."

Elínborg thought she noticed a smile, but there was no smile on her face.

The official from the British embassy greeted Erlendur with such perfect courtesy and decorum that Erlendur almost thanked him with a bow. He said he was a secretary. Impeccably dressed in a suit and squeaky black leather shoes, he was unusually tall and thin, and spoke very precise Icelandic, much to the delight of Erlendur, who spoke English badly and understood little of it. He sighed with relief when he realised that if one of them was to give a slightly stilted impression in their conversation, it would be the secretary.

The office was as impeccable as the secretary himself, and Erlendur thought about his own workplace which always looked like a bomb had hit it. The secretary – "Just call me Jim," he said – offered him a seat.

"I love the way you are so informal here in Iceland," Jim said.

"Have you lived here for long?" Erlendur asked, not exactly sure why he was behaving like an old lady at a tea party.

"Yes, almost 20 years now," Jim nodded. "Thank you for asking. And as it happens, World War II is a particular interest of mine. I mean World War II in Iceland. I did an MA on the subject at the London School of Economics. When you rang about those barracks I thought I might be able to help."

"You've got a good command of the language."

"Thank you, my wife's Icelandic."

"So what about those barracks?" Erlendur asked, getting to the point.

"Well, I haven't had much time, but I did find some embassy

reports about the camps we built during the war. We might need to send for more information. That's for you to judge. There were a couple of barracks on what is now Grafarholt golf course."

Jim picked up some papers from the table and browsed through them.

"There was also, what do you call it, a fortification there. Or a bunker? A tower. A huge cannon. A platoon from the 12th Tyneside Scottish Battalion manned the cannon, but I still haven't found out who was in the barracks. It looks like a depot to me. Why it was located on the hill I'm not sure, but there were barracks and bunkers all over the place there, on the way to Mosfellsdalur, in Kollafjördur and Hvalfjördur."

"We were wondering about a missing person from the hill, as I told you over the phone. Do you know whether any soldiers who were there were lost or reported missing?"

"Do you think the skeleton you found might be a British soldier?"

"Perhaps it's not very likely, but we think that the body was buried during the war and if the British were in the area it's a good idea to be able to rule them out, at least."

"I'll check it for you, but I don't know how long they keep such records. I think the Americans took over the camp like everything else when we left in 1941. Most of our troops were sent to other countries, but not all of them."

"So the Americans ran that camp?"

"I'll check that too. I can talk to the American embassy about it and see what they say. That will save you the bother."

"You had military police here."

"Precisely. That might be the best place to start. It will take a few days. Maybe weeks."

"We have plenty of time," Erlendur said, thinking of Skarphédinn.

Rummaging around in Benjamín's possessions, Sigurdur Óli was bored stiff. Elsa had greeted him at the front door, shown him down to the cellar and left him there, and he had spent four hours turning out cupboards, drawers and countless boxes, without knowing exactly what he was looking for. Bergthóra was preoccupying his thoughts. He wondered whether she would be as much of a nymphomaniac when he got home as she had been over the past few weeks. He made up his mind to ask her straight out whether there was any particular reason for her sudden appetite for him, and whether that reason might just be that she wanted a baby. But that question, he knew, would mean broaching another matter that they had sometimes discussed without reaching any conclusion: wasn't it time to get married with all the appropriate ceremony and trimmings?

That was the question burning on her lips between the passionate kisses that she smothered him with. He still had to make his mind up about that issue and always dodged answering. His train of thought was: their life together was going smoothly, their love was flourishing, why ruin it by getting married? All the fuss. A stag party. Walking down the aisle. All those guests. Inflated condoms in the bridal suite. Unspeakably naff. Bergthóra did not want any civil ceremony bullshit. She talked about fireworks and beautiful memories to keep herself warm in her old age. Sigurdur Óli mumbled. Thought it was too early to think about old age. The problem was unresolved, it was clearly up to him to settle it and he had no idea what he wanted, apart from no church wedding and not hurting Bergthóra either.

Like Erlendur, when he read the letters he sensed Benjamín's genuine love and fondness for the girl who had vanished from the streets of Reykjavík one day and was said to have thrown herself into the sea. *My lovely. Dearest. How I miss you.*

All that love, Sigurdur Óli thought.

Was it capable of killing?

The bulk of the papers concerned Knudsen's shop, and Sigurdur Óli had given up all hope of finding anything remotely constructive when he pulled a note out of an old filing cabinet and read:

Höskuldur Thórarinsson.
Rent in advance for Grafarholt.
8 krónur.
Signed *Benjamín Knudsen.*

Erlendur was leaving the embassy when his mobile rang.

"I found a tenant," Sigurdur Óli said. "I think."

"For what?" Erlendur said.

"For the chalet. I'm on my way out of Benjamín's cellar. Never seen such a bloody mess in my life. I found a note implying that a certain Höskuldur Thórarinsson paid rent for Grafarholt."

"Höskuldur?"

"Yes. Thórarinsson."

"What's the date on the note?"

"No date. No year. Actually it's only an invoice from Knudsen's shop. The rent receipt is written on the back. And I also found invoices for what might well be construction materials for the chalet. It's all charged to the shop and the invoices are dated 1938. He may have started building the chalet around that time or been working on it."

"What year did we say his fiancée went missing?"

"Hang on, I jotted that down." Erlendur waited while Sigurdur Óli checked. He took notes at meetings, a practice Erlendur had never managed to make a habit of. He could hear Sigurdur Óli flick through papers and return to the telephone.

"She disappeared in 1940. In the spring."

"So Benjamín is building his chalet up to that time, then gives up and rents it out instead."

"And Höskuldur is one of the tenants."

"Have you found out anything else about this Höskuldur character?"

"No, not yet. Shouldn't we start with him?" Sigurdur Óli asked, hoping to escape from the cellar.

"I'll check him out," Erlendur said, and to Sigurdur Óli's chagrin added: "See if you can find anything more about him or anyone else in all that rubbish. If there's one note, there may well be more."

14

Erlendur sat by Eva Lind's bedside for quite a while after arriving from the embassy, and he turned over in his mind what to talk about. He had no idea what to say to her. He made several attempts, in vain. Ever since the doctor mentioned that it would help if he talked to her, he had repeatedly wondered what to say, but never reached any conclusion.

He began talking about the weather, but soon gave that up. Then he described Sigurdur Óli and told her how tired he had been looking recently. But there was not much else to say about him. He tried to find something to say about Elínborg, but gave up on that too. Then he told her about Benjamín Knudsen's fiancée, who was supposed to have drowned herself, and about the love letters he found in the merchant's cellar.

He told Eva Lind he had seen her mother sitting at her bedside. Then he fell silent.

"What's with you and Mum?" Eva Lind had once asked when she was visiting him. "Why don't you talk?"

Sindri Snaer had come with her, but did not stay long, leaving the two of them together as darkness fell. It was December and there were Christmas songs on the radio, which Erlendur switched off and Eva Lind turned back on, saying she wanted to listen to them. She was several months pregnant and had gone straight for the time being, and as usual when she sat down with him she began to talk about the family she did not have. Sindri Snaer never talked about that, nor about his mother or sister or all that never happened. He was silent and withdrawn when Erlendur spoke to him. Didn't care for his father. That was the difference between the sister and brother. Eva Lind wanted to get to know her father and did not baulk at holding him responsible.

"Your mother?" Erlendur said. "Can't we turn off those Christmas jingles?"

He was trying to win time. Eva's probing into the past always threw him into a quandary. He didn't know the answers to give about their short-lived marriage, the children they had, why he had walked out. He didn't have answers to all her questions, and sometimes that enraged her. She had a short fuse as far as her family was concerned.

"No, I want to hear Christmas songs," Eva Lind said, and Bing Crosby went on dreaming of a white Christmas. "I've never ever heard her say a good thing about you, but she must have seen something in you all the same. At first. When you met. What was it?"

"Have you asked her?"

"Yes."

"And what did she say?"

"Nothing. That would mean she'd have to say something positive about you and she can't handle that. Can't handle the idea of there being anything good about you. What was it? Why the two of you?"

"I don't know," Erlendur said, and meant it. He tried to be honest. "We met at a dance. I don't know. It wasn't planned. It just happened."

"What was going on in your head?"

Erlendur did not reply. He thought about children who never

126

knew their parents; never found out who they really were. Entered their life when it was as much as halfway through and did not have a clue about them. Never got to know them except as father and mother and authority and protector. Never discovered their shared and separate secrets, with the result that the parents were just as much strangers as everyone else the children met during the course of their lives. He pondered how parents managed to keep their children at arm's length until all that remained was acquired, polite behaviour, with an artificial sincerity that sprang from common experience rather than real love.

"What was going on in your head?" Eva Lind's questions opened wounds that she picked at constantly.

"I don't know," Erlendur said, keeping her at a distance as he had always done. She felt that. Maybe she acted in this way to produce such a reaction. Gain one more confirmation. Feel how remote he was from her and how far away she was from understanding him.

"You must have seen *something* in her."

How could she understand when he sometimes did not understand himself?

"We met at a dance," he repeated. "I don't expect there was any future in that."

"And then you just left."

"I didn't just leave," Erlendur said. "It wasn't like that. But in the end I did leave and it was over. We didn't do it . . . I don't know. Maybe there is no right way. If there is, we didn't find it."

"But it wasn't over," Eva Lind said.

"No," Erlendur said. He listened to Bing Crosby on the radio. Through the window he watched the big snowflakes drifting to earth. Looked at his daughter. The rings pierced through her eyebrows. The metal stud in her nose. Her army boots up on the coffee table. The dirt under her fingernails. The bare stomach that showed beneath her black T-shirt and was beginning to bulge.

"It's never over," he said.

Höskuldur Thórarinsson lived in a flat in the basement of his daughter's elegant detached house in Árbaer and gave the impression of being pleased with his lot. He was a small, nimble man with silvery hair and a silver beard around his little mouth, wearing a checked labourer's shirt and beige corduroys. Elínborg tracked him down. There weren't many people in the national registry named Höskuldur and past retirement age. She telephoned most of them, wherever they lived in Iceland, and this particular Höskuldur from Árbaer told her, you bet he rented from Benjamín Knudsen, that poor, dear old chap. He remembered it well although he did not spend long in the chalet on the hill.

They sat in his living room, Erlendur and Elínborg, and he had made coffee and they talked about this and that. He told them he was born and bred in Reykjavík, then started complaining how those bloody conservatives were throttling the life out of pensioners as if they were a bunch of layabouts who couldn't provide for themselves. Erlendur decided to cut the old man's ramblings short.

"Why did you move out to the hill? Wasn't it rather rural for someone from Reykjavík?"

"You bet it was," Höskuldur said as he poured coffee into their cups. "But there was no alternative. Not for me. You couldn't find housing anywhere in Reykjavík at that time. People crammed into the tiniest rooms during the war. All of a sudden all the yokels could come to town and earn hard cash instead of getting paid with a bowl of curds and a bottle of booze. Slept in tents if they had to. The price of housing went sky high and I moved out to the hill. What are those bones you found there?"

"When did you move to the hill?" Elínborg asked.

"It would have been some time around 1943, I reckon. Or '44. I think it was autumn. In the middle of the war."

"How long did you live there?"

"I was there for a year. Until the following autumn."

"Did you live alone?"

"With my wife. Dear old Ellý. She's passed away now."

"When did she die?"

"Three years ago. Did you think I buried her up on the hill? Do I look like the type, dearie?"

"We can't find the records of anyone who lived in that house," Elínborg said without answering his remark. "Neither you nor anyone else. You didn't register as domiciled there."

"I can't remember how it was. We never registered. We were homeless. Others were always prepared to pay more than us, then I heard about Benjamín's chalet and spoke to him. His tenants had just moved out and he took pity on me."

"Do you know who the tenants were? The ones before you?"

"No, but I remember the place was spotless when we moved in." Höskuldur finished his cup of coffee, refilled it and took a sip. "Spick and span."

"What do you mean, spick and span?"

"Well, I remember Ellý specifically commenting on it. She liked that. Everything scrubbed and polished and not a speck of dust to be seen. It was just like moving into a hotel. Not that we were rough, mind you. But that place was exceptionally well kept. Clearly a housewife who knew her business, my Ellý said."

"So you never saw any signs of violence or the like?" Erlendur asked, having kept silent until now. "Bloodstains on the walls for example."

Elínborg looked at him. Was he teasing the old man?

"Blood? On the walls? No, there was no blood."

"Everything in order then?"

"Everything in order. Definitely."

"Were there any bushes by the house when you were there?"

"There were a couple of redcurrant bushes, yes. I remember them clearly because they were laden with fruit that autumn and we made jam from the berries."

"You didn't plant them? Or your wife, Ellý?"

"No, we didn't plant them. They were there when we moved in."

"You can't imagine who the bones belonged to that we found buried up there?" Erlendur asked.

"Is that really why you're here? To find out if I killed anyone?"

"We think a human body was buried there some time during the war or thereabouts," Erlendur said. "But you're not suspected of murder. Far from it. Did you ever talk to Benjamín about the people who lived in the chalet before you?"

"As it happens, I did," Höskuldur said. "Once when I was paying the rent and praised the immaculate condition the previous tenants had left the house in. But he didn't seem interested. A mysterious man. Lost his wife. Threw herself in the sea, I heard."

"Fiancée. They weren't married. Do you remember British troops camped on the hill? Or Americans rather, that late in the war?"

"It was crawling with British after the occupation in 1940. They set up barracks on the other side of the hill and had a cannon to defend Reykjavík against an attack. I always thought it was a joke, but Ellý told me not to make fun of it. Then the British left and the Americans took over. They were camped on the hill when I moved there. The British had left years before."

"Did you get to know them?"

"Hardly at all. They kept themselves to themselves. They didn't smell as bad as the British, my Ellý said. Much cleaner and smarter.

Elegant. So much more elegant than them. Like in the films. Clark Gable. Or Cary Grant."

Cary Grant was British, Erlendur thought, but didn't bother to correct a know-it-all. He noticed that Elínborg ignored it as well.

"Built better barracks too," Höskuldur went on undaunted. "Much better barracks than the British. The Americans concreted the floors, didn't use rotten planks like the British did. Much better places to live. Everything the Americans touched. All much better and smarter."

"Do you know who took over the chalet when you and Ellý moved out?" Erlendur asked.

"Yes, we showed them around the place. He worked on the farm at Gufunes, had a wife and two kids and a dog. Lovely people, but I can't for the life of me remember their names."

"Do you know anything about the people who lived there before you, who left it in such good condition?"

"Only what Benjamín told me when I started talking about how nicely his house had been kept and telling him that Ellý and I set our standards just as high."

Erlendur pricked up his ears and Elínborg sat up in her seat. Höskuldur said nothing.

"Yes?" Erlendur said.

"What he said? It was about the wife." Höskuldur paused again and sipped his coffee. Erlendur waited impatiently for him to finish his story. His eagerness had not escaped Höskuldur, who knew he had the detective begging now.

"It was very interesting, you can be sure of that," Höskuldur said. The police wouldn't go away from him empty-handed. Not from Höskuldur. He sipped his coffee yet again, taking his time about it.

My God, Elínborg thought. Won't the old bore ever get round to it? She had had enough of old fogeys who either died on her or put on airs.

"He thought the husband battered her."

"Battered her?" Erlendur repeated.

"What's it called these days? Domestic violence?"

"He beat his wife?" Erlendur said.

"That's what Benjamín said. One of that lot who beat their wives and their kids too. I never lifted a finger against my Ellý."

"Did he tell you their names?"

"No, or if he did, I forgot it long ago. But he told me another thing that I've often thought about since. He said that she, that man's wife, was conceived in the old Gasworks on Raudarárstígur. Down by Hlemmur. At least that was what they said. Just like they said Benjamín killed his wife. His fiancée, I mean."

"Benjamín? The Gasworks? What are you talking about?" Erlendur had completely lost his thread. "Did people say Benjamín killed his fiancée?"

"Some thought so. At the time. He said so himself."

"That he killed her?"

"That people thought he'd done something to her. He didn't say that he killed her. He'd never have told me that. I didn't know him in the slightest. But he was sure that people suspected him and I remember there was some talk of jealousy."

"Gossip?"

"All gossip of course. We thrive on it. Thrive on saying nasty things about other people."

"And wait a minute, what was that about the Gasworks?"

"That's the best rumour of all. Haven't you heard it? People thought the end of the world was nigh so they had an all-night orgy in the Gasworks. Several babies were born afterwards and this woman was one of them, or so Benjamín thought. They were called the doomsday kids."

Erlendur looked at Elínborg, then back at Höskuldur.

"Are you pulling my leg?"

Höskuldur shook his head.

"It was because of the comet. People thought it would collide with Earth."

"What comet?"

"Halley's comet, of course!" the know-it-all almost shouted, outraged by Erlendur's ignorance. "Halley's comet! People thought the Earth would collide with it and be consumed in hellfire!"

15

Earlier that day Elínborg had located Benjamín's fiancée's sister, and when she and Erlendur left Höskuldur she told him she wanted to talk to her. Erlendur nodded, saying that he was going to the National Library to try to find newspaper articles about Halley's comet. Like most know-it-alls, as it turned out, Höskuldur did not know much about what really happened. He went round in circles until Erlendur could not be bothered to listen any more and took his leave, rather curtly.

"What do you think about what Höskuldur was saying?" Erlendur asked her when they got back to the car.

"That Gasworks business is preposterous," Elínborg said. "It'll be interesting to see what you can find out about it. But of course what he said about gossip is perfectly true. We take a special delight in telling nasty stories about other people. The rumour says nothing about whether Benjamín was actually a murderer, and you know that."

"Yes, but what's that idiom again? No smoke without fire?"

"Idioms," Elínborg muttered. "I'll ask his sister. Tell me another thing. How's Eva Lind doing?"

"She's just lying in bed. Looks as though she's peacefully sleeping. The doctor told me to talk to her."

"Talk to her?"

"He thinks she can hear voices through her coma, and that's good for her."

"So what do you talk to her about?"

"Nothing much," Erlendur said. "I have no idea what to say."

The sister of Benjamín's fiancée had heard the rumours, but flatly denied that there was any truth in them. Her name was Bára and she was considerably younger than the one who had gone missing. She lived in a large detached house in Grafarvogur, still married to a wealthy wholesaler and living in luxury, which was manifested in flamboyant furniture, the expensive jewellery she wore and her condescending attitude towards the detective who was now in her sitting room. Elínborg, who had outlined over the phone what she wanted to talk about, thought that this woman had never had to worry about money, always granted herself whatever she pleased and never had to associate with anyone but her own type. Probably gave up caring for anything else long ago. She had the feeling that this was the life that had awaited Bára's sister, around the time she disappeared.

"My sister was extremely fond of Benjamín, which I never really understood. He struck me as a crushing bore. No lack of breeding, of course. The Knudsens are the oldest family in Reykjavík. But he wasn't the exciting type."

Elínborg smiled. She didn't know what she meant. Bára noticed.

"A dreamer. Hardly ever came down to earth, what with his big ideas for the retailing business, which actually all came to pass years ago, although he didn't live to benefit from them. And he was kind to ordinary people. His maids didn't need to call him Sir. People have stopped that now. No courtesy any more. And no maids."

Bára wiped imaginary dust from the coffee table. Elínborg noticed some large paintings at one end of the room, separate portraits of

Bára and her husband. The husband looked quite glum and worn out, his thoughts miles away. Bára seemed to have an insinuating grin on her strict face and Elínborg could not help thinking that she had emerged from this marriage the victor. She pitied the man in the painting.

"But if you think he killed my sister, you're barking up the wrong tree," Bára said. "Those bones you said were found by the chalet are not hers."

"How can you be sure of that?"

"I just know. Benjamín would never have hurt a fly. An awful wimp. A dreamer, as I said. That was obvious when she disappeared. The man fell apart. Stopped caring about his business. Gave up socialising. Gave up everything. Never got over it. My mother gave him back the love letters he sent to my sister. She read some of them, said they were beautiful."

"Were you and your sister close?"

"No, I can't say that. I was so much younger. She already seemed grown-up in my earliest memories of her. Our mother always said she was like our father. Whimsical and tetchy. Depressive. He went the same way."

Bára gave the impression she had let out the last sentence by mistake.

"The same way?" Elínborg said.

"Yes," Bára said peevishly. "The same way. Committed suicide." She spoke the words with complete detachment. "But he didn't go missing like her. Oh no. He hanged himself in the dining room. From the hook for the chandelier. In full view of everyone. That was how much he cared about the family."

"That must have been difficult for you," Elínborg said for the sake of saying something. Bára glared accusingly at Elínborg from where she sat facing her, as if blaming her for having to recall it all.

"It was hardest for my sister. They were very close. It leaves its mark on people, that sort of thing. The dear girl."

For a moment there was a trace of sympathy in her voice.

"Was it . . . ?"

"This was a few years before she herself went missing," Bára said, and Elínborg could tell that she was concealing something. That her story was rehearsed. Purged of all emotion. But perhaps the woman was simply like that. Bossy, cold-hearted and dull.

"To his credit, Benjamín treated her well," Bára continued. "Wrote her love letters, that sort of thing. In those days, people in Reykjavík would go for long walks when they were engaged. A very ordinary courtship really. They met at Hótel Borg, which was *the* place in those days, they called on each other and went for walks and travelled, and it developed from there just as with young people everywhere. He proposed to her and the wedding was only a fortnight away, I would guess, when she disappeared."

"I'm told that people said she threw herself into the sea," Elínborg said.

"Yes, people made quite a meal of that story. They looked for her all over Reykjavík. Dozens of people took part in the search, but they didn't find so much as a hair. My mother broke the news to me. My sister left us that morning. She was going shopping and went to a few places, there weren't as many shops in those days, but she didn't buy anything. She met Benjamín in his shop, left him and was never seen again. He told the police, and us, that they quarrelled. That's why he blamed himself for what happened and took it so badly."

"Why the talk of the sea?"

"Some people thought they'd seen a woman heading towards the beach where Tryggvagata ends today. She was wearing a coat like my sister's. Similar height. That was all."

"What did they argue about?"

"Some petty matter. To do with the wedding. The preparations. Or at least that's what Benjamín said."

"You don't think it was something else?"

"I have no idea."

"And you don't think it possible that it's her skeleton we found on the hill?"

"Out of the question, yes. I have nothing to base that claim on, of course, and I can't prove it, but I find it just so far-fetched. I simply can't conceive of it."

"Do you know anything about the tenants in Benjamín's chalet in Grafarholt? Maybe people who were there during the war? Possibly a family of five, a couple with three children. Does that ring a bell?"

"No. But I know people lived in his chalet all throughout the war. Because of the housing shortage."

"Do you have a keepsake from your sister, such as a lock of hair? In a locket maybe?"

"No, but Benjamín had a lock of her hair. I saw her cut it off for him. He asked her for a memento one summer when my sister went up north to Fljót for a couple of weeks to visit some relatives."

When Elínborg got into her car she phoned Sigurdur Óli. He was on his way out of Benjamín's cellar after a long, boring day, and she told him to keep his eyes open for a lock of hair from Benjamín's fiancée. It might be inside a pretty locket, she said. She heard Sigurdur Óli groan.

"Come on," Elínborg said. "We can prove whether it's her if we find the lock of hair. It's as simple as that."

She rang off and was about to drive away when she had a sudden thought and switched off the engine. After pondering for a moment, nervously biting her lower lip, she decided to act.

When Bára answered the door she was surprised to see Elínborg again.

"Did you forget something? she asked.

"No, just one question," Elínborg said awkwardly. "Then I'll leave."

"Well, what is it?" Bára said impatiently.

"You said your sister was wearing a coat the day she went missing."

"So?"

"What sort of coat was it?"

"What sort? Just an ordinary coat that my mother gave her."

"I mean, what colour? Do you know?"

"Why do you ask?"

"I'm curious," Elínborg said, not wanting to go into explanations.

"I don't remember."

"No, of course not," Elínborg said. "I understand. Thank you and sorry for bothering you."

"But my mother said it was green."

*

So many things changed during those strange years.

Tómas had stopped wetting the bed. Stopped enraging his father and in some way which eluded Símon, Grímur had started showing the younger boy more attention. He thought Grímur might have changed after the troops arrived. Or maybe Tómas was changing.

Símon's mother never talked about the Gasworks which Grímur had teased her about so much, so eventually he got bored with it. You little bastard, he used to say, and called her Gashead and talked about the big gas tank and the orgy in it the night that the Earth was supposed to perish, smashed to smithereens in a collision with a comet. Although he understood little of what his father was saying,

139

Símon noticed that it upset his mother. Símon knew that his words hurt her as much as when he beat her up.

Once when he went to town with his father they walked past the Gasworks and Grímur pointed to the big tank, laughing, saying that was where his mother came from. Then he laughed even more. The Gasworks was one of the largest buildings in Reykjavík and Símon found it disturbing. He decided to ask his mother about the building and the big gas tank that aroused his curiosity.

"Don't listen to the nonsense he talks," she said. "You ought to know by now the way he rants and raves. You shouldn't believe a word he says. Not a word."

"What happened at the Gasworks?"

"As far as I know, nothing. He's making it all up. I don't know where he got that story from."

"But where are your mum and dad?"

She looked at her son in silence. She had wrestled with this question all her life and now her son had innocently put it to her and she was at a loss as to what to tell him. She had never known her parents. When she was younger she had asked about them, but never made any headway. Her first memory was of being in a household full of children in Reykjavík, and as she grew up she was told that she was no-one's sister and no-one's daughter; the council paid for her to be there. She mulled over those words, but did not find out what they meant until much later. One day she was taken from the home and went to live with an elderly couple as a kind of domestic servant, and when she reached adulthood she went to work for the merchant. That was her entire life before she met Grímur. She missed not having parents or a place to call home, a family with cousins, aunts and uncles, grandparents and siblings, and in between girlhood and womanhood she went through a phase of incessantly puzzling over who she was and who her parents were. She did not know where to look for the answers.

She imagined they had been killed in an accident. This was her consolation, because she could not bear the thought that they had left her, their child. She fantasised they had saved her life and died in the process. Even sacrificed their lives for her. She always saw them in that light. As heroes battling for their lives and hers. She could not conceive of her parents being alive. For her, that was unthinkable.

When she met the fisherman, Mikkelína's father, she enlisted him to help find the answer, and they called at a succession of offices without learning anything about her, except that she was an orphan; her parents' names were missing from her entry in the national register. She was described as an orphan. Her birth certificate could not be located. She and the fisherman called on the family where she lived with all the other children, and they talked to the woman who had been her foster mother as far back as she could remember, but she had no answers either. "They paid for you," she said. "We needed the money." She had never enquired into the girl's background.

She had long given up wondering about her parents by the time Grímur came home claiming to have discovered who they were and how she came into the world, and she saw the morbid pleasure on his face when he talked about the orgy in the gas tank.

All these thoughts passed through her mind as she looked at Símon, and for a moment she seemed to be on the brink of telling him something important before suddenly she told him to stop asking those endless questions.

War was raging in much of the world and it had reached all the way up to the other side of the hill where British occupying forces had begun erecting buildings shaped like loaves of bread, which they called barracks. Símon did not understand the word. Inside the barracks there was supposed to be something with another incomprehensible name. A depot.

Sometimes he ran over the hill with Tómas to watch the soldiers. They had transported timber up the hill, roofing beams, corrugated iron and fencing, rolls of barbed wire, bags of cement, a cement mixer and a bulldozer to clear the ground for the barracks. And they built the bunker overlooking Grafarvogur, and one day the brothers saw the British bringing a huge cannon up the hill. The cannon was installed in the bunker with its gigantic barrel sticking several metres out through a slit, ready to blow the enemy to pieces. They were defending Iceland from the Germans, who had started the war and killed everyone they got their hands on, even little boys like Símon and Tómas.

The soldiers erected the fencing around what turned out to be eight barracks in total, which went up in no time at all, and they put up a gate and signs in Icelandic saying that unauthorised access was strictly prohibited. A soldier with a rifle was always on guard in a sentry post at the gate. The soldiers ignored the boys, who made sure to keep a safe distance. When the weather was fine Símon and Tómas carried their sister over the hill, put her down on the moss and let her see what the soldiers were building and showed her the barrel projecting from the bunker. Mikkelína lay looking at everything around her, but was silent and contemplative, and Símon had the feeling that she was scared of what she saw. The soldiers and the big cannon.

All the troops wore khaki uniforms with belts, and heavy-duty black boots laced up to their calves, and some had helmets and carried rifles or guns in holsters. In warm weather they took off their jackets and shirts and lay bare-chested in the sunshine. Every so often there were military exercises on the hill, when the soldiers would lie concealed, run from their hiding places, throw themselves to the ground and fire their weapons. Noise and music came from the camp at night. Sometimes they had a machine that made scratchy music with tinny singing. At other times the soldiers sang into the night, songs from their own country which Símon knew was called Britain and Grímur said was an empire.

They told their mother all that was happening on the other side of the hill, but she showed little interest. Once, though, they took her with them to the top of the hill and she had a long look over the British camp, then back home she talked about all the bother and danger there and banned the boys from snooping around the soldiers, because they could never tell what might happen when men had guns and she did not want them to come to any harm.

Time passed and one day the camp filled up with Americans; almost all the British left. Grímur said they were all being sent away to be killed but the Americans would have an easy time in Iceland, without a care in the world.

Grímur gave up shovelling coal and started working for the Americans on the hill because there was plenty of money and work to be had at the camp. One day he had strolled over the hill and asked for work at the depot, and without further ado he was given a job in the quartermaster's stores and the mess. Afterwards, the diet at their home changed for the better. Grímur produced a red can with a key on the side. He opened the lid with the key and turned the can upside-down, and a lump of pink meat plopped onto the plate covered in clear jelly. It wobbled and tasted deliciously salty.

"Ham," Grímur said. "From America, no less."

Símon had never tasted anything so good in his life.

At first he did not wonder how the new food found its way onto their table, but he did notice the anxious look on his mother's face once when Grímur brought home a boxful of cans and hid them in the house. Sometimes Grímur set off for Reykjavík with a sack full of those cans and other goods that Símon did not recognise. When he came back he counted out money onto the table, and Símon saw him happy in a way he had never witnessed before. Grímur ceased being so spiteful to their mother. Stopped talking about the Gasworks. Stroked Tómas on the head.

As time passed, the house was swamped with merchandise. American cigarettes, delicious canned food, fruit and even nylon stockings that their mother said all the women in Reykjavík yearned to have.

None of it stayed in their house for long. Once Grímur brought back a little packet with the most wonderful scent Símon had ever smelt. Grímur opened it and let them all have a taste, telling them that the Americans chewed it all the time, like cows with cud. You weren't allowed to swallow it, but after a while you should spit it out and take a fresh strip. Símon, Tómas – and even Mikkelína, who was given a pink, scented piece to chew – chomped away for all they were worth, then spat it out and took some more.

"It's called gum," Grímur said.

Grímur soon learned to get by in English and befriended the troops. If they were off duty he occasionally invited them to his house, and then Mikkelína had to lock herself in the little store room, the boys combed their hair and their mother put on a dress and made herself presentable. The soldiers would arrive and act politely, greet the family with handshakes, introduce themselves and give the children sweets. Then they sat around drinking. They left in their jeep for Reykjavík and everything fell quiet again in the chalet which, otherwise, no-one ever visited.

Normally, however, the soldiers went straight to Reykjavík and came back at night singing. The hill resounded with their shouts and calls, and once or twice there was a sound like guns being fired, but not the cannon because, as Grímur put it, that would mean "the fucking Nazis are in Reykjavík and they'll kill us all in seconds". He often went for a night on the town with the soldiers and when he came back he was singing American songs. Símon had never heard Grímur sing before that summer.

And once Símon witnessed something strange.

One day one of the American solders walked over the hill with a fishing rod, stopped on the shore of Lake Reynisvatn and cast for trout. Then he walked down the hill with his rod and whistled all the way over to Lake Hafravatn, where he spent most of the day. It was a beautiful summer's day and he strolled around the lake, casting whenever he felt the urge. Instead of fishing with much motivation, he just seemed to enjoy being on the lakeside in the good weather. Sat down, smoked and sunbathed.

Around three o'clock he seemed to have had enough, gathered up his rod and a bag containing the three trout he had caught that day and strolled as casually as ever from the lake and up the hill. But instead of walking past the house he stopped and said something incomprehensible to Símon, who had been keeping a close watch on his movements and was now standing at the front door.

"Are your parents in?" the smiling soldier asked Símon in English and looked inside the house. The door was always kept open in good weather. Tómas had helped Mikkelína over to the sunny spot behind the house, and was lying there with her. Their mother was indoors, doing the housework.

Símon did not understand the soldier.

"You don't understand me?" The soldier said. "My name is Dave. I'm American."

Gathering that his name was Dave, Símon nodded. Dave held out the bag in front of the boy, put it down on the ground, opened it, took out the three trout and laid them beside it.

"I want you to have this. You understand? Keep them. They should be great."

Símon stared at Dave, uncomprehending. Dave smiled, his white teeth gleaming. He was short and thin, bony-faced, his thick, dark hair slicked over to one side.

"Your mother, is she in?" he asked. "Or your father?" Símon looked blank. Dave unbuttoned his shirt pocket, took out a black notebook and flicked through it to the place he wanted. He walked up to Símon and pointed to a sentence in the book.

"Can you read?" he asked.

Símon read the sentence that Dave was pointing to. He could understand it because it was in Icelandic, but was followed by something foreign that he could not fathom. Dave read the Icelandic sentence out loud, as carefully as he could.

"*Ég heiti Dave*," he said. "My name is Dave," he said again in English. Pointed once more, then handed the book to Símon, who read out loud.

"My name is . . . Símon," he said with a smile. Dave smiled even wider. Found another sentence and showed it to the boy.

"How are you, miss?" Símon read.

"Yes, but not miss, just you," Dave laughed, but Símon did not understand. Dave found another word and showed it to Símon. "Mother," Símon read out loud, and Dave pointed to him with a nod.

"Where is?" he asked in Icelandic, and Símon understood he was asking about his mother. Símon beckoned to Dave to follow him and he took him into the kitchen where his mother was sitting at the table darning socks. She smiled when she saw Símon enter, but when she saw Dave behind him her smile froze, she dropped the sock and leapt to her feet, knocking over the chair. Dave, equally taken aback, stepped forward waving his arms.

"Sorry," he said. "Please, I'm so sorry. I didn't want to scare you. Please."

Símon's mother rushed over to the kitchen sink and stared down at it as if not daring to look up.

"Please take him out, Símon," she said.

"Please, I will go," Dave said. "It's okay. I'm sorry. I'm going. Please, I . . ."

"Take him out, Símon," his mother repeated.

Puzzled by her reaction, Símon looked at them in turn, and saw Dave backing out of the kitchen and into the yard.

"Why did you do that to me?" she said and turned to Símon. "Bringing a man in here. Why would you do that?"

"Sorry," Símon said. "I thought it was all right. His name is Dave."

"What did he want?"

"He wanted to give us his fish," Símon said. "That he caught in the lake. I thought that was all right. He only wanted to give us some fish."

"God, what a shock! Good Lord, what a shock! You must never do that again. Never! Where are Mikkelína and Tómas?"

"Out the back."

"Are they all right?"

"All right? Yes, Mikkelína wanted to be in the sunshine."

"You must never do that again," she repeated as she walked out to check on Mikkelína. "Do you hear! Never."

She walked round the corner of the house and saw the soldier standing over Tómas and Mikkelína, staring down at the girl in bewilderment. Mikkelína pulled faces and craned her neck to see who was standing over them. She could not see the soldier's face because the sun was behind his head. The soldier looked at her mother, then back at Mikkelína writhing in the grass.

"I . . ." Dave said falteringly. "I didn't know," he said. "I'm sorry. Really I am. This is none of my business. I'm sorry."

Then he turned round and hurried away, and they watched him disappear slowly over the hill.

"Are you all right?" their mother asked, kneeling down beside Mikkelína and Tómas. She was calmer now that the soldier had left without apparently wanting to cause them any harm. She picked up Mikkelína, carried her into the house and put her down on the divan in the kitchen. Símon and Tómas ran in behind her.

"Dave isn't bad," Símon said. "He's different."

"Is his name Dave?" their mother said vacantly. "Dave," she repeated. "Isn't that the same as Davíd in Icelandic?" she asked, directing the question more at herself than anyone else. And then it happened, something that struck Símon as very strange.

His mother smiled.

Tómas had always been mysterious, reticent, a loner, a little nervous and shy, the silent type. The previous winter Grímur seemed to notice something in him that aroused his interest more than in Símon. He would pay attention to Tómas and take him into another room. When Símon asked his brother what they had talked about Tómas said nothing, but Símon insisted and wheedled out of him that they had been talking about Mikkelína.

"What was he saying to you about Mikkelína?" Símon asked.

"Nothing," Tómas said.

"Yes he was, what?" Símon said.

"Nothing," Tómas said with an embarrassed look, as if he was trying to conceal something from his brother.

"Tell me."

"I don't want to. I don't want him to talk to me. I don't want him to."

"You don't want him to talk to you? So you mean you don't want him to say the things he says? Is that what you mean?"

"I don't want anything, that's all," Tómas said. "And you stop talking to me too."

The weeks and months passed by and Grímur displayed his favour for his younger son in various ways. Although Símon was never party to their conversations, he found out what they were doing one evening towards the end of the summer. Grímur was getting ready to take some goods from the depot into Reykjavík. He was waiting for a soldier named Mike who was going to help him. Mike had a jeep at his disposal and they planned to fill it with goods to sell in town. The children's mother was cooking the food, which was from the depot as well. Mikkelína was lying in her bed.

Símon noticed Grímur pushing Tómas towards Mikkelína, whispering in his ear and smiling the way he did when he made snide remarks at the boys. Their mother noticed nothing and Símon had no real idea what was going on until Tómas went up to Mikkelína, urged on by Grímur, and said:

"Bitch."

Then he went back to Grímur, who laughed and patted him on the head.

Símon looked over to the sink where his mother was standing. Although she could not have helped overhearing, she did not move and showed no reaction at first, as if trying to ignore it. Except that he saw she was holding a knife in one hand, peeling potatoes, and her knuckles whitened as she gripped the handle. Then she turned slowly with the knife in her hand and stared at Grímur.

"That's one thing you shall never do," she said in a quavering voice.

Grímur looked at her and the grin froze on his face.

"Me?" Grímur said. "What do you mean, never do? I didn't do anything. It was the lad. It was my boy Tómas."

Their mother moved a step closer to Grímur, still wielding the knife.

"Leave Tómas alone."

Grímur stood up.

"Are you going to do anything with that knife?"

"Don't do that to him," she said, and Símon sensed she was beginning to back down. He heard a jeep outside the house.

"He's here," Símon shouted. "Mike's here."

Grímur looked out of the kitchen window then back at their mother, and the tension eased for a moment. She put down the knife. Mike appeared in the doorway. Grímur smiled.

When he got back that night he beat their mother senseless. The next morning she had a black eye and a limp. They heard the grunts when Grímur was pummelling her. Tómas crawled into Símon's bed and looked at his brother through the darkness of night, in shock, continually muttering to himself as if that could erase what had happened.

". . . sorry, I didn't mean to, sorry, sorry, sorry . . ."

16

Elsa opened the door for Sigurdur Óli and asked him to join her for a cup of tea. As he watched Elsa in the kitchen, he thought about Bergthóra. They had argued that morning before leaving for work. After rejecting her amorous advances he had begun clumsily to describe his concerns, until Bergthóra became seriously agitated.

"Oh, just a minute," she said. "So we're never supposed to get married? Is that your plan? Is the idea that we just live in limbo with nothing on paper and our children bastards? For ever."

"Bastards?"

"Yes."

"Are you thinking about the big wedding again?"

"Sorry if it bothers you."

"You really want to walk down the aisle? In your wedding dress with a posy in your hand and ..."

"You have such contempt for the idea, don't you?"

"And what's this about children anyway?" Sigurdur Óli said, and immediately regretted it when he saw Bergthóra's face turn ever darker.

"Do you never want to have children?"

"Yes, no, yes, I mean, we haven't discussed it," Sigurdur Óli said. "I think we need to discuss that. You can't decide on your own whether we have children or not. That's not fair and it's not what I want. Not now. Not straight away."

"The time will come," Bergthóra said. "Hopefully. We're both 35. It won't be long until it's too late. Whenever I try to talk about it you change the subject. You don't want to discuss it. Don't want children or a marriage or anything. Don't want anything. You're getting as bad as that old fart Erlendur."

"Eh?" Sigurdur Óli was thunderstruck. "What was that?"

But Bergthóra had already set off for work, leaving him with an horrific vision of the future.

Elsa noticed Sigurdur Óli's thoughts were elsewhere as he sat in her kitchen staring down at his cup.

"Would you like some more tea?" she asked quietly.

"No, thank you," Sigurdur Óli said. "Elínborg, who's working on this case with me, wanted me to ask if you know whether your uncle Benjamín kept a lock of his fiancée's hair, maybe in a locket or a jar or the like."

Elsa thought about it.

"No," she said, "I don't remember a lock of hair, but I'm not a hundred per cent sure what's down there."

"Elínborg says there should be one. According to the fiancée's sister, who told her yesterday that she gave Benjamín a lock of hair when she went on a trip somewhere, I believe."

"I've never heard about a lock of her hair, or anyone else's for that matter. My family aren't particularly romantic and never have been."

"Are any possessions of hers in the basement? The fiancée's?"

"Why do you want a lock of her hair?" Elsa asked instead of answering his question. She had a prying look on her face which made Sigurdur Óli hesitate. He didn't know how much Erlendur had told her. She saved him the bother of asking.

"You can prove that it's her buried up on the hill," she said. "If you have something from her. You can do a DNA test to find out whether it's her, and if it is, you'll claim my uncle murdered her and left her there. Is that the idea?"

"We're just investigating all the possibilities," Sigurdur Óli said, wanting at all costs to avoid provoking Elsa into a rage on the scale of that he had sparked with Bergthóra just half an hour before. This day was not getting off to a very good start. Definitely not.

"That other detective came here, the sad one, and implied that Benjamín was responsible for his fiancée's death. And now you can all confirm that if you find a lock of her hair. I just don't understand it. That you could think Benjamín capable of killing that girl. Why should he do it? What motive could he have had? None. Absolutely none."

"No, of course not," Sigurdur Óli said to calm her down. "But we need to know who the bones belong to and so far we don't have much to go on apart from the fact that Benjamín owned the house and his fiancée disappeared. Surely you're curious about it yourself. You must want to know whose bones they are."

"I'm not certain I do," Elsa said, somewhat calmer now.

"But I can go on looking in the cellar, can't I?" he said.

"Yes, of course. I can hardly stop you doing that."

He finished his tea and went down to the cellar, still thinking about Bergthóra. He did not keep a lock of her hair in a locket, and did not feel he needed anything to remind him of her. Not even her photograph in his wallet, like the pictures of wife and children that some men he knew carried around. He felt bad. He needed to talk things over with Bergthóra. Sort it all out.

He didn't want to be like Erlendur at all.

Sigurdur Óli looked through Benjamín Knudsen's belongings until midday, then popped out to a fast-food joint, bought a hamburger that he barely nibbled at, and read the papers over coffee. Around two he headed back to the cellar, cursing Erlendur for his obstinacy. He had not found the slightest clue as to why Benjamín's fiancée had disappeared, nor any evidence of wartime tenants apart from Höskuldur. He had not found the lock of hair that Elínborg was so convinced about after reading all those romances. It was Sigurdur Óli's second day in the cellar and he was at the end of his tether.

Elsa was at the door when he returned, and she invited him in. He tried to find an excuse to turn down the invitation, but was not quick enough to manage it without sounding rude, so he followed Elsa into the sitting room.

"Did you find anything down there?" she asked, and Sigurdur Óli knew that behind this helpful-sounding remark she was in fact actually trying to wheedle information out of him. It didn't occur to him that she might be lonely, which was the impression Erlendur had just minutes after entering her gloomy house.

"I haven't found that lock of hair, anyway," Sigurdur Óli said, nursing his tea. She had been waiting for him. He looked at her, wondering what was in the offing.

"No," she said. "Are you married? Sorry, of course that's none of my business."

"No, that's . . . yes, no, not married but living with my partner," Sigurdur Óli said, awkwardly.

"Any children?"

"No, no children," Sigurdur Óli said. "Not yet."

"Why not?"

"Pardon?"

"Why haven't you had any children?"

What's going on here? Sigurdur Óli thought, sipping his tea to win time.

"Stress, I suppose. So busy at work all the time. We're both in demanding jobs and, well, there's no time."

"No time for children? Have you really got anything better to do with your time? What does your girlfriend do?"

"She's a partner in a computer firm," Sigurdur Óli said, poised to thank her for the tea and say he needed to get going. He did not plan to be interrogated about his private life by some posh old maid who had clearly gone strange from living alone, the way women like her eventually do – until they end up snooping around everyone's private business.

"Is she a good woman?" Elsa asked.

"Her name's Bergthóra," said Sigurdur Óli, on the verge of becoming impolite. "She's a terribly good woman." He smiled. "Why are you . . . ?"

"I've never had a family," Elsa said. "Never had any children. Nor a husband for that matter. I don't care about that, but I would have liked children. They'd be 30 today, perhaps. In their thirties. I sometimes think about that. Grown-up. With their own children. I don't really know what happened. Suddenly you're middle-aged. I'm a doctor. Not many women studied medicine when I enrolled. I was like you, I didn't have the time. Didn't have time for a life of my own. What you're doing now isn't your own life. It's just work."

"Yes, well, I suppose I should . . ."

"Benjamín didn't have a family either," Elsa went on. "That was all he wanted, a family. With that girl."

Elsa stood up and so did Sigurdur Óli. He expected her to say goodbye, but instead she went over to a large oak cabinet with beautiful glass doors and carved drawers, opened one of them, took out a little Chinese trinket box, lifted the lid and pulled out a silver locket on a slender chain.

"He did keep a lock of her hair," she said. "There's a photograph

155

of her in the locket too. Her name was Sólveig." Elsa gave a hint of a smile. "The apple of Benjamín's eye. I don't think that's her buried on the hill. The thought is unbearable. That would mean Benjamín harmed her. He didn't. Couldn't. I'm convinced of that. This lock of hair will prove it."

She handed Sigurdur Óli the locket. He sat down again, opened it carefully and saw a tiny lock of black hair on top of a photograph of its owner. Without touching the hair he manoeuvred it onto the lid of the necklace to be able to see the photograph. It showed the petite face of a girl of 20, dark-haired with beautifully curved eyebrows above big eyes staring enigmatically into the lens. Lips that suggested determination, a small chin, her face slender and pretty. Benjamín's fiancée. Sólveig.

"Please excuse me for holding back," Elsa said. "I've thought the matter over and weighed it up and I couldn't bring myself to destroy that lock of hair. Whatever emerges from the investigation."

"Why did you conceal it?"

"I needed to think things over."

"Yes, but even . . ."

"It gave me quite a shock when your colleague – Erlendur, isn't it? – started insinuating that it might be her up there, but once I'd thought more about it . . ." Elsa shrugged as if in resignation.

"Even if the DNA test proves positive," Sigurdur Óli said, "that doesn't necessarily mean that Benjamín murdered her. The analysis won't give any answers to that. If that is his fiancée up on the hill, there could be another reason besides Benjamín . . ."

Elsa interrupted him.

"She . . . what's it called these days . . . she dumped him. 'Broke off their engagement' is probably the old phrase. Back when people used to get engaged. She did it the day that she disappeared. Benjamín didn't reveal that until much later. To my mother, on his deathbed.

She told me. I've never told anyone before. And I would have taken it to my grave if you hadn't found those bones. Do you know yet whether it's a male or a female?"

"Not yet, no," Sigurdur Óli said. "Did he say anything about why she broke off their engagement? Why she left him?"

He sensed Elsa hesitating. They looked each other in the eye and he knew she had already given too much away to back down now. He felt that she wanted to tell him what she knew. As if she were bearing a heavy cross and the time had come to put it down. At last, after all these years,

"It wasn't his child," she said.

"Not Benjamín's child?"

"No."

"She wasn't pregnant by him?"

"No."

"So whose was it?"

"You have to understand that times were different then," Elsa said. "Today women have abortions like going to the dentist. Marriage has no special meaning even if people want to have children. They live together. They separate. Start living with someone else. Have more children. Split up again. It wasn't like that. Not in those days. Having a child out of wedlock used to be unthinkable for women. It brought shame, they would be outcasts. People were merciless, they called them tarts."

"So I gather," Sigurdur Óli said. His mind turned to Bergthóra and it gradually dawned on him why Elsa had been asking about his private life.

"Benjamín was prepared to marry her," Elsa continued. "Or at least that's what he later told my mother. Sólveig didn't want that. She wanted to break off their engagement and told him so straight out. Just like that. Without any warning."

"Who was the father then?"

"When she left Benjamín she asked him to forgive her. For leaving him. But he didn't. He needed more time."

"And she disappeared?"

"She was never seen again after she said goodbye to him. When she didn't return home that evening they started looking for her and Benjamín wholeheartedly took part in the search. But she was never found."

"What about the father of her child?" Sigurdur Óli asked again. "Who was he?"

"She didn't tell Benjamín. She left without ever letting him know. That's what he told my mother, at least. If he did know, he certainly never told her."

"Who could it have been?"

"Could have been?" Elsa repeated. "It doesn't matter who it *could* have been. The only important thing is who it *was*."

"Do you mean the father was involved in her disappearance?"

"What do you think?" Elsa asked.

"You and your mother never suspected anyone?"

"No, no-one. Nor did Benjamín, as far as I know."

"Could he have fabricated the whole story?"

"I can't say for sure, but I don't think Benjamín told a lie in his life."

"I mean, to detract attention from himself."

"I'm not aware that he ever came under any suspicion, and it was quite a long time later that he told my mother all this. It was just before he died."

"He never stopped thinking about her."

"That's what my mother said."

Sigurdur Óli thought for a moment.

"Could the shame have led her to suicide?"

"Definitely. She not only betrayed Benjamín, she was pregnant and refused to say whose child it was."

"Elínborg, the woman I work with, talked to her sister. She said their father committed suicide. Hanged himself. That it was tough for Sólveig because they were particularly close."

"Tough for Sólveig?"

"Yes."

"That's odd!"

"How so?"

"He did hang himself, but it could hardly have upset Sólveig."

"What do you mean?"

"They said he was driven to it by grief."

"Grief?"

"Yes, that's the impression I got."

"Grief over what?"

"His daughter's disappearance," Elsa said. "He hanged himself after she went missing."

17

At long last, Erlendur found something to talk to his daughter about. He had done a lot of research at the National Library, gathering information from newspapers and journals that were published in Reykjavík in 1910, the year that Halley's comet passed the Earth with its tail supposedly full of cyanide. He obtained special permission to browse through the papers instead of running them through the microfilm reader. He loved poring over old newspapers and journals, hearing them rustle and inhaling the scent of yellowed paper, experiencing the atmosphere of the time they preserved on their crisp pages, then, now and for ever.

Evening had set in when he sat down at Eva Lind's bedside and began telling her about the discovery of the skeleton in Grafarholt. He told her about how the archaeologists demarcated small areas above the site of the bones, and about Skarphéðinn with his fangs which prevented him from closing his mouth completely. He told her about the redcurrant bushes and Róbert's strange description of the crooked, green lady. He told her about Benjamín Knudsen and his fiancée, who vanished one day, and the effect her disappearance had on her lover as a young man, and he told her about Höskuldur, who had rented the chalet during the war, and of Benjamín's mention of the woman who lived on the hill and who had been conceived in the gas tank the night that everyone thought the world would be destroyed.

"It was the year Mark Twain died," Erlendur said.

Halley's comet was heading towards Earth at an unimaginable speed with its tail full of poisonous gases. Even if the Earth escaped being smashed to smithereens in a collision, people believed, it would pass through the comet's tail and all life would perish; those who feared the worst imagined themselves consumed by fire and acid. Panic broke out, not only in Iceland but all over the world. In Austria, in Trieste and Dalmatia, people sold all they owned for next to nothing, to go on a spree for the short time they assumed they had left to live. In Switzerland, the young ladies' finishing schools stood empty because families thought they should be together when the comet destroyed Earth. Clergymen were instructed to talk about astronomy in laymen's terms to allay people's fears.

In Reykjavík, it was claimed that women took to their beds from fear of doomsday and many seriously believed that, as one of the papers phrased it, "the cold spring that year was caused by the comet". Old people talked of how terrible the weather had been the last time the comet approached Earth.

Around that time, in Reykjavík, gas was hailed as the key to the future. Gas lamps were widely used in the city, although not so extensively as to provide proper street lighting, but people lit their homes with gas as well. The next step planned was to erect a modern gasworks on the outskirts of town to meet the population's entire gas requirement for decades to come. The Mayor of Reykjavík negotiated with a German firm, and Carl Franke, an engineer, duly arrived in Iceland from Bremen and with a team of experts began building the Reykjavík Gasworks. It was opened in the autumn of 1910.

The tank itself was a huge contraption, with a volume of 1500 cubic metres, and was known as the "bell jar" because it floated in water, rising or sinking according to how much gas it contained. Never having beheld such a spectacle, people flocked to watch its construction.

When the tank was nearing completion, a group of people assembled inside it on the night of May 18. They believed that the tank was the only place in Iceland to offer any hope of protection from the comet's poisonous gases. Word spread that there was a party in the tank and people swarmed to take part in a night of wild abandon before doomsday.

Accounts of what went on in the tank that night spread like wildfire for the next few days. It was claimed that drunken revellers held an orgy till dawn, until it was obvious that the Earth would not perish, neither in a collision with Halley's comet nor in the hellfire of its tail.

It was also rumoured that a number of babies were conceived in the tank that night, and Erlendur wondered whether one of them might have met her fate in Grafarholt many years later and been buried there.

"The Gasworks manager's office still stands," he told Eva Lind, unaware whether she could hear him or not. "But apart from that, all sign of the Gasworks has gone. In the end, the power source of the future turned out to be electricity, not gas. The Gasworks was on Raudarárstígur, where Hlemmur bus station is now, and it still performed a useful function despite being a thing of the past; in biting frost and bad weather, homeless people would go inside to warm themselves by the burners, especially at night, and it was often crowded in the tank house in the darkest part of winter."

Eva Lind made no movement while Erlendur told his story. Nor did he expect her to; he did not expect miracles.

"The Gasworks was built on a plot of land called Elsumýrarblettur," he continued, smiling at the irony of Providence. "Elsumýrar-blettur stood undeveloped for years after the Gasworks was demolished and the tank was removed. Then a block of offices was built on the site, opposite the bus station. That block now houses the Reykjavík police force. My office is there. Precisely where the tank once stood."

Erlendur paused.

"We're all waiting for the end of the world," he said. "Whether it's a comet or something else. We all have our private doomsday. Some bring it upon themselves. Others avoid it. Most of us fear it, show it respect. Not you. You could never show respect for anything. And you don't fear your own little doomsday."

Erlendur sat quietly watching his daughter and wondered whether it meant anything, talking to her when she did not seem to hear a word he uttered. He thought back to what the doctor said and even felt a hint of relief, talking to his daughter this way. He had seldom been able to talk to her calmly and at ease. The tension between them had coloured their entire relationship and they had not often had the chance to sit down for a quiet conversation.

But they were hardly talking together. Erlendur smiled wryly. He was talking and she was not listening.

In that respect, nothing had changed between them.

Maybe this was not what she wanted to hear. The discovery of the skeleton, the Gasworks, the comet and the orgy. Maybe she wanted him to talk about something completely different. Himself. Them.

He stood up, bent down and kissed her on the forehead and left the room. Engrossed in his thoughts, instead of turning right down the corridor and out of the ward, without noticing it he went in the opposite direction, into intensive care, past dimly lit rooms where other patients lay, their lives in the balance, connected to all the latest equipment. He only snapped out of his trance at the end of the corridor. He was about to turn round when a small woman came out of the innermost room and bumped straight into him.

"Excuse me," she said in a slightly squeaky voice.

"No, excuse me," he said in a fluster, looking all around. "I didn't mean to come this way. I was leaving the ward."

"I was called here," the little woman said. She had very thin hair and was plump with a huge bosom just barely contained by a violet T-shirt, and she was round with a friendly face. Erlendur noticed a wisp of dark moustache over her upper lip. A glance into the room she had emerged from revealed an elderly man lying under a sheet, his face thin and pallid. On a chair beside his bed sat a woman draped in a luxurious fur coat, dabbing a handkerchief to her nose with a gloved hand.

"There are still some people who believe in mediums," the woman said in a low voice, as if to herself.

"Excuse me, I didn't quite catch . . ."

"I was asked to come here," she said, gently leading Erlendur away from the room. "He's dying. They can't do a thing. His wife is with him. She asked me to find out if I could make contact with him. He's in a coma and they say nothing can be done, but he refuses to die. Like he doesn't want to go. She asked me to help, but I couldn't detect him."

"Detect him?" Erlendur said.

"In the afterlife."

"The after . . . are you a medium?"

"She doesn't understand that he's dying. He went out a few days ago and the next thing she knew the police called to tell her about a car crash on the West Road. He was heading for Borgarfjördur. A lorry swerved into his path. They say there's no hope of saving him. Brain-dead."

She looked up at Erlendur, who stared blankly back.

"She's my friend."

Erlendur had no idea what she was talking about or why she was telling him all this in the dimly lit corridor, whispering conspiratorially. He said a rather curt farewell to this woman whom he had never seen before, and was about to walk away when she grabbed his arm.

"Wait," she said.

"I beg your pardon?"

"Wait."

"Excuse me, but this is none of my busi . . ."

"There's a boy out there," the little woman said.

Erlendur did not hear properly what she said.

"There's a little boy in the blizzard," she went on.

Erlendur looked at her in astonishment and jerked his arm away from her as if he had been stabbed.

"What are you talking about?" he said.

"Do you know who it is?" the woman asked, looking up at Erlendur.

"I don't have the faintest idea what you're going on about," Erlendur snapped, turned round and strode down the corridor towards the exit sign.

"You have nothing to fear," she called after him. "He accepts it. He's reconciled to what happened. It was nobody's fault."

Erlendur stopped in his tracks, turned slowly round and stared at the little woman at the other end of the corridor. Her persistence was beyond his comprehension.

"Who is that boy?" she asked. "Why is he with you?"

"There is no boy," Erlendur snorted. "I don't know what you mean. I don't know you from Adam and I have no idea what boy you're talking about. Leave me alone!" he shouted.

Then he spun round and stormed out of the ward.

"Leave me alone," he hissed through clenched teeth.

18

Edward Hunter had been an officer with the American wartime forces in Iceland, one of the few members of the military who did not leave when peace was restored. Jim, the secretary at the British embassy, had located him without any great difficulty through the American embassy. He was looking for members of the British and American occupying forces, but according to the Home Office in London, few were still alive. Most of the British troops who went to Iceland lost their lives in combat in North Africa and Italy or on the western front, in the invasion of Normandy in 1944. Only a few Americans stationed in Iceland subsequently went into battle; most stayed for the duration of the war. Several remained behind, married Icelandic women and eventually became Icelandic nationals. One of them was Edward Hunter.

Erlendur received a call from Jim early in the morning.

"I talked to the American embassy and they directed me to this man Hunter. I talked to him myself to save you the bother. I hope that was in order."

"Thank you," Erlendur said.

"He lives in Kópavogur."

"Has he been there since the war?"

"Unfortunately I don't know that."

"But he still lives here, in other words, this Hunter," Erlendur said, rubbing the sleep from his eyes.

He had not slept well that night, he dozed and had bad dreams. The words of the little thin-haired woman at the hospital the previous evening were preying on his mind. He had no faith in mediums acting as go-betweens for the afterlife, and he did not believe that they could see what was hidden to others. On the contrary, he dismissed them as frauds, every one of them: clever at winkling information out of people and reading body language to establish details about the individual in question, which in half the cases might fit and in the other half might be plain wrong – simple probability. Erlendur scoffed at the subject as bloody nonsense when it had arisen at the office once, to Elínborg's great chagrin. She believed in mediums and life after death, and for some reason she expected him to be open to such ideas. Possibly because he was from the countryside. That turned out to be a huge misunderstanding. He was certainly not open to the supernatural. Yet there was something about the woman at the hospital and what she said that Erlendur could not stop thinking about, and it had disturbed his sleep.

"Yes, he still lives here now," Jim said, with profuse apologies for having woken Erlendur; he thought all Icelanders got up early. He did so himself, the endless spring daylight showed him no mercy.

"Hang on, so he's married to an Icelander?"

"I've spoken to him," Jim said again in his English accent as if he had not heard the question. "He's expecting your call. Colonel Hunter served for a while with the military police in Reykjavík and he remembers an incident in the depot on the hill that he's prepared to tell you about."

"What incident?" Erlendur asked.

"He'll tell you about it. And I'll go on trying to dig up something about soldiers who died or went missing here. You ought to ask Colonel Hunter about that too."

They said goodbye and Erlendur lumbered into the kitchen to make coffee. He was still deep in thought. Could a medium say which side people were on if they were halfway between life and death? Without accepting it in the slightest, he thought to himself that if it offered consolation to people who had lost loved ones, he was not going to oppose it. It was consolation that mattered, not where it came from.

The seething coffee burned his tongue when he sipped it. He avoided thinking about what was really haunting him that night and morning, and managed to keep it at bay.

More or less.

Ex-US army colonel Edward Hunter cut more an Icelandic than an American figure when, dressed in a buttoned-up woollen sweater and sporting a scraggy white beard, he welcomed Erlendur and Elínborg to his detached house in Kópavogur. His hair was unkempt and a little scruffy, but he was both friendly and polite when he shook them by the hand and told them just to call him Ed. In that respect he reminded Erlendur of Jim. He told them his wife was in the States, visiting his sister. Himself, he went there less and less.

On their way to visit Ed, Elínborg told Erlendur that, according to Bára, Benjamín's fiancée was wearing a green coat when she went missing. Elínborg thought this interesting, but Erlendur stifled any further discussion by saying rather brashly that he did not believe in ghosts. Elínborg had the feeling the subject was closed.

Ed showed them into a large sitting room and Erlendur saw scant evidence of the military life as he took a look around: in front of him were two gloomy Icelandic landscape paintings, Icelandic ceramic statues and framed family photographs. Nothing that reminded Erlendur of military service or World War II.

Having expected them, Ed had coffee, tea and biscuits ready, and after a polite chat, which rather bored all three of them, the old soldier went into action and asked how he could help. He spoke almost flawless Icelandic, in short, concise phrases as if the discipline of the army had taught him to keep to the bare essentials.

"Jim at the British embassy told us you served here during the war, including a spell with the military police, and were involved in a case concerning the depot at the present site of Grafarholt golf course."

"Yes, I play golf there regularly now," Ed said. "I heard the news of the bones on the hill. Jim told me you thought they might belong to one of our men. British or American."

"Was there some kind of incident at the depot?" Erlendur asked.

"They used to steal," Ed said. "It happens at most depots. I guess you'd call it 'wastage'. A group of soldiers stole provisions and sold them to the Icelanders. It started on a very small scale, but gradually they got more confident and in the end it became quite a large operation. The quartermaster was in on it with them. They were all sentenced. Left the country. I remember it well. I kept a diary and browsed through it after Jim phoned. It all came back to me, the theft. I also rang my friend from that time, Phil, who was my superior. We went over it together."

"How was the theft discovered?" Elínborg asked.

"Greed got the better of them. Theft on the scale they were practising is difficult to conceal, and rumours about irregularities spread."

"Who was involved?" Erlendur took out a cigarette and Ed nodded to show that he did not mind him smoking. Elínborg gave Erlendur a reproachful look.

"Civilians. Mostly. The quartermaster was the highest ranked. And at least one Icelander. A man who lived on the hill. On the other side from the depot."

"Do you remember his name?"

"No. He lived with his family in an unpainted shack. We found a lot of merchandise there. From the depot. I wrote in my diary that he had three children, one of them handicapped, a girl. The other two were boys. The mother ..."

Ed fell silent.

"What about the mother?" Elínborg said. "You were going to say something about the mother."

"I think she had a pretty rough time." Ed fell silent again and grew pensive, as if trying to transport himself back to that distant time when he investigated the theft, walked into an Icelandic house and encountered a woman whom he could tell was the victim of violence. And not only the victim of a single, recent attack; it was obvious that she suffered persistent and systematic abuse, both physical and psychological.

He barely noticed her when he entered the house with four other military policemen. The first thing he saw was the handicapped girl lying on her makeshift bed in the kitchen. He saw the two boys standing side by side next to her, transfixed and terrified as the soldiers burst in. He saw the man leap up from the kitchen table. They had arrived unannounced and clearly he was not expecting them. They could tell at a glance whether people were tough. Whether they posed a threat. This man would not give them any trouble.

Then he saw the woman. It was very early spring and gloomy, and it took him a moment to adjust to the dark inside. As if hiding, the woman stood where he thought he could see a passage leading to other rooms. At first he took her for one of the thieves, trying to make a getaway. He marched up to the passage, drawing his gun from its holster. Shouted down the passage and pointed his gun into the darkness. The crippled girl started screaming at him. The two boys pounced on him as one, shouting something he did not understand. And out of the darkness came the woman, whom he would never forget as long as he lived.

Immediately he realised why she was hiding. Her face was badly bruised, her upper lip puffed up and one eye so swollen that she could not open it. She looked at him in fear with the other eye, then bowed her head as if by instinct. As if she thought he was going to hit her. She was wearing one tattered dress on top of another, her legs bare but for socks and scruffy old shoes. Her dirty hair hung down to her shoulders in thick knots. For all he could tell, she limped. She was the most miserable creature he had ever seen in his life.

He watched her trying to calm her sons and understood that it was not her appearance that she was trying to hide.

She was hiding her shame.

The children fell silent. The older boy huddled up against his mother. Ed looked over at the husband, walked up to him and hit him round the face with a resounding slap.

"And that was that," Ed concluded his account. "I couldn't control myself. Don't know what happened. Don't know what came over me. It was incomprehensible, really. You were trained, you know, trained to face anything. Trained to keep calm whatever happened. As you can imagine, it was crucial to keep your self-control at all times, with a war going on and all that. But when I saw that woman ... when I saw what she'd had to put up with – and clearly not just that once – I could visualise her life at that man's hands, and something snapped inside me. Something happened that I just couldn't control."

Ed paused.

"I was a policeman in Baltimore for two years before war broke out. It wasn't called domestic violence then, but it was just as ugly all the same. I came across it there too and I've always been repelled by it. I could tell right away what was going on, and he'd been stealing from us too . . . but, well, he was sentenced by your courts," Ed said, as if trying to shake out of his mind the memory of the woman on the hill. "I don't think he got much of a sentence. He was sure to be back home beating up his poor wife before a couple of months were up."

"So you're talking about serious domestic violence," Erlendur said.

"The worst imaginable. It was appalling, the sight of that woman," Ed said. "Plain appalling. As I say, I could see straight away what was going on. Tried to talk to her, but she couldn't understand a word of English. I told the Icelandic police about her, but they said there wasn't a lot they could do. That hasn't changed much, I understand."

"You don't remember their names, do you?" Elínborg asked. "They're not in your diary?"

"No, but you ought to have a report on it. Because of the theft. And he worked in the depot. There are bound to be lists of the employees, of Icelandic workers in the camp on the hill. But maybe it's too long ago."

"What about the soldiers?" Erlendur asked. "The ones your courts sentenced."

"They spent time in military prison. Stealing supplies was a very serious crime. Then they were sent to the front. A death sentence of sorts."

"And you caught them all."

"Who knows? But the thieving stopped. The inventories returned to normal. The matter was resolved."

"So you don't think any of this is connected with the bones we found?"

"I couldn't say."

"You don't recall anyone who went missing from your ranks, or the British?"

"You mean a deserter?"

"No. An unexplained disappearance. Because of the skeleton. If you know who it might be. Maybe an American soldier from the depot?"

"I simply don't have a clue. Not a clue."

They talked to Ed for a good while longer. He gave the impression that he enjoyed talking to them. Seemed to enjoy reminiscing about the old days, armed with his precious diary, and soon they were discussing the war years in Iceland and the impact of the military presence, until Erlendur came to his senses. Mustn't waste time like that. He stood up, and so did Elínborg, and they both thanked him warmly.

Ed stood up to show them out.

"How did you discover the theft?" Erlendur asked at the door.

"Discover it?" Ed repeated.

"What was your lead?"

"Oh, I see. A phone call. Someone phoned the police headquarters and reported a sizeable theft from the depot."

"Who blew the whistle?"

"We never found out, I'm afraid. Never knew who it was."

*

Símon stood by his mother's side and watched, dumbfounded, when the soldier spun round with a mixture of astonishment and rage, walked directly across the kitchen and slapped Grímur around the face so hard that he knocked him to the floor.

The three other soldiers stood motionless in the doorway while Grímur's assailant stood over him and shouted at him something the Icelanders did not understand. Símon could not believe his eyes. He looked at Tómas, transfixed on what was happening, and then at Mikkelína, who stared in horror at Grímur lying on the floor. He looked over at their mother and saw tears in her eyes.

Grímur was off his guard. When they heard two jeeps pull up outside the house the mother had hurried into the passage so that no-one would see her. The sight of her with her black eye and burst lip. Grímur had not even stood up from the table, as if he had no worries that what he was doing with the pilferers from the depot would ever be discovered. He was expecting his soldier friends with a batch of merchandise that they planned to store in the house and that evening they were going into town to sell some of the booty. Grímur had plenty of money and had started talking about moving away from the hill, buying a flat, and even talked of buying a car, but only when he was in particularly high spirits.

The soldiers led Grímur out. Put him in one of the jeeps and drove him away. Their leader, the one who knocked Grímur to the floor without the slightest effort – who just walked up to him and hit him as if he did not know how strong Grímur was – said something to their mother and then said goodbye, not with a salute, but with a handshake, and got into the other jeep.

Silence soon returned to the little house. Their mother remained standing in the passage as if the intrusion was beyond her comprehension. She stroked her eye gingerly, fixated on something only she could see. They had never seen Grímur lying on the floor. They had never seen him knocked flat. Never heard anyone shout at him. Never seen him so helpless. They could not fathom what had happened. How it could happen. Why Grímur did not attack the soldiers and beat them to pulp. The children looked at each other. Inside the house, the silence was stifling. They looked at their mother as a strange noise was heard. It came from Mikkelína. She was squatting on her bed and they heard the noise again, and saw that she was beginning to giggle, and the giggling built up into a snigger which she tried to repress at first, but could not, and she erupted into laughter. Símon smiled and started laughing too, and Tómas followed suit, and before long all three were howling with uncontrollable spasms that echoed around the house and carried out onto the hill in the fine spring weather.

Two hours later a military truck pulled up and emptied the house of all the booty that Grímur and his colleagues had stashed indoors. The boys watched the truck drive away, and they ran over the hill and saw it go back to the depot where it was unloaded.

Símon did not know exactly what had happened and he was not sure that his mother did either, but Grímur had received a prison sentence and would not come home for the next few months. At first life continued as normal on the hill. They didn't seem to take in that Grímur was no longer around. At least, not for the time being. Their mother went about her chores as she always had, and had no qualms about using Grímur's ill-gotten gains to provide for herself and her children. Later she found herself a job on the Gufunes farm, about half an hour's walk from the house.

Weather permitting, the boys carried Mikkelína out into the sunshine. Sometimes they took her along when they went fishing in Reynisvatn. If they caught enough trout their mother would fry it in a pan and make a delicious meal. Gradually they were liberated from the grip that Grímur still exerted over them even while he was away. It was easier to wake up in the mornings, the day rushed past care free, and the evenings passed in an unfamiliar calm which was so comfortable that they stayed up well into the night, talking and playing, until they couldn't keep their eyes open.

Grímur's absence, however, had the greatest effect on their mother. One day, when she had finally realised that he would not be coming back in the immediate future, she washed every inch of their double bed. She aired the mattresses in the yard and beat the dust and dirt out of them. Then she took out the quilts and beat them too, changed the bed linen, bathed her children in turn with green soap and hot water from a big tub that she put on the kitchen floor, and ended by carefully washing her own hair and her face – which still bore the marks from Grímur's last assault – and her whole body. Hesitantly she picked up a mirror and looked into it. She stroked her eye and lip. She had grown thinner and her expression was tougher, her teeth protruding a little, her eyes sunk deep and her nose, which had been broken once, had an almost imperceptible curve.

Towards midnight she took all her children into her bed and the four of them slept there together. After that the children slept in the big bed with their mother, Mikkelína by herself on her right and the two boys on her left, happy.

She never visited Grímur in prison. They never mentioned his name all the time he was away.

One morning, shortly after Grímur had been led away, Dave the soldier strolled over the hill with his fishing rod, walked past their house and winked at Símon, who was standing in front of the house, and continued all the way to Hafravatn. Símon set off in pursuit, lying down at a suitable distance to spy on him. Dave spent the day by the lake, relaxed as ever, without apparently minding whether he caught any fish or not. He landed three.

When evening set in he went back up the hill and stopped by their house with his three fish tied together by their tails with a piece of string. Dave was unsure of himself, or so it appeared to Símon, who had run back home to watch him through the kitchen window, where he made sure that Dave could not see him. At last the soldier made up his mind, walked over to the house and knocked on the door.

Símon had told his mother about the soldier, the same one who had given them the trout before, and she went out and glanced around for him, went back in, looked in the mirror and tidied her hair. She seemed to sense that he would drop in on his way back to the barracks. She was ready to greet him when he did.

She opened the door and Dave smiled, said something she didn't understand and handed her the fish. She took them and invited him inside. He entered the house and stood awkwardly in the kitchen. Nodded to the boys and to Mikkelína, who stretched and strained for a better look at this soldier who had come all that way just to stand in their kitchen in his uniform with a funny hat shaped like an upturned boat, which he suddenly remembered he had forgotten to take off when he came inside and snatched from his head in embarrassment. He was of medium height, certainly older than 30, slim with nicely shaped hands, which fiddled with the upturned boat, twisting it as if they were wringing out the washing.

She gestured to him to sit at the kitchen table, and he sat with the boys beside him while their mother made coffee, real coffee from the depot, coffee that Grímur had stolen and the soldiers had not discovered. Dave knew Símon's name, and found out that Tómas was called Tómas, which was easy for him to pronounce. Mikkelína's name amused him and he said it over and again in such a funny way that they all laughed. He said his name was Dave Welch, from a place called Brooklyn in America. He told them he was a private. They had no idea what he was talking about.

"A private," he repeated, but they just stared at him.

He drank his coffee and seemed very pleased with it. The mother sat facing him at the other end of the table.

"I understand your husband is in jail," he said. "For stealing."

He got no response.

With a glance at the children he took a piece of paper out of his

177

breast pocket and twiddled it between his fingers as if uncertain what to do. Then he passed the note across the table to their mother. She picked it up, unfolded it and read what it said. She looked at him in astonishment, then back at the note. Then she folded up the note and put it in the pocket of her apron.

Tómas managed to make Dave understand that he ought to have another try at saying Mikkelína's name, and when he did they all started laughing again, and Mikkelína crinkled up her face in sheer joy.

Dave Welch visited their house regularly all that summer and made friends with the children and their mother. He fished in the two lakes and gave his catches to them, and he brought them little things from the depot that came in useful. He played with the children, who took a special delight in having him there, and he always carried his notebook in his pocket to make himself understood in Icelandic. They rolled around laughing when he spluttered out a phrase in Icelandic. His serious expression was completely at odds with what he said, and the way he said it sounded like a three-year-old child talking.

But he was a quick learner and it soon became easier for them to understand him and for him to know what they were talking about. The boys showed him the best places to fish and walked proudly with him over the hill and around the lake, and they learned English words from him and American songs that they had heard before from the depot.

He formed a special relationship with Mikkelína. Before long he had won her over entirely, and would carry her outside in good weather and test what she was capable of achieving. His approach was similar to her mother's: moving her arms and legs for her, supporting her while she walked, helping her with all kinds of exercises. One day he brought over an army doctor to look at

Mikkelína. The doctor shone a torch into her eyes and down her throat, moved her head round and felt her neck and down her spine. He had wooden blocks of different shapes with him, and made her fit them into matching holes. That took her no time at all. He was told that she had fallen ill at the age of three and understood what people said to her, but could barely speak a word herself. That she could read and that her mother was teaching her to write. The doctor nodded as if he understood, a meaningful expression on his face. He had a long talk with Dave after the examination and when he left Dave managed to make them understand that Mikkelína's mind was completely healthy. They already knew that. But then he said that, with time, the proper exercises and a lot of effort, Mikkelína would be able to walk unaided.

"Walk!" Her mother slumped onto her chair.

"And even speak normally," Dave added. "Perhaps. Has she never been to a doctor before?"

"All this is beyond me," she said sadly.

"She's okay," Dave said. "Just give her time."

Their mother had ceased to hear what he was saying.

"He's a terrible man," she said all of a sudden, and her children pricked up their ears, because they had never heard her talk about Grímur the way she did that day. "A terrible man," she continued. "A wretched little creature that doesn't deserve to live. I don't know why they're allowed to live. I don't understand. Why they're allowed to do what they please. What makes people like that? What is it that turns him into a monster? Why does he behave like an animal year after year, attacking his children and humiliating them, attacking me and beating me until I want to die and think about how to . . ."

She heaved a deep sigh and went to sit beside Mikkelína.

"It makes you feel ashamed for being the victim of a man like that, you disappear into total loneliness and bar everyone from entering your world, even your own children, because you don't want anyone to set foot in there, least of all them. And you sit bracing yourself for the next attack that comes out of the blue and is full of hatred for something or other, you don't know what, and you spend your whole life waiting for the next attack, when is it coming, how bad will it be, what's the reason, how can I avoid it? The more I do to please him, the more I repulse him. The more submissiveness and fear I show, the more he loathes me. And if I resist, all the more reason for him to beat the living daylights out of me. There's no way to do the right thing. None.

"Until all you think about is how to get it over with. It doesn't matter how. Just get it over with."

A deathly silence fell. Mikkelína lay motionless in her bed and the boys had inched closer to their mother. They listened, dumbstruck, to every word. Never before had she opened a window into the torment that she had grappled with for so long that she had forgotten everything else.

"It'll be okay," Dave said.

"I'll help you," Símon said in a serious voice.

She looked at him.

"I know, Símon," she said. "I always have known, my poor Símon."

The days went by and Dave devoted all his spare time to the family on the hill and spent longer and longer with the children's mother, either indoors or walking around Reynisvatn and over to Hafravatn. The boys wanted to see more of him, but he had stopped going fishing with them and had less time for Mikkelína. But they did not mind. They noticed the change in their mother, they associated it with Dave and were happy for her.

One beautiful autumn day, almost half a year after Grímur was marched away from the hill in the arms of the military police, Símon saw Dave and his mother in the distance, walking towards the house. They were walking close together and for all he could see they were holding hands. As they drew closer they stopped holding hands and moved apart, and Símon realised they did not want to be seen.

"What are you and Dave going to do?" Símon asked his mother one evening that autumn, after dusk had fallen on the hill. They sat in the kitchen. Tómas and Mikkelína were playing cards. Dave had spent the day with them then gone back to the depot. The question had been in the air all summer. The children had discussed it amongst themselves and imagined all kinds of situations that ended with Dave becoming a father to them and expelling Grímur from their sight for ever.

"What do you mean, do?" his mother said.

"When he comes back," Símon said, noticing that Mikkelína and Tómas had stopped playing cards and were now watching him.

"There's plenty of time to think about that," their mother said. "He won't be back for a while."

"But what are you going to do?" Mikkelína and Tómas turned their heads from Símon to their mother.

She looked at Símon, then at the other two.

"He's going to help us," she said.

"Who?" Símon said.

"Dave. He's going to help us."

"What's he going to do?" Símon looked at his mother, trying to work out what she meant. She looked him straight in the eye.

"Dave knows about that sort of person. He knows how to get rid of them."

"What's he going to do?" Símon repeated.

"Don't worry about it," his mother replied.

"Is he going to get rid of him for us?"

"Yes."

"How?"

"I don't know. The less we know, the better, he says, and I shouldn't even be telling you this. Maybe he'll talk to him. Scare him into leaving us alone. He says he has friends in the army who can help him if need be."

"But what if Dave leaves?"

"Leaves?"

"If he leaves Iceland," Símon said. "He won't always be here. He's a soldier. They're always sending troops away. Posting new ones to the barracks. What if he leaves? What will we do then?"

She looked at her son.

"We'll find a way," she said in a low voice. "We'll find a way then."

19

Sigurdur Óli phoned Erlendur, told him about his meeting with Elsa and how she thought that another man – who had got Benjamín's fiancée pregnant – was involved; his identity was unknown. They talked the matter over for a while and Erlendur told Sigurdur Óli what he had found out from the ex-serviceman, Ed Hunter, about the theft from the depot and how a family man from the hill had been arrested for his part in it. Ed believed that the man's wife had been the victim of domestic violence, which corroborated the account given by Höskuldur, who had heard it from Benjamín.

"All those people are dead and buried long ago," Sigurdur Óli said wearily. "I don't know why we're chasing them. It's like hunting ghosts. We'll never meet any of them and talk to them. They're all just part of a ghost story."

"Are you talking about the green woman on the hill?" Erlendur asked.

"Elínborg said Róbert had seen Sólveig's ghost wearing a green coat, so we're involved in a genuine ghost hunt."

"But don't you want to know who's in that grave with one hand sticking up in the air as if they were buried alive?"

"I've spent two days locked in a filthy cellar and I couldn't care less," Sigurdur Óli said. "Couldn't care less about all this old bollocks," he growled, and hung up.

As ever, Erlendur's mind was on Eva Lind, who was lying in intensive care and scarcely expected to live. He was deep in thought about the last argument they had had in his flat, two months before. It was still winter then, with heavy snow, dark and cold. He was not intending to argue with her. He hadn't planned to lose his temper. But she would not give an inch. Any more than usual.

"You can't do that to the baby," he said in yet another effort to persuade her. He assumed that she was five months pregnant. She had pulled herself together when she found out she was pregnant and, after two attempts, looked as though she would manage to kick her drug habit. He gave her all the support he could, but they both knew that it carried little weight and that their relationship was such that the less he involved himself, the more likely she was to succeed. Eva Lind had an ambivalent attitude towards her father. She sought his company, but found fault with everything about him.

"What do you know about that?" she said. "What do you know about children? Sure I can have my baby. And I'm going to have my baby by myself."

He did not know whether she was using drugs or alcohol or a combination of the two, but she was hardly in her right mind when he opened the door for her and let her in. She did not sit on his sofa, she fell onto it. Her belly protruded beneath the unzipped leather jacket, her pregnancy was becoming visible. She was only wearing a thin T-shirt underneath. Outside, the temperature was at least −10°C.

"I thought we'd ..."

"We haven't anything," she interrupted. "You and me. We haven't anything."

"I thought you'd decided to take care of your baby. Make sure nothing happened to it. Make sure the drugs didn't affect it. You were going to quit, but you're probably above that. You're probably above taking proper care of your child."

"Shut up."

"Why did you come here?"

"I don't know."

"It's your conscience. Isn't it? Your conscience is gnawing at you, and you expect my sympathy for the awful state you're in. That's why you come here. To get some pity and to feel better about yourself."

"Right on. This is just the place to come if you want a conscience, Saint Arsehole."

"You'd decided the name. You remember? If it's a girl."

"You decided it. Not me. You. Like always. You decide everything. If you want to leave then you just leave, don't give a shit about me or anyone else."

"She's supposed to be called Audur. You wanted that."

"Don't you think I know your game? Don't you think I can see through you? You're shit scared . . . I know what I've got in my stomach. I know it's a human being. I know that. You don't have to remind me. There's no need."

"Good," Erlendur said. "Sometimes you seem to forget. Forget there's not just you to think about any more. It's not just you getting stoned. When you get stoned your baby does too, and gets much more damaged by it than you."

He paused.

"Maybe it was a mistake," he said. "Not having an abortion."

She looked at him.

"Fuck you!"

"Eva . . . "

"Mum told me. I know exactly what you wanted."

"What?"

"And you can call her a cheap liar, but I know it's true."

"What are you talking about?"

"She said you'd deny it."

"Deny what?"

"That you didn't want me."

"What?"

"You didn't want me. When you got her pregnant."

"What did your mother say?"

"That you didn't want me."

"She's lying."

"You wanted her to have an abortion . . ."

"That's a lie . . ."

". . . then you pass judgment on me, no matter how I try. Always judging me."

"That's not true. That wasn't even considered. I don't know why she told you that, but it's not true. It wasn't an option. We never even mentioned it."

"She knew you'd say that. She warned me."

"Warned you? When did she tell you all this?"

"When she knew I was pregnant. She said you wanted to send her for an abortion and she said you'd deny it. She said you'd say everything that you've just said."

Eva Lind stood up and walked over towards the door.

"She's lying, Eva. Believe me. I don't know why she said that. I know she hates me, but surely not that much. She's manipulating you against me. You must see that. Saying that sort of thing is . . . is . . . it's repulsive. You can tell her that."

"Tell her yourself," Eva Lind shouted. "If you dare."

"It's repulsive to tell you that. Making up a story just to poison our relationship."

"Actually, I believe her."

"Eva . . ."

186

"Shut up."

"I'll tell you why it can't be true. Why I could never ..."

"I don't believe you!"

"Eva ... I had ..."

"Shut your gob. I don't believe a word you say."

"Then you ought to get out of here," he said.

"Yeah, right," she provoked him. "Get rid of me."

"Get out!"

"You're repulsive!" she shouted, and stormed out.

"Eva!" he called after her, but she was gone.

He neither heard from her nor saw her until his mobile rang when he was standing over the skeleton on the hill two months later.

Erlendur sat in his car, smoking and thinking that he should have reacted differently, swallowed his pride and tracked Eva down when his anger abated. Told her again that her mother was lying, he would never have suggested an abortion. Never could have. And not leave her to send him an SOS. She was simply not mature enough to go through all this, did not realise what she had got herself into and had no sense of her responsibility.

Erlendur feared breaking the news to her when she regained consciousness. If she regained consciousness. For the sake of doing something, he picked up the phone and called Skarphédinn.

"Just show a little patience," the archaeologist said, "and stop phoning me all the time. We'll let you know when we've got down to the bones."

Skarphédinn was acting as though he had taken over the investigation, he became more arrogant by the day.

"When will that be?"

"Difficult to say," he said, and Erlendur imagined his yellow teeth beneath his beard. "We'll just have to see. Leave us in peace to get on with the job."

"You must be able to tell me *something*. Was it a man? A woman?"

"Patience is the key to every puzzle . . ."

Erlendur hung up on him. He was lighting another cigarette when the phone rang. It was Jim from the British embassy. Ed and the US embassy had discovered a list with the names of Icelandic employees at the depot and Jim had just received it by fax. He had not found anything himself about Icelandic employees while the British ran the depot. There were nine names on the list and Jim read them to Erlendur over the phone. Erlendur did not recognise any of them and gave Jim the fax number at his office so that he could send it there.

He drove into Vogar and parked, as before, some distance from the basement that he had burst into in search of Eva Lind. He waited, wondering what it was that made men behave the way that this one did towards his wife and child, but the conclusion he reached was the usual one: they were bloody idiots. He couldn't articulate what he wanted to do with that man. Whether he intended anything more than spying on him from his car. He couldn't erase from his mind the memory of the little girl with cigarette burns on her back. The man denied having done anything to the child and the mother backed up his claim, so the authorities could do little else apart from take the child away from them. The man's case was with the Director of Public Prosecutions. Maybe he would be charged. Maybe not.

Erlendur pondered the options available to him. There weren't many, and all of them were bad. If the man had gone back to the flat the night he was looking for Eva Lind and the baby was sitting on the floor with burns on its back, Erlendur would have attacked the sadist. Several days had elapsed since then and he could not attack him out of the blue for what he had done. Could not go straight up and thump him, although that was what he most wanted to do. Erlendur knew he could not talk to him. Men like that laughed at threats. He would laugh in Erlendur's face.

Erlendur didn't see anyone entering or leaving the building for the two hours he sat in his car smoking.

In the end he gave up and drove to the hospital to see his daughter. Tried to forget all this, like so much else he had needed to forget in the past.

20

Elínborg got a call from Sigurdur Óli when she reached her office. He told her that Benjamín was probably not the father of the child his fiancée had been expecting, which brought their engagement to an end. Plus Sólveig's father had hanged himself after his daughter disappeared, and not before as her sister Bára had at first said.

Elínborg called in at the National Statistics Office and browsed through the death certificates before driving up to Grafarvogur. She didn't like being lied to, especially by condescending posh women.

Bára listened to Elínborg recount what Elsa had said about the unidentified father of Sólveig's child and she remained as stony faced as ever.

"Have you heard this before?" Elínborg asked.

"That my sister was a whore? No, I haven't heard that before and I don't understand why you're serving it up to me now. After all these years. I don't understand it. You ought to let my sister rest in peace. She doesn't deserve being gossiped about. Where did this . . . this Elsa woman get her story from?"

"From her mother," Elínborg said.

"And she heard it from Benjamín?"

"Yes. He didn't tell anyone about it until he was on his deathbed."

"Did you find a lock of her hair at his house?"

"We did, as it happens."

"And you'll send it for tests with the bones?"

"I expect so."

"So you think he killed her. That Benjamín, that weed, killed his fiancée. I think it's ridiculous. Absolutely ridiculous. It's beyond me how you can believe it."

Bára stopped talking and grew thoughtful.

"Will it be in the papers?" she asked.

"I have no idea," Elínborg said. "The bones have been given a lot of publicity."

"That my sister was murdered, I mean?"

"If that's the conclusion we come to. Do *you* know who could have been the father of her child?"

"Benjamín was the only one."

"Was there never mention of anyone else? Didn't your sister talk to you about any other man?"

Bára shook her head.

"My sister was not a tart."

Elínborg cleared her throat.

"You told me your father committed suicide some time before your sister disappeared."

They fleetingly looked each other in the eye.

"I think you should be leaving now," Bára said, standing up.

"I wasn't the one who started talking about your father. I checked his death certificate at the National Statistics Office. Unlike some people, the Statistics Office rarely tells lies."

"I have nothing more to say to you," Bára said, but without her earlier arrogance.

"I don't think you would have mentioned him unless you wanted to talk about him. Deep down inside."

"Bloody rubbish!" she spat out. "Are you playing the psychologist now?"

"He died six months after your sister went missing. His death certificate doesn't specify that he killed himself. No cause of death is given. Probably too posh to use the word suicide. Died suddenly at his home, it says."

Bára turned her back on Elínborg.

"Is there any chance that you could start telling me the truth?" Elínborg said, standing up as well. "What did your father have to do with it? Why did you mention him? Who got Sólveig pregnant? Was it him?"

She received no response. The silence between them was almost tangible. Elínborg looked around the spacious lounge, at all the beautiful articles, the paintings of her and her husband, the expensive furniture, the black pianoforte, a prominently placed photograph of Bára with the leader of the Progressive Party. What an empty life, she thought.

"Doesn't every family have its secrets?" Bára said eventually, her back still turned on Elínborg.

"I imagine so," Elínborg said.

"It wasn't my father," Bára said reluctantly. "I don't know why I lied to you about his death. It just slipped out. If you want to play the psychologist you can say that deep down inside I wanted to confess everything to you. That I'd kept silent for so long that when you started talking about Sólveig the floodgates opened. I don't know."

"Who was it then?"

"His nephew," Bára said. "His brother's son, from Fljót. It happened on one of her summer visits."

"How did your family find out?"

"She was completely different when she came back. Mum ... our mother noticed immediately, and of course it would have been impossible to conceal for long."

"Did she tell your mother what happened?"

"Yes. Our father went up north. I don't know any more about that. By the time he came back, the boy had been sent abroad. So the local people said. Grandfather ran a large farm. There were only two brothers. My father moved south here, set up a business and became wealthy. A pillar of society."

"What happened to the nephew?"

"Nothing. Sólveig said he'd had his way with her. Raped her. My parents didn't know what to do, they didn't want to press charges with all the legal fuss and gossip it would bring. The boy came back several years later and settled here in Reykjavík. Had a family. He died about 20 years ago."

"What about Sólveig and the baby?"

"Sólveig was ordered to have an abortion but she refused. Refused to get rid of the baby. Then one day she disappeared."

Bára turned round to face Elínborg.

"You could say it destroyed us, that summer trip to Fljót. Destroyed us as a family. It has certainly shaped my whole life. Covering up. Family pride. It was taboo. We could never mention it. My mother made sure of that. I know that she talked to Benjamín, later. Explained the matter to him. That made Sólveig's death nobody's business but her own. Sólveig's, that is. Her secret, her choice. We were all right. We were pure and respectable. She went mad and threw herself into the sea."

Elínborg looked at Bára and suddenly felt pity for the lie that she had been forced to live.

"She did it by herself," Bára went on. "Nothing to do with us. It was her business."

Elínborg nodded.

"She's not lying up there on the hill," Bára said. "She's lying on the bottom of the sea and she's been there for more than 60 terrible years."

Erlendur sat down beside Eva Lind after talking to her doctor, who said the same as before: her condition was unchanged, only time could tell the outcome. He sat at his daughter's bedside, wondering what to talk to her about this time, but could not make up his mind.

Time went by. The intensive care ward was quiet. Occasionally a doctor walked past the door, or a nurse in soft white shoes that squeaked against the linoleum.

That squeaking.

Erlendur watched his daughter and, almost automatically, started to talk to her in a low voice, telling her about a missing person that he had puzzled over for a long time and perhaps, even after all those years, had yet to understand fully.

He started telling her about a young boy who moved to Reykjavík with his parents, but always missed his countryside home. The boy was too young to understand why they had moved to the city, which at that time was not a city, but a large town by the sea. Later he realised that the decision was a combination of many factors.

His new home felt strange from the start. He had been brought up in simple rural life and isolation – with warm summers, harsh winters and tales about his family who had lived in the countryside all around, most of them crofters and desperately poor for centuries. Those people were his heroes. He heard about them in stories of everyday life that had been told for years and decades, accounts of hazardous journeys or disasters, or tales that were so hilarious that the storytellers would gasp for breath through their laughter or burst into fits of coughing that left them curled up, spluttering and shaking from sheer joy. All these stories were about people he had lived with and known, or those who had lived in the countryside, generation after generation: uncles and nieces, grandmothers and great-grand-mothers, grandfathers and great-grandfathers way back in time. He knew all these characters from stories, even those who were long dead and buried in the little cemetery beside the parish church: midwives who waded icy glacial rivers to help women in childbirth; farmers who heroically rescued their flocks in raging storms; farmhands who froze to death on their way to the sheepcote; drunken clergymen, ghosts and monsters; tales of lives that were part of his own life.

He brought all these tales with him when his parents moved to the city. They bought a wartime bathhouse built by the British military on the outskirts of the city, and converted it into a tiny house because that was all they could afford. Urban life did not suit his father, who had a weak heart and died not long after he moved. His mother sold the bathhouse, bought a cramped little basement flat not far from the harbour and worked in a fish factory. The son did not know what to do when he finished his compulsory schooling. Did manual labour. Building sites. Fishing boats. Saw a vacancy advertised with the police force.

He no longer heard any tales, and they became lost to him. All his people were gone, forgotten and buried in deserted rural areas. He, in turn, drifted through a city that he had no business being in. Knew that he was not the urban type. Could not really tell what he was. But he never lost his yearning for a different life, felt rootless and uncomfortable, and sensed how his last links with the past evaporated when his mother died.

He went to dancehalls. At one of them, Glaumbaer, he met a woman. He had known others, but never for more than casual meetings. This one was different, more steadfast, and he felt that she took control of him. Everything happened too quickly for him to grasp. She made demands of him which he fulfilled without any particular motivation and before he knew it, he had married her and they had a daughter. They rented a small flat. She had big plans for their future and talked about having more children and buying an apartment, quick and tense with a tone of expectation in her voice as if she saw her life on a safe track that nothing would ever overshadow. He looked at her and it dawned on him that he did not really know this woman at all.

They had another child and she became increasingly aware of how distant he was. When their baby son entered the world he was only moderately happy to be a father again and had already begun mentioning that he wanted to put an end to all this, he wanted to leave. She felt it. She asked whether there was another woman, but he just stared blankly without the question even registering. He had never contemplated it. "There must be another woman," she said. "It's not that," he said, and started to explain to her his feelings and his thoughts, but she did not want to hear. She had two children by him and he could not seriously be talking about leaving her. Them. His children.

His children. Eva Lind and Sindri Snaer. Pet names that she chose for them. He did not regard them as part of him. Lacked all paternal feeling, but recognised the responsibility he bore. His duty towards them, which had absolutely nothing to do with their mother or his relationship with her. He said he wanted to provide for the children and divorce amicably. She said there would be nothing amicable about it, as she picked up Eva Lind and clutched her. His impression was that she would use the children to keep hold of him, and that only strengthened the resolution that he could not live with this woman. It had all been one huge mistake from the outset and he should have acted long ago. He had no idea what he had been thinking all that time, but now it had to come to an end.

He tried to get her to agree to him having the children for part of the week or month, but she flatly refused and told him that he would never see them again if he left her. She would see to that.

And then he disappeared. Disappeared out of the life of the little girl of two who was in her nappy and holding a dummy as she watched him walk out of the door. A little, white dummy that squeaked when she bit it.

"We're going about this the wrong way," Erlendur said.

That squeaking.

He bowed his head. He thought the nurse was walking past the door again.

"I don't know what became of that man," Erlendur said in a barely audible voice, looking at his daughter's face, which was more peaceful than he had ever seen it. The outlines clearer. Looked at the equipment that was keeping her alive. Then looked back down at the floor.

A long time passed in this way until he stood up, bent over Eva Lind and kissed her on the forehead.

"He disappeared and I think he's still lost and has been for a long time, and I'm not certain he'll ever be found. It's not your fault. It happened before you came into the world. I think he's looking for himself, but he doesn't know why or exactly what he's searching for, and obviously he'll never find it."

Erlendur looked down at Eva Lind.

"Unless you help him."

Her face like a cold mask in the lamplight from the table next to her bed.

"I know you're searching for him and I know that if there's anyone who can find him, it's you."

He turned away from her, poised to leave, when he saw his ex-wife standing in the doorway. He did not know how long she had been standing there. Did not know how much she had heard of what he had told Eva Lind. She was wearing the same brown coat as before, on top of a jogging suit, but now she wore stilettos too, an outfit which made her look ridiculous. Erlendur had barely seen her for more than two decades, and he noticed how she had aged during that time, how her facial features had lost their sharpness, her cheeks fattened and a double chin started to form.

"That was a repulsive lie you told Eva Lind about the abortion." Erlendur seethed with rage.

"Leave me alone," Halldóra said. Her voice had aged too. Grown hoarse. Smoking too much. Too long.

"What other lies did you tell the kids?"

"Get out," she said, moving away from the door so that he could get past.

"Halldóra . . ."

"Get out," she repeated. "Just go and leave me in peace."

"We both wanted the children."

"Don't you regret it?" she said.

Erlendur didn't follow.

"Do you think they had any business coming into this world?"

"What happened?" Erlendur said. "What made you like this?"

"Get out," she said. "You're good at leaving. So leave! Leave me in peace with her."

Erlendur stared at her.

"Halldóra . . ."

"Leave, I said." She raised her voice. "Get out of here. This minute. Leave! I don't want you around! I never want to see you again!"

Erlendur walked past her and out of the room, and she closed the door behind him.

21

Sigurdur Óli finished searching the cellar that evening without discovering any more about Benjamín's tenants in the chalet on the hill. He did not care. He was relieved to escape from that task. Bergthóra was waiting for him when he got home. She had bought some red wine and was in the kitchen sipping it. Took out another glass and handed it to him.

"I'm not like Erlendur," Sigurdur Óli said. "Never say anything so nasty about me."

"But you want to be like him," Bergthóra said. She was cooking pasta and had lit candles in the dining room. A beautiful setting for an execution, Sigurdur Óli thought.

"All men want to be like him," Bergthóra said.

"Aei, why do you say that?"

"Left to their own devices."

"That's not right. You can't imagine what a pathetic life Erlendur leads."

"I need to work out our relationship at least," Bergthóra said, pouring wine into Sigurdur Óli's glass.

"Okay, let's work out our relationship." Sigurdur Óli had never met a more practical woman than Bergthóra. This conversation was not going to be about the love in their lives.

"We've been together now for, what, three or four years, and nothing's happening. Not a thing. You pull faces as soon as I start talking about anything that vaguely resembles commitment. We still have completely separate finances. A church wedding seems out of the question; I'm not clear about any other type. We're not registered as cohabiting. Having children is as remote to you as a distant galaxy. So I ask: What's left?"

There was no hint of anger in Bergthóra's words. So far, she was still only seeking to understand their relationship and where it was heading. Sigurdur Óli decided to capitalise on this before matters got out of hand. There had been ample time to ponder such questions over his drudgery in Benjamín's cellar.

"We're left," Sigurdur Óli said. "The two of us."

He found a CD, put it in the player and selected a track that had haunted him ever since Bergthóra started to pressurise him about commitment. Marianne Faithfull sang about Lucy Jordan, the housewife who, at the age of 37, dreamed of riding through Paris in a sports car with the cool wind in her hair.

"We've talked about it for long enough," Sigurdur Óli said.

"What?" Bergthóra said.

"Our trip."

"You mean to France?"

"Yes."

"Sigurdur . . ."

"Let's go to Paris and rent a sports car," Sigurdur Óli said.

Erlendur was trapped in a swirling, blinding blizzard. The snow pounded him and lashed his face, the cold and the darkness enveloped him. He battled against the storm, but he made no headway, so he turned his back to the wind and huddled up while the snow piled up against him. He knew he would die and there was nothing he could do about it.

The telephone started to ring and kept on, penetrating the blizzard, until suddenly the weather cleared, the howling storm fell silent and he woke up at home in his chair. On his desk, the telephone rang with increasing intensity, showing him no mercy.

Stiffly he got to his feet and was poised to answer when the ringing stopped. He stood over the telephone, waiting for it to start again, but nothing happened. The telephone was too old to have a caller ID, so Erlendur had no idea who could be trying to contact him. Imagined it was a cold caller trying to sell him a vacuum cleaner with a toaster thrown in for good measure. He silently thanked the telesales person for bringing him in from the blizzard.

He went into the kitchen. It was eight in the evening. He tried to shut the bright spring evening out with the curtains, but it forced its way past them in places, dust-filled sunbeams that lit up the gloom in his flat. Spring and summer were not Erlendur's seasons. Too bright. Too frivolous. He wanted heavy, dark winters. Finding nothing edible in the kitchen, he sat down at the table with his chin resting in his hand.

He was still dazed from sleeping. After returning from a visit to Eva Lind at the hospital at around six, he sat down in the chair, fell asleep and dozed until eight. He thought about the blizzard from his dream and how he turned his back on it, waiting for death. He had often dreamed this dream, in different versions. Yet there was always the unrelenting, freezing blizzard that pierced him to the bone. He knew how the dream would have continued if his sleep had not been broken by the telephone.

The ringing began again and Erlendur wondered whether to ignore it. Eventually he lounged out of the chair, went into the sitting room and picked up the receiver.

"Yes, Erlendur?"

"Yes," Erlendur said, clearing his throat. He recognised the voice at once.

"Jim from the British embassy here. Forgive me for calling you at home."

"Did you ring just now?"

"Just now? No. Only this time. Well, I just spoke to Ed and I thought I needed to get in touch with you."

"Really, is there anything new?"

"He's working on the case for you and I just wanted to keep you in the picture. He's phoned America, looked through his diary and talked to people, and he thinks he knows who blew the whistle on the theft from the depot."

"Who was it?"

"He didn't say. Asked me to let you know and said he was expecting your call."

"This evening?"

"Yes, no, or in the morning. Tomorrow morning might be better. He was off to sleep. Goes to bed early."

"Was it an Icelander? Who grassed on them?"

"He'll tell you about it. Good night, and my apologies for disturbing you."

Erlendur was still standing by the phone when it started ringing again. It was Skarphédinn. He was on the hill.

"We'll uncover the bones tomorrow," Skarphédinn said without any preamble.

"About time too," Erlendur said. "Did you call me just now?"

"Yes, did you just get in?"

"Yes," Erlendur lied. "Have you found anything useful up there?"

"No, nothing, I just wanted to tell you that . . . good evening,

evening, ehmm, let me help you, there you go ... er, sorry, where were we?"

"You were telling me that you'll reach the bones tomorrow."

"Yes, some time towards evening, I expect. We haven't uncovered any clues as to how the body ended up being buried. Maybe we'll find something under the bones."

"See you tomorrow, then."

"Goodbye."

Erlendur put the phone down. He was not fully awake. He thought about Eva Lind and whether any of what he said got through to her. And he thought about Halldóra and the hatred she still felt for him after all those years. And he contemplated for the millionth time what his life and their lives would have been like had he not decided to leave. He never came to any conclusion.

He stared at nothing in particular. An occasional ray of evening sun broke past the sitting-room curtains, slashing a bright wound into the gloom around him. He looked into the curtains. They were made of thick corduroy, hanging right down to the floor. Thick, green curtains to keep the brightness of spring at bay.

Good evening.

Evening.

Let me help you.

Erlendur peered into the green of the curtains.

Crooked.

Green.

"What was Skarphédinn ... ?" Erlendur leaped to his feet and snatched up the phone. Not remembering Skarphédinn's mobile number, he desperately called directory enquiries. Then he rang the archaeologist.

"Skarphédinn. Skarphédinn?" He blared down the phone.

"What? Is that you again?"

"Who did you say good evening to just then? Who were you helping?"

"Eh?"

"Who were you talking to?"

"What are you so worked up about?"

"Who's there with you?"

"You mean who I said hello to?"

"This isn't a videophone. I can't see you up there on the hill. I heard you say good evening to someone. Who's there with you?"

"Not with me. She went somewhere, wait, she's standing by the bush."

"The bush? You mean the redcurrant bushes? Is she by the redcurrant bushes?"

"Yes."

"What does she look like?"

"She's . . . do you know her then? What's all this panic about?"

"What does she look like?" Erlendur repeated, trying to keep calm.

"Take it easy."

"How old is she?"

"Seventyish. No, maybe more like 80. Difficult to say."

"What's she wearing?"

"She's got on a long green coat, ankle-length. A lady of about my height. And she's lame."

"In what way, lame?"

"She's limping. More than that really. She's sort of, I don't know . . ."

"What?! What! What are you trying to say?"

"I don't know how to describe it . . . I . . . it's like she's crooked."

Erlendur threw down the phone and ran out into the spring evening, forgetting to tell Skarphédinn to keep the lady on the hill there with him at all costs.

*

The day that Grímur returned home, Dave had not been with them for several days.

Autumn had arrived with a piercing north wind and a thin blanket of snow on the ground. The hill stood high above sea level and winter came earlier there than in the lowland, where Reykjavík was beginning to take on some kind of urban shape. Símon and Tómas took the school bus to Reykjavík in the mornings and came back in the evening. Every day their mother walked to Gufunes, where she tended the milk cows and did other routine farm work. She left before the boys, but was always back when they returned from school. Mikkelína stayed at home during the day, excruciatingly bored by her solitude. When her mother came home from work Mikkelína could hardly control herself for glee, and her delight was all the greater when Símon and Tómas burst in and threw their school books into one corner.

Dave was a regular visitor to their home. Their mother and Dave found it increasingly easy to understand each other, and they sat at length at the kitchen table, wanting the boys and Mikkelína to leave them in peace. Occasionally, when they wanted to be left entirely to themselves, they went into the bedroom and closed the door.

Símon sometimes saw Dave stroke his mother's cheek or sweep back a lock of hair if one fell across her face. Or he stroked her hand. They went on long walks around Reynisvatn and up the surrounding hills, and some days even strolled over to Mosfellsdalur and Helgufoss, taking food with them because such an outing could last a whole day. Sometimes they took the children along and Dave carried Mikkelína on his back without the slightest effort. Símon and Tómas were amused that he called their outings a "picnic", and they clucked the word at each other: pic-nic, pic-nic, pic-nic.

Sometimes Dave and their mother sat talking seriously, on their picnics or at the kitchen table, and in the bedroom once when Símon opened the door. They were sitting on the edge of the bed, Dave was holding her hand and they looked over to the door and gave Símon a smile. He did not know what they were talking about, but he knew it could not be pleasant, because he recognised his mother's expression when she felt bad.

And then, one cold autumn day, it all ended.

Grímur came home early one morning when their mother had gone to the farm and Símon and Tómas were on their way to take the school bus. It was piercing cold on the hill and they met Grímur as he walked up the track to the house, clutching his tattered jacket close to him to fend off the north wind. He ignored them. They could not see his face clearly in the dim autumn morning, but Símon imagined he wore a hard, cold expression as he headed towards their house. The boys had been expecting him for the past few days. Their mother had told them he would be released from prison after serving his sentence and would come back to the hill to them; they could expect him at any time.

Símon and Tómas watched Grímur walk up to the house, and looked at each other. Both were thinking the same thing. Mikkelína was home alone. She always woke up when they and their mother got up, but went back to sleep for much of the morning. She would be alone to greet Grímur. Símon tried to calculate their father's reaction when he discovered that their mother was not at home, nor the boys, only Mikkelína, whom he had always hated.

The school bus arrived and beeped twice. Although the driver saw the boys on the hill, when he could not wait for them any longer he drove away and the bus disappeared down the road. They stood motionless, not saying a word, then set off slowly and inched their way towards the house.

They did not want to leave Mikkelína at home by herself.

Símon contemplated running after his mother or sending Tómas to fetch her, but told himself that there was no hurry for them to meet again; their mother could have this last day of peace. The boys saw Grímur enter the house and close the door behind him, and they broke into a run. They did not know what to expect inside the house. All they thought about was Mikkelína asleep in the double bed where she must not be found under any circumstances.

Cautiously opening the door, they crept inside: Símon leading the way but Tómas close behind, holding his hand. When they went into the kitchen they saw Grímur standing at the worktop. He had his back turned to them. Sniffed and spat into the sink. He had turned on the light over the table and they could see only his outline beyond it.

"Where's your mother?" he said, his back still turned.

Símon thought that he had noticed them on the way up the hill after all and heard them enter the house.

"She's working," Símon said.

"Working? Where's she working?" Grímur said.

"At Gufunes dairy," Símon said.

"Didn't she know I was coming today?" Grímur turned round to face them and stepped into the light. The brothers stared at him as he emerged from the darkness and their eyes turned like saucers when they saw his face in the dull glow. Something had happened to Grímur. Along one of his cheeks, a burn mark stretched all the way up to his eye, which was half closed because his eyelid had fused with the skin.

Grímur smiled.

"Doesn't Dad look pretty?"

The brothers stared at his disfigured face.

"First they make you coffee, then they throw it in your face."

He moved closer to them.

"Not because they want you to confess. They know it all already because someone's told them. That's not why they throw boiling coffee over you. That's not why they destroy your face."

The boys did not understand what was going on.

"Fetch your mother," Grímur ordered, looking at Tómas, who was cowering behind his brother. "Go to that fucking cow shop and bring the cow back."

Out of the corner of his eye Símon saw a movement in the bedroom, but he did not dare for the life of him to look inside. Mikkelína was up and about. She was able to stand on one leg and could move about if she supported herself, but she did not risk going into the kitchen.

"Out!" Grímur shouted. "Now!"

Tómas jumped. Símon was uncertain that his brother would find the way. Tómas had been to the farm with his mother once or twice in the summer, but it was darker and colder outside now and Tómas was still very much a child.

"I'll go," Símon said.

"You're not bloody going anywhere," Grímur snarled. "Piss off!" he shouted at Tómas, who staggered away from behind Símon, opened the door into the cold air and closed it carefully behind him.

"Come on, Símon my boy, come and sit down with me," Grímur said, his rage seeming suddenly to have vanished.

Símon fumbled his way into the kitchen and sat on a chair. He saw a movement in the bedroom again. He hoped Mikkelína would not come out. There was a pantry in the passageway and he thought that she could sneak in there without Grímur noticing her.

"Didn't you miss your old dad?" Grímur said, sitting down facing him. Símon couldn't take his eyes off the burn on his face. He nodded.

"What have you all been up to this summer?" Grímur asked, and Símon stared at him without saying a word. He did not know where to start telling lies. He could not tell him about Dave, about the visits and mysterious meetings with his mother, the trips, the picnics. He could not say that they all slept in the big bed together, always. He could not say how his mother had become a completely different person since Grímur left, which was all thanks to Dave. Dave had brought back her zest for life. He could not tell him how she made herself look pretty in the mornings. Her changed appearance. How her expression grew more beautiful each day that she spent with Dave.

"What, nothing?" Grímur said. "Hasn't anything happened the whole summer?"

"The ... the ... weather was great," Símon whimpered, his eyes glued to the burn.

"Great weather. The weather was great," Grímur said. "And you've been playing here and by the barracks. Do you know anyone from the barracks?"

"No," Símon blurted out. "No-one."

Grímur smiled.

"You've learned to tell lies this summer. Amazing how quickly people learn to tell lies. Did you learn to tell lies this summer, Símon?"

Símon's lower lip was beginning to tremble. It was a reflex beyond his control.

"Just one," he said. "But I don't know him well."

"You know one. Well, well. You should never tell lies, Símon. People like you who tell lies just end up in trouble and can get others into trouble too."

"Yes," Símon said, hoping this would soon come to an end. He hoped that Mikkelína would come out and disturb them. Wondered

209

whether to tell Grímur that Mikkelína was in the passage and had slept in his bed.

"Who do you know from the barracks?" Grímur said, and Símon could feel himself sinking deeper and deeper into the swamp.

"Just one," he said.

"Just one," Grímur repeated, stroking his cheek and lightly scratching the burn with his index finger. "Who's this one? I'm glad there's not more than one."

"I don't know. He sometimes goes fishing in the lake. Sometimes he gives us trout that he catches."

"And he's good to you kids?"

"I don't know," Símon said, well aware that Dave was the best man he had ever met. Compared with Grímur, Dave was an angel sent from heaven to save their mother. Where was Dave? Símon thought. If only Dave were here. He thought about Tómas out in the cold on his way to Gufunes, and about their mother who did not even know that Grímur was back on the hill. And he thought about Mikkelína in the passage.

"Does he come here often?"

"No, just every now and again."

"Did he come here before I was put in the nick? When you're put in the nick, Símon, it means you're put in the nick. It doesn't have to mean you're guilty of anything bad if you go prison, just that someone put you there. In the nick. And it didn't take them long. They talked a lot about making an example. The Icelanders mustn't steal from the army. Awful business. So they had to sentence me, hard and fast. So no-one else would copy me and go stealing too. You get it? Everyone was supposed to learn from my mistakes. But they all steal. They all do it, and they're all making money. Did he come here before I was put in the nick?"

"Who?"

"That soldier. Did he come here before I was put in the nick? That one."

"He used to fish in the lake sometimes before you went away."

"And he gave your mother the trout he caught?"

"Yes."

"Did he catch a lot of trout?"

"Sometimes. But he wasn't a good fisherman. He just sat down by the lake, smoking. You catch a lot more than he did. With your nets too. You always catch so much with your nets."

"And when you gave your mother the trout, did he stop by? Did he come in for coffee? Did he sit down at this table?"

"No," Símon said, unable to decide whether the lie he was telling was too obvious. He was scared and confused, he kept his finger pressed against his lip to stop it trembling, and tried to answer the way he thought Grímur wanted him to, but without incriminating his mother if he said something Grímur was not supposed to know. Símon was discovering a new side to Grímur. His father had never talked to him so much before and it caught him off his guard. Símon was floundering. He was not sure exactly what Grímur was not supposed to know, but he tried his utmost to safeguard his mother.

"Didn't he ever come in here?" Grímur said, and his voice transposed from soft and cunning to strict and firm.

"Just twice, something like that."

"And what did he do then?"

"Just came in."

"Oh, it's like that. Have you started telling lies again? Are you lying to me again? I come back here after months of being treated like shit and all I get to hear are lies. Are you going to tell me lies again?"

His questions lashed Símon's face like a whip.

"What did you do in prison?" Símon asked hesitantly in the weak hope of being able to talk about something other than Dave and his

211

mother. Why didn't Dave come? Didn't they know that Grímur was out of prison? Hadn't they discussed this at their secret meetings when Dave stroked her hand and tidied up her hair?

"In prison?" Grímur said, changing his voice to soft and cunning again. "I listened to stories in prison. All sorts of stories. You hear so much and want to hear so much because no-one comes to visit you and the only news you get from home is what you hear there, because they're always sending people to prison and you get to know the wardens who tell you a thing or two as well. And you have loads and loads of time to think about all those stories."

A floorboard creaked inside the passageway and Grímur paused, then went on as if nothing had happened.

"Of course, you're so young ... wait, how old are you anyway, Símon?"

"I'm 14, I'll be 15 soon."

"You're almost an adult, so maybe you understand what I'm talking about. Everyone hears about how all the Icelandic girls just throw their legs over the soldiers. It's like they lose control of themselves when they see a man in uniform, and you hear about what gentlemen the soldiers are and how they open doors for them and they're polite and want to dance and never get drunk and have cigarettes and coffee and all sorts of things and come from places that all the girls want to go to. And us, Símon, we're crummy. Just yokels, Símon, that the girls won't even look at. That's why I want to know a bit more about this soldier who goes fishing in the lake, Símon, because you've disappointed me."

Símon looked at Grímur and all the strength seemed to sap from his body.

"I've heard so much about that soldier on the hill here and you've never heard of him. Unless of course you're lying to me, and I don't think that's very nice, lying to your dad when a soldier comes here every day and goes out for walks with your dad's wife all summer. You don't know anything about it?"

Símon said nothing.

"You don't know anything about it?" Grímur repeated.

"They sometimes went for walks," Símon said, tears welling in his eyes.

"See," Grímur said. "I knew we were still friends. Did you go with them maybe?"

It seemed that this would never end. Grímur looked at him with his burnt face and one eye half closed. Símon felt he could not hold back much longer.

"We sometimes went to the lake and he took a picnic. Like you sometimes brought in those cans you open with a key."

"And did he kiss your mother? Down by the lake?"

"No," Símon said, relieved at not having to answer with a lie. He had never seen Dave and his mother kissing.

"What were they doing then? Holding hands? And what were you doing? Why did you let that man take your mother for walks down by the lake? Didn't it ever occur to you that I might object? Didn't that ever occur to you?"

"No," Símon said.

"No-one was thinking about me on those walks. Were they?"

"No," Símon said.

Grímur leaned forward under the light and his burning red scar stood out even more.

"And what's the name of this man who steals other people's families and thinks that's okay and no-one does a thing about it?"

Símon did not answer him.

"The one who threw the coffee, Símon, the one who made my face like this, do you know his name?"

"No," Símon said in a barely audible voice.

"He attacked me and burned me, but they never put him in the nick for that. What do you reckon to that? Like they're holy, all those soldiers. Do you think they're holy?"

"No," Símon said.

"Has your mother got fatter this summer?" Grímur asked as if a new idea had suddenly entered his head. "Not because she's a cow from the dairy, Símon, but because she's been going for walks with soldiers from the barracks. Do you think she's got fatter this summer?"

"No," he said.

"I think it's likely though. We'll find out later. This man who threw the coffee over me. Do you know his name?"

"No," Símon said.

"He had some strange idea, I don't know where he got it from, that I wasn't treating your mother properly. That I did nasty things to her. You know I've had to teach her to behave sometimes. He knew about it, but he didn't understand why. Couldn't understand that tarts like your mother need to know who's in charge, who they're married to and how they ought to behave. He couldn't understand you have to push them around a bit sometimes. He was really angry when he was talking to me. I know a bit of English because I've had some good friends at the barracks and I understood most of what he was saying, and he was very angry with me about your mother."

Símon's eyes were transfixed on the scald.

"This man, Símon, his name's Dave. I don't want you to lie to me: the soldier who was so kind to your mother, has been ever since the spring and all summer and well into the autumn, could his name be Dave?"

Símon racked his brains, still staring at the burn.

"They're going to sort him out," Grímur said.

"Sort him out?" Símon didn't know what Grímur meant, but it couldn't be nice.

"Is the rat in the passage?" Grímur said, nodding towards the door.

"What?" Símon did not catch on to what he was talking about.

"The moron? Do you think it's listening to us?"

"I don't know about Mikkelína," Símon said. That was some kind of truth.

"Is his name Dave, Símon?"

"It might be," Símon said tentatively.

"It might be? You're not sure. What does he call you, Símon? When he talks to you, or maybe he cuddles you and strokes you, what does he call you then?"

"He never strokes . . ."

"What's his name?"

"Dave!" Símon said.

"Dave! Thank you, Símon."

Grímur leaned back and moved out of the light. He lowered his voice.

"You see, I heard he was fucking your mum."

At that moment the door opened and the children's mother came in with Tómas following behind her, and the cold gust of wind that accompanied them sent a chill running down Símon's sweating back.

22

Erlendur was at the hill 15 minutes after talking to Skarphédinn.

He did not have his mobile with him. Otherwise he would have called Skarphédinn and told him to keep the woman waiting until he arrived. He felt sure it had to be the lady that Róbert had seen by the redcurrant bushes, the crooked lady in green.

The traffic on Miklabraut was light and he drove up the slope on Ártúnsbrekka as fast as his car could manage, then along the road out of Reykjavík where he took a right turn for Grafarholt. Skarphédinn was about to drive away from the excavation site, but stopped. Erlendur got out of his car and the archaeologist wound down his window.

"What, so you're here? Why did you slam the phone down on me? Is something wrong? What are you looking at me like that for?"

"Is the woman still here?" Erlendur asked.

"What woman?"

Erlendur looked in the direction of the bushes and thought he saw a movement.

"Is that her?" he asked, squinting. He could not see well from that distance. "The lady in green. Is she still there?"

"Yes, she's over there," Skarphédinn said. "What's going on?"

"I'll tell you later," Erlendur said, walking off.

The redcurrant bushes came into focus as he approached them and the green figure took shape. As if expecting the woman to disappear at any moment, he quickened his pace. She was standing by the leafless bushes, holding one branch and looking over towards Mount Esja, apparently deep in thought.

"Good evening," Erlendur said when he was within earshot of her.

The woman turned round.

"Good evening," she said.

"Nice weather tonight," Erlendur said for the sake of saying something.

"Spring was always the best time up here on the hill," the lady said. She had to make an effort to speak. Her head dangled, and Erlendur could tell that she had to concentrate hard on every word. They did not come of their own accord. One of her arms was hidden inside her sleeve. He could see that she had a club foot protruding from her long, green coat, and her shoulder-length hair was thick and grey. Her face was friendly but sorrowful. Erlendur noticed that her head moved gently on reflex, with regular spasms. It never seemed to stay completely still.

"Are you from these parts?" Erlendur asked.

"And now the city's spread all the way out here," she said without answering him. "You never would have expected that."

"Yes, this city crawls everywhere," Erlendur said.

"Are you investigating those bones?" she suddenly said.

"I am," Erlendur said.

"I saw you on the news. I come up here sometimes, especially in spring. Like now, in the evenings when everything's quiet and we still have this lovely spring light."

"It's beautiful up here," Erlendur said. "Are you from here, or somewhere nearby maybe?"

"Actually, I was on my way to see you," the lady said, still not answering him. "I was going to contact you tomorrow. But it's good that you found me. It's about time."

"About time?"

"That the story came out."

"What story?"

"We used to live here, by these bushes. The chalet's long gone now. I don't know what happened to it. It just gradually fell apart. My mother planted the redcurrant bushes and made jam in the autumn, but she didn't want them only for jam. She wanted a hedge for shelter where she could grow vegetables and nice flowers facing south at the sun, wanted to use the chalet to block off the north wind. He wouldn't let her. It was the same as with everything else."

She looked at Erlendur, her head jerking as she spoke.

"They used to carry me out here when the sun shone," she smiled. "My brothers. There was nothing I loved more than to sit outside in the sunshine, and I used to squeal with joy when I came out into the garden. And we played games. They were always inventing new games to play with me, because I couldn't move much. Due to my disability, which was much worse in those days. They tried to include me in everything they did. That they got from their mother. Both the brothers, at first."

"What did they get from her?"

"Kindness."

"An old man told us about a lady in green who sometimes comes here to tend the bushes. His description fits you. We thought it might be someone from the chalet that was here once."

"You know about the chalet."

"Yes, and some of the tenants, but not all. We think a family of five lived here during the war, possibly the victims of violence from the father. You mentioned your mother and both brothers, two of them, and if you're the third child in the family, that fits the information we have."

"Did he talk about a lady in green?" she smiled.

"Yes. The lady in green."

"Green's my colour. Always has been. For as long as I can remember."

"Don't they say that people who like green are down-to-earth types?"

"That could be true," she smiled. "I'm terribly down-to-earth."

"Do you know of this family?"

"We lived in the house that was here."

"Domestic violence?"

She looked at Erlendur.

"Yes, domestic violence."

"It would have been . . ."

"What's your name?" she interrupted Erlendur.

"My name's Erlendur," he said.

"Do you have a family?"

"No, yes, well, a kind of family, I think."

"You're not sure. Do you treat your family well?"

"I think . . ." Erlendur hesitated. He had not anticipated being questioned and did not know what to say. Had he treated his family well? Hardly, he thought to himself.

"Maybe you're divorced," the woman said, looking at Erlendur's tatty clothes.

"As it happens, I am," he said. "I was going to ask you . . . I think I was asking you about domestic violence."

"Such a convenient term for soul murder. Such a harmless term for people who don't know what lies behind it. Do you know what it's like, living in constant fear your whole life?"

Erlendur said nothing.

"Living with hatred every single day, it never stops no matter what you do, and you can never do anything to change it, until you lose your independent will and just wait and hope that the next beating won't be as bad as the one before."

Erlendur did not know what to say.

"Gradually the beatings turn into sadism, because the only power that the violent man has in the world is his power over the one woman who is his wife, and that power is absolute because he knows she can do nothing. She is totally helpless and totally dependent on him because he doesn't just threaten her, doesn't torment her only with his hatred and anger for her, but with his loathing for her children too, and makes it clear that he'll harm them if she tries to break free from his power. All the physical violence, all the pain and the beatings, the broken bones, the wounds, the bruises, the black eyes, the split lips – they're nothing compared to the mental torment. Constant fear that never goes away. For the first years, when she still shows some sign of life, she tries to find help and she tries to flee, but he catches her and whispers to her that he'll kill her daughter and bury her on the mountainside. And she knows he's capable of that, so she gives up. Gives up and commits her life into his hands."

The woman looked over towards Esja and to the west, where the outline of Snaefellsnesjökull glacier could be seen.

"And her life becomes a mere shadow of his life," she continued. "Her resistance ebbs and with it her will to live, her life becomes his life and she is no longer alive, she's dead, and she goes around like a creature of darkness in an endless search for a way out. A way out from the beatings and the torment and his life, because she no longer lives her own life, but only exists as the object of his hatred.

"In the end he destroys her. And she's all but dead. One of the living dead."

She became silent and stroked her hand across the bare branches of the bushes.

"Until that spring. During the war."

Erlendur said nothing.

"Who passes sentence on anyone for soul murder?" she went on. "Can you tell me that? How can you charge a man for soul murder, take him to court and have him sentenced?"

"I don't know," Erlendur said, not altogether following.

"Have you got down to the bones?" she asked, almost as if her mind was elsewhere.

"We will tomorrow," Erlendur replied. "Do you know anything about who's buried there?"

"She turned out to be like these bushes," the woman said faintly.

"Who?"

"Like the redcurrant bushes. They don't need tending to. They're particularly hardy, they withstand all kinds of weather and the harshest winters, but they're always green and beautiful again in the summer, and the berries they produce are just as red and juicy as if nothing had ever happened. As if winter had never come."

"Pardon me, but what's your name?" Erlendur asked.

"The soldier brought her back to life."

The woman stopped talking and stared into the bushes as if transported to a different place and a different time.

"Who are you?" Erlendur asked.

"Mum loved green. She said green was the colour of hope."

She snapped out of her trance.

"My name's Mikkelína," she said. Then she seemed to falter. "He was a monster," she said. "Full of uncontrollable hatred and rage."

23

It was approaching 10 p.m., the temperature was dropping on the hill and Erlendur asked Mikkelína whether they ought not to get in his car. Or they could talk some more tomorrow. It was late and . . .

"Let's get in your car," she said, and set off. She moved slowly and lurched to one side with every step that she took with her club foot. Erlendur walked just ahead of her and showed her to his car, opened the door and helped her in. Then he walked round the front of the car. He couldn't work out how Mikkelína had got to the hill. She didn't seem to have driven.

"Did you take a taxi here?" he asked as he sat down behind the wheel. He started the engine, which was still hot, and they soon warmed up.

"Símon gave me a lift," she said. "He'll be back to collect me soon."

"We've tried to gather information about the people who lived on the hill – I presume it's your family – and some of what we've heard, mostly from old people, sounds strange. One story is about the Gasworks by Hlemmur."

"He teased her about the Gasworks," Mikkelína said, "but I don't think she was the product of some doomsday orgy there as he said. It could just as easily have been him. I think that insult was levelled at him once, he might even have been teased about it, maybe when he was younger, maybe later, and he transferred it to her."

"So you think your father was one of the Gasworks kids?"

"He wasn't my father," Mikkelína said. "My father was lost at sea. He was a fisherman and my mother loved him. That was my only consolation in life when I was a child. That he was not my father. He hated me in particular. The cripple. Because of my condition. I had an illness at the age of three that left me paralysed and I lost my power of speech. He thought I was retarded, but my mind was normal. I never had any therapy, which people take for granted nowadays. And I never told anyone, because I lived forever in fear of that man. It's not unusual for children who experience a trauma to become reticent and even dumb. I presume that happened to me. It wasn't until later that I learned to walk and started talking and got an education. I've got a degree now. In psychology."

She paused.

"I've found out who his parents were," she went on. "I've searched. To understand what happened and why. I tried to dig up something about his childhood. He worked as a farmhand here and there, the last place was in Kjós around the time he met Mum. The part of his upbringing that interests me most was in Mýrarsýsla, at a little croft called Melur. It doesn't exist any more. The couple who lived there had three children of their own and the parish council paid them to take others into their home. There were still paupers in the countryside at that time. The couple had a reputation for treating the poor children badly. People on neighbouring farms talked about it. His foster parents were taken to court after a child in their care died from malnutrition and neglect. An autopsy was performed on the farm under very primitive conditions, even by the standards of the time. It was a boy of eight. They took a door off its hinges and conducted the autopsy on that. Rinsed his innards in the brook on the farm. Discovered he was subjected to 'unnecessarily harsh treatment', as they used to call it, but they couldn't prove that he'd died from it. He would have seen it all. Perhaps they were friends. He was in care at Melur around the same time. He's mentioned in the case documents: undernourished with injuries on his back and legs."

She paused.

"I'm not trying to justify what he did to us and the way he treated us," she said. "There's no justification for that. But I wanted to know who he was."

She stopped again.

"And your mother?" Erlendur asked, though he sensed that Mikkelína intended to tell him everything she considered important and would go about it her own way. He did not want to put pressure on her. She had to tell the story at her own pace.

"She was unlucky," Mikkelína said forthrightly, as if this was the only sensible conclusion to draw. "She was unlucky to end up with that man. It's as simple as that. She had no family, but by and large she had a decent upbringing in Reykjavík and was a maid in a respectable household when she met him. I haven't managed to find out who her parents were. If it ever was written down, the papers are lost."

Mikkelína looked at Erlendur.

"But she found true love before it was too late. He entered her life at the right moment, I think."

"Who? Who entered her life?"

"And Símon. My brother. We didn't realise how he felt. The strain he was under for all those years. I felt the treatment that my stepfather dished out to my mother and I suffered for her, but I was tougher than Símon. Poor, poor Símon. And then Tómas. There was too much of his father in him. Too much hatred."

"Sorry, you've lost me. Who entered your mother's life?"

"He was from New York. An American. From Brooklyn."

Erlendur nodded.

"Mum needed love, some kind of love, admiration, recognition that she existed, that she was a human being. Dave restored her self-respect, made her human again. We always used to wonder why he spent so much time with Mum. What he saw in her when no-one else would even look at her apart from my stepfather, and then only to beat her up. Then he told Mum why he wanted to help her. He said he sensed it the moment he saw her the first time he brought over some trout; he used to go fishing in Reynisvatn. He recognised all the signs of domestic violence. He could see it in her eyes, in her face, her movements. In an instant he knew her entire history."

Mikkelína paused and looked across the hill to the bushes.

"Dave was familiar with it. He was brought up with it just like Símon, Tómas and me. His father was never charged and never sentenced, and never punished for beating his wife until her dying day. They lived in awful poverty, she contracted TB and died. His father beat her up just before she passed away. Dave was a teenager then, but he was no match for his father. He left home the day of his mother's death and never went back. Joined the army a few years later. Before the war broke out. They sent him to Reykjavík during the war, up here where he walked inside a shack and saw his mother's face again."

They sat in silence.

"By then he was big enough to do something about it," Mikkelína said.

A car drove slowly past them and stopped by the foundations of the house. The driver stepped out and looked around towards the redcurrant bushes.

"Símon's come to fetch me," Mikkelína said. "It's late. Do you mind if we continue tomorrow? You can call on me at home if you want."

She opened the car door and called out to the man, who turned round.

"Do you know who's buried there?" Erlendur asked.

"Tomorrow," Mikkelína said. "We'll talk tomorrow. There's no rush," she said. "No rush about anything."

The man had walked over to the car by now to help Mikkelína.

"Thank you, Símon," she said and got out of the car. Erlendur stretched over the seat to take a better look at him. Then he opened his door and got out.

"That can't be Símon," he said to Mikkelína, looking at the man who was supporting her. He could not have been older than 35.

"What?" Mikkelína said.

"Wasn't Símon your brother?" Erlendur asked, looking at the man.

"Yes," Mikkelína said, then seemed to understand Erlendur's bewilderment. "Oh, he's not that Símon," she said with a smile. "This is my son, whom I named after him."

24

The next morning Erlendur held a meeting with Elínborg and Sigurdur Óli at his office, told them about Mikkelína and what she had said, and that he would meet her again later that day. He was certain she would tell him who was buried on the hill, who had put him there and why. Then the bones would be excavated towards evening.

"Why didn't you get it out of her yesterday?" asked Sigurdur Óli, who had woken replenished after a quiet evening with Bergthóra. They had discussed the future, including children, and agreed about the best arrangement for everything; likewise the trip to Paris and the sports car they would rent.

"Then we can stop this fucking around," he added. "I'm fed up with these bones. Fed up with Benjamín's cellar. Fed up with the two of you."

"I want to go with you to see her," Elínborg said. "Do you think she's the handicapped girl Ed saw in the house when he arrested that man?"

"It's highly likely. She had two half-brothers, Símon and Tómas. That fits with the two boys he saw. And there was an American soldier by the name of Dave, who helped them in some way. I'll talk to Ed about him. I don't have his surname.

"I thought a soft approach was the right way to handle her, she'll tell us what we need to know. There's no point in rushing this matter."

He looked at Sigurdur Óli.

"Have you finished in Benjamín's cellar?"

"Yes, finished it yesterday. Didn't find a thing."

"Can you rule out that it's his fiancée buried up there?"

"Yes, I think so. She threw herself in the sea."

"Is there any way to confirm the rape?" Elínborg wondered.

"I think the confirmation's on the bottom of the sea," Sigurdur Óli said.

"How did they put it, a summer trip to Fljót?" Erlendur asked.

"A real countryside romance," Sigurdur Óli said with a smile.

"Arsehole!" Erlendur said.

Ed welcomed Erlendur and Elínborg at the front door and showed them into the sitting room. The table was covered with documents relating to the depot. There were faxes and photocopies on the floor and open diaries and books spread all over the room. Erlendur had the feeling he had conducted a major investigation. Ed flicked through a pile of papers on the table.

"Somewhere here I have a list of the Icelanders who worked at the depot," he said. "The embassy found it."

"We've located one of the tenants from the house you went to," Erlendur said. "I think she's the handicapped girl you were talking about."

"Good," Ed said, engrossed in his search. "Good. Here it is."

He gave Erlendur a handwritten list of the names of nine Icelanders who worked at the depot. Erlendur recognised the list. Jim had read it out to him over the phone and was going to send him a copy. Erlendur remembered he had forgotten to ask Mikkelína her stepfather's name.

"I found out who blew the whistle," Ed said. "Informed on the thieves. My old colleague from the military police in Reykjavík lives in Minneapolis now. We've stayed in touch off and on so I phoned him. He remembered the matter, phoned someone else and found the name of the informant."

"And who was it?" Erlendur asked.

"His name was Dave, David Welch, from Brooklyn. Private."

The same name Mikkelína mentioned, Erlendur thought.

"Is he alive?" he asked.

"We don't know. My friend's trying to trace him through the Pentagon. He might have been sent to the front."

Elínborg enlisted Sigurdur Óli's help in investigating the identity of the depot workers and the whereabouts of them and their descendants. Erlendur asked her to meet him again that afternoon before they went to see Mikkelína. First he was going to the hospital to see Eva Lind.

He walked down the corridor in intensive care and looked in at his daughter, who lay motionless as ever, her eyes closed. To his enormous relief, Halldóra was nowhere to be seen. He looked down the ward to where he had accidentally wandered when he'd had the bizarre conversation with the little woman about the boy in the blizzard. Inching his way down the corridor to the innermost room, he noticed that it was empty. The woman in the fur coat had gone and there was no-one in the bed where the man had been lying between this world and the next. The self-styled medium was gone too, and Erlendur wondered whether it ever actually happened, or whether it was a dream. He stood in the doorway for a second, then turned and went into his daughter's room, softly closing the door behind him. He wanted to lock it, but there was no lock. He sat down beside Eva Lind. Sat silently at her bedside, thinking about the boy in the blizzard.

A good while passed before Erlendur finally plucked up the courage, and heaved a deep sigh.

"He was eight years old," he said to Eva Lind. "Two years younger than I was."

He thought about how the medium had said that he accepted it, that it was no-one's fault. Such simple words out of the blue told him nothing. He had been battling against that blizzard all his life, and all the passage of time did was intensify it.

"I lost my grip," he said to Eva Lind.

He heard the scream in the storm.

"We couldn't see each other," he said. "We held hands so there was no distance between us, but still I couldn't see him for the blizzard. And then I lost my grip."

He paused.

"That's why you mustn't let go. That's why you have to survive this and come back and get healthy again. I know your life hasn't been easy, but you destroy it as if it were worthless. As if you were worthless. But that's not right. You're not right to think that. And you mustn't think that."

Erlendur looked at his daughter in the dull glow from the bedside lamp.

"He was eight. Did I say that? A boy, just like any other boy, fun to be with and always smiling, we were friends. You can't take that for granted. Normally there's some rivalry. Fighting, bragging and arguments. But not between us. Maybe because we were completely different. He impressed people. Unconsciously. Some people are like that. I'm not. There's something in those people that breaks down all the barriers, because they act completely the way they are, have nothing to hide, never shelter behind anything, are just themselves, straightforward. Kids like that ..."

Erlendur fell silent.

"You remind me of him sometimes," he continued. "I didn't see it until later. When you tracked me down after all those years. There's something about you that reminds me of him. Something you're destroying, and that's why I'm hurt by the way you treat your life and yet I don't seem able to do anything about it. I'm as helpless with you as when I stood in that blizzard and felt my grip slipping. We were holding hands and I lost my grip and I could feel it happening and sensed it was the end. We would both die. Our hands were frozen and we couldn't hold on. I couldn't feel his hand, apart from that split second when I lost hold of it."

Erlendur paused and looked down at the floor.

"I don't know whether that's the reason for all of this. I was ten and I've blamed myself ever since. I couldn't shake it off. Don't want to shake it off. The pain is like a fortress around a sorrow I don't want to release. Maybe I should have done that long ago, to come to terms with the life that was saved and give it a purpose. But that didn't happen and hardly will at this stage. We all have our burdens. Maybe I don't suffer more than anyone else who has lost a loved one, but I can't deal with it at all.

"Something switched off in me. I never found him again and I dream about him all the time and I know he's still there somewhere, roaming around in the blizzard, alone and abandoned and cold, until he drops down where he can't be found and never will be, and the storm rages against his back and he's buried by the snow in the twinkling of an eye, and no matter how I search and shout, I can't find him and he can't hear me, and he's lost to me for ever."

Erlendur looked at Eva Lind.

"It was like he'd gone straight to God. I was found. I was found

231

and I survived and I lost him. I couldn't tell them a thing. Couldn't say where I'd been when I lost him. Couldn't see out of my eyes for that bloody blizzard. I was ten years old and almost frozen to death and couldn't tell them a thing. They mounted a search party and people combed the moor carrying lamps from dawn to dark for days on end, shouting for him and prodding the snow with sticks, and they split up and took dogs and we could hear the shouts and the barking, but nothing happened. Never.

"He was never found.

"Then in the ward here I met a woman who said she had a message for me from the boy in the blizzard. And she said it wasn't my fault and I had nothing to fear. What does it mean? I don't believe in that sort of thing, but what am I supposed to think? All my life it's been my fault, although I'm well aware, and have been for a long time, that I was too young to shoulder any blame. But the guilt torments you like a cancer that eventually kills you.

"Because that was no ordinary boy I lost my grip on.

"Because the boy in the blizzard . . . was my brother."

*

Their mother slammed the door on the cold autumn wind and in the dim light of the kitchen she could see Grímur sitting opposite Símon at the table. She could not see Grímur's face clearly. This was the first time she had seen him since he had been led away, but as soon as she sensed his presence in the house and saw him again in the twilight, fear enveloped her. She had been expecting him all autumn, but she did not know exactly when he would be released. When she saw Tómas running up to her she realised at once what had happened.

Símon did not dare move, but, keeping his back rigid, he turned his head to look in the direction of the front door and saw his mother staring at them. She had let go of Tómas, who sneaked into the passage where Mikkelína was standing. She saw the terror in Símon's eyes.

Grímur sat on the kitchen chair and made no sign of moving. Several moments passed and the only sounds to be heard were the howling of the wind and their mother panting for breath after running up the hill. Her fear of Grímur, which had diminished since the spring, erupted again with full force and in an instant she was back to her old state. As if nothing had happened all the while he was away. Her legs went weak, the ache gnawed harder and harder at her stomach, her expression lost its new-found dignity, she hunched up, made herself as small as she could. Submissive. Obedient. Ready for the worst.

The children saw the change that came over her as she stood in the kitchen doorway.

"Símon and I were having a talk," Grímur said, thrusting his head back into the light to reveal his burn. Their mother flinched when she looked him in the face and saw the glaring red scar. She opened her mouth as if to speak or scream, but nothing came out and she stared at Grímur, dumbstruck.

"Don't you think it's pretty?" he said.

There was something strange about Grímur. Something that Símon couldn't quite pin down. More self-confident. More smug. He was a tyrant, that was obvious from his whole attitude towards his family and always had been, but there was something else, something dangerous, and Símon was wondering what it could be when Grímur stood up from the table.

He walked over to the children's mother.

"Símon told me about the soldier called Dave who brings fish here."

Their mother said nothing.

"It was a soldier called Dave who did this to me," he said, pointing to his scar. "I can't open my eye properly because he thought it was all right to throw coffee over me. First he heated it in a jug until it was so hot that he had to hold it with a cloth, and when I thought he was going to pour a cup for us, he emptied the jug over my face."

Their mother averted her glance from Grímur to the floor, but did not move.

"They let him in when my hands were handcuffed behind my back. I think they knew what he was going to do."

He walked menacingly towards Mikkelína and Tómas in the passageway. Símon sat at the table as if nailed to his seat. Grímur turned back to their mother and walked over to her.

"It was like they were rewarding him," he said. "Do you know why?"

"No," their mother said in a low voice.

"No," Grímur mimicked her. "Too busy fucking him."

He smiled.

"I wouldn't be surprised if he turns up floating in the lake. As if he'd fallen in the water fishing for trout."

Grímur stood right up close to their mother and roughly placed his hand on her stomach.

"Do you reckon he left something behind?" he asked in a quiet, threatening voice. "Something from the picnics down by the lake? Do you think so? Do you reckon he left something? I can tell you that if he's left anything, I'll kill it. Who knows, I might burn it, like he burned my face."

"Don't talk like that," their mother said.

Grímur looked at her.

"How did that bastard know we were pilfering?" he asked. "Who do you suppose told him what we were doing? Do you know anything about that? Maybe we weren't careful enough. Maybe he saw us. Or maybe he gave someone some trout and saw all the stuff in here, wondered where it came from and asked the little tart who lives here if she knew."

Grímur tightened his grip on her stomach.

"You can't look at a uniform without dropping your knickers."

Silently, Símon stood up behind his father.

"What do you say to a cup of coffee?" Grímur said to the children's mother. "What do you say to some piping hot, refreshing coffee for breakfast? If Dave lets us. Do you reckon he'll let us?"

Grímur laughed.

"Maybe he'll have a drop with us. Are you expecting him? Do you think he'll come and rescue you?"

"Don't," Símon said behind him.

Grímur released his grip on their mother and turned to Símon.

"Don't do that," Símon said.

"Símon!" his mother snapped. "Stop it!"

"Leave Mum alone," Símon said in a trembling voice.

Grímur turned back to their mother. Mikkelína and Tómas watched from the passage. He leaned over to her and whispered in her ear.

"Maybe you'll just go missing one day like Benjamín's girlfriend."

Their mother watched Grímur, ready for an attack that she knew could not be avoided.

"What do you know about that?" she asked.

"People disappear. All kinds of people. Posh people too. So scum like you can go missing. Who'd ask about you? Unless your mother from the Gasworks is looking for you. Do you think she might be?"

"Leave her alone," Símon said, still standing by the kitchen table.

"Símon?" Grímur said. "I thought we were friends. You and me and Tómas."

"Leave her alone," Símon said. "You have to stop hurting her. You have to stop it and go away. Go away and never come back."

Grímur had walked up to him and stared at him as if he were a total stranger.

"I've been away. I was away for six months and this is the welcome I get. The missus shagging soldiers and little Símon wants to throw his dad out. Are you big enough to handle your dad, Símon? Do you think so? Do you reckon you'll ever be big enough to fight me?"

"Símon!" his mother said. "It's all right. Take Tómas and Mikkelína down to Gufunes and wait for me there. Do you hear, Símon? Do as you're told."

Grímur grinned in Símon's face.

"And now the missus is running the whole show. What does she think she is? Funny how everyone's changed in this short time."

Grímur looked down the passage to the rooms.

"And what about the freak? Is the cripple going to answer back too? Da, da, da, da, that fucking cripple that I should have strangled years ago. Is this all the thanks I get? Is this my thanks?" he shouted down the passage.

Mikkelína scuttled away from the doorway to the dark passage. Tómas stayed there watching Grímur, who smiled at him.

"But me and Tómas are friends," Grímur said. "Tómas would never betray his dad. Come here, son. Come to Daddy."

Tómas went up to him.

"Mum phoned," he said.

"Tómas!" their mother shouted.

25

"I don't think Tómas intended to help him. It's more likely that he thought he was helping Mum. Perhaps he wanted to scare him to do her a favour. But I think it's most likely he didn't know what he was doing. He was so small, the dear child."

Mikkelína looked at Erlendur. He and Elínborg were in her sitting room and had listened to her account of the mother from the hill and Grímur, how they met and the first time he hit her, how the violence gradually intensified and twice she tried to flee from him, how he threatened to kill her children. She told them about life on the hill, the soldiers, the depot, the thefts and the soldier called Dave who went fishing in the lake, and about the summer their father was imprisoned and her mother and the soldier fell in love, how her brothers carried Mikkelína out into the sunshine, how Dave took them for picnics, and about the cold autumn morning when her stepfather returned.

Mikkelína took all the time she needed to tell her story, and tried not to omit any part of the family's history that she thought might be relevant. Erlendur and Elínborg sat and listened, drinking the coffee Mikkelína had made for them and eating the cake she had baked because, she said, she knew Erlendur would be coming. She greeted Elínborg sincerely and asked if there were many women detectives.

"Next to none," Elínborg smiled.

"Sinful," said Mikkelína, offering her a seat. "Women should be in the forefront everywhere."

Elínborg looked at Erlendur, who gave a half smile. She had picked him up from the office in the afternoon, aware that he had come from the hospital, and found him exceptionally glum. She asked about Eva Lind's condition, thinking it might have worsened, but he said it was stable, and when she asked how he was feeling and whether she could do anything for him, he just shook his head and told her there was nothing to do but wait. She had the impression that the waiting was proving a terrible strain on him, but did not risk broaching the subject. Long experience had taught her that Erlendur had no need to talk about himself to others.

Mikkelína lived on the ground floor in a small block of flats in Breidholt. Her home was small but cosy and while she was in the kitchen making coffee Erlendur walked around the sitting room looking at pictures of what he assumed to be her family. There were not many photographs and none seemed to be from the hill.

She began with a short account of herself while she was going about her business in the kitchen and they listened to her from the sitting room. She started school late, approaching 20 – at the same time as she had her first therapy for her handicap – and she made enormous progress. Erlendur felt she rather skated over her own story, but did not remark on it. In the course of time Mikkelína completed secondary school with extramural classes, enrolled at the university and graduated in psychology. By then she was in her forties. Now she was retired.

She had adopted the boy she called Símon before she went to university. Starting a family would have been difficult for reasons she did not need to go into, she said, with a sardonic smile.

She visited the hill regularly in spring and summer, to look at the

238

redcurrant bushes, and in the autumn she picked berries to make jam. She still had a jar with a little left in it from last autumn's batch and let them have a taste. Elínborg, a doyenne of cooking, praised her for it. Mikkelína told her to keep the rest and apologised for how little there was.

Then she told them how she had seen the city growing over the years and decades, first stretching out to Breidholt and then Grafarvogur, then at lightning speed along the road to Mosfellsbaer and finally up to Grafarholt, the hill where she had once lived and acquired some of her most painful memories.

"I really only have bad memories of that place," she said. "Apart from that short summer."

"Were you born with this disability?" Elínborg asked. She tried to phrase the question as politely as possible, but she decided there was no way of doing so.

"No," Mikkelína said. "I fell ill when I was three. Went to hospital. Mum told me that parents were forbidden to stay in the wards with their children. She couldn't understand such a heartless and repulsive rule: not being allowed to stay with a child that was seriously ill or even on the verge of death. It took her several years to realise I could regain what I had lost with therapy, but my stepfather never let her care for me, send me to the doctor or find out about cures. I have a memory from before I was ill, I don't know whether it's a dream or real – the sun is shining and I'm in the garden of a house, probably where my mother was a maid, and I'm running at full pelt, squealing, and Mum seems to be chasing me. I don't remember anything else. Just that I could run around as I pleased."

Mikkelína smiled.

"I often have that sort of dream. Where I'm healthy and can move as I want, not wagging my head all the time I talk, and I have control over my facial muscles, they don't pull my features all over the place."

Erlendur put down his cup.

"You told me yesterday you named your son after your half-brother, Símon."

"Símon was a wonderful boy. There was none of his father in him. At least I never saw it. He was like Mum. Kind, understanding and helpful. He had endless pity, that child. Hated his father, and his hatred did him harm. He should never have needed to hate anything. And like the rest of us he was smitten with fear throughout his childhood. Terrified when his father went on the rampage. He watched our mother being beaten to a pulp. I used to hide my head under the quilt, but I noticed that Símon sometimes stood watching the attacks, as if he was steeling himself to tackle it, later, when he was strong enough to stand up to his father. When he was big enough to sort him out.

"Sometimes he tried to intervene. Stood in front of our mother, defying him. Mum feared that more than the beatings. She couldn't bear the thought that anything would happen to her children.

"Such an amazingly kind boy, that Símon."

"You talk about him as though he's still a child," Elínborg said. "Did he die?"

Mikkelína smiled, but said nothing.

"And Tómas?" Erlendur said. "There were only three of you."

"Yes, Tómas," Mikkelína said. "He was different from Símon. Their father could tell that."

Mikkelína fell silent.

"Where did your mother phone?" Erlendur asked. "Before she went back to the hill?"

Without answering him either, Mikkelína stood up and went into her bedroom. Elínborg and Erlendur exchanged glances. A moment later Mikkelína came back holding a piece of paper. She unfolded the note, read it and handed it to Erlendur.

"Mum gave me this note," she said. "I clearly remember Dave sliding it across the table to her, but we were never allowed to know what it said. Mum didn't show me it until later. Years later."

Erlendur read the message.

"Dave got an Icelander or a soldier who spoke Icelandic to write the note for him. Mum always kept it, and, of course, I'll take it to the grave with me."

Erlendur looked at the note. Although written in clumsy capitals, the words were very clear.

I KNOW WHAT HE DOES TO YOU.

"Mum and Dave talked about her contacting him as soon as my stepfather got out of prison, and he would come to help her. I don't know the exact arrangements."

"Couldn't anyone at Gufunes help her?" Elínborg asked. "Plenty of people must have worked there."

Mikkelína looked at her.

"My mother had suffered abuse at his hands for a decade and a half. It was physical violence, he beat her, often so brutally that she was bedridden for days afterwards. And it was psychological too, which was maybe a worse form of violence because, as I told Erlendur yesterday, it reduced my mother to nothing. She started to despise herself as much as her husband despised her; she thought for a long time of suicide, but partly because of us, her children, she never went further than contemplating it. Dave made up for some of this in the six months he spent with her, and he was the only person she could have asked for help. She never mentioned to anyone what she'd been through in all those years and I think she was prepared to suffer the beatings again if need be. At worst he'd attack her and everything would be back to normal."

Mikkelína looked at Erlendur.

"Dave never came."

She looked at Elínborg.

"And nothing went back to normal."

*

"So she phoned, did she?"

Grímur put his arm around Tómas.

"Who did she phone, Tómas? We shouldn't keep secrets. Your mother might think she can keep secrets, but that's a big misunderstanding. Keeping secrets can be dangerous."

"Don't use the boy," their mother said.

"Now she's starting to order me around," Grímur said, rubbing Tómas' shoulders. "How things change. Whatever next?"

Símon positioned himself beside his mother. Mikkelína edged her way towards them. Tómas started crying. A dark stain spread out from the crotch of his trousers.

"And did anyone answer?" Grímur asked. The smile had left his face, the sarcastic tone gone, his expression serious. They could not take their eyes off his scar.

"No-one answered," the mother said.

"No Dave who's coming to save the day?"

"No Dave," the mother said.

"I wonder who grassed on me," Grímur said. "They sent a ship off this morning. Jam-packed with soldiers. Apparently there's a need for soldiers in Europe. They can't all have it cushy in Iceland where there's nothing else to do than shag our wives. Or maybe they've got him. It was a much bigger matter than even I imagined. Heads rolled. Much more important heads than mine. Officers' heads. They weren't very pleased with that."

He pushed Tómas away.

"They weren't very pleased with that at all."

Símon stood up close to his mother.

"There's just one thing in this whole business that I don't understand," Grímur said. By now he was right up against their mother and they could smell the acrid stench he gave off. "I just can't understand it. It's beyond me. I quite understand you dropping your knickers for the first bloke who looked at you when I was gone. You're just a whore. But what was he thinking?"

They almost touched.

"What did he see in you?"

He grabbed her head with both hands.

"You ugly fucking slut."

*

"We thought he was going to attack her and kill her this time. We were ready for it. I was quivering with fear and Símon was no better. I wondered whether I could get the knife from the kitchen. But nothing happened. They looked each other in the eye and instead of attacking her he backed away."

Mikkelína paused.

"I'd never been so afraid in my life. And Símon was never the same afterwards. He grew more and more distant from us after that. Poor Símon."

She looked down at the floor.

"Dave left our life as suddenly as he entered it," she said. "Mum never heard from him again."

"His surname was Welch," Erlendur said. "And we're investigating what happened to him. What was your stepfather's name?"

"His name was Thorgrímur," Mikkelína said. "He was always called Grímur."

"Thórgrímur," Erlendur repeated. He remembered the name from the list of Icelanders who worked at the depot.

His mobile phone rang in his coat pocket. It was Sigurdur Óli, who was at the excavation on the hill.

"You ought to come up here," Sigurdur Óli said.

"Here?" Erlendur said. "Where is 'here'?"

"On the hill, of course," Sigurdur Óli said. "They've reached the bones and I think we've found out who's buried there."

"Who is it?"

"Benjamín's fiancée."

"Why? What makes you think it's her?" Erlendur had stood up and gone into the kitchen for some privacy.

"Come up and see," Sigurdur Óli said. "It can't be anyone else. Just come and see for yourself."

Then he rang off.

26

Fifteen minutes later, Erlendur and Elínborg were in Grafarholt. They said a hurried farewell to Mikkelína, who watched in surprise as they walked out of the door. Erlendur did not tell her what Sigurdur Óli had said over the phone about Benjamín's fiancée, only that he had to go to the hill because the skeleton was finally being uncovered, and he asked her to save her story for now. Apologised. They would talk more later.

"Shouldn't I come with you?" Mikkelína asked from the hallway, where she stood watching them through the doorway. "I have ..."

"Not now," Erlendur interrupted her. "We'll have a better talk later. There's a new development."

Sigurdur Óli was waiting for them on the hill and took them to Skarphédinn, who was standing by the grave.

"Erlendur," the archaeologist greeted him. "We're getting there. It didn't take so long in the end."

"What have you found?" Erlendur asked.

"It's a female," Sigurdur Óli said self-importantly. "No question about it."

"How come?" Elínborg said. "Are you a doctor all of a sudden?"

"This doesn't call for a doctor," Sigurdur Óli said. "It's obvious."

"There are two skeletons in the grave," Skarphédinn said. "One of an adult, probably a woman, the other of a baby, a tiny baby, maybe even unborn. It's lying like that, in the skeleton."

Erlendur looked at him in astonishment.

"Two skeletons?"

He glanced at Sigurdur Óli, took two steps forward and peered down into the grave where he saw at once what Skarphédinn meant. The large skeleton was almost unearthed and it lay exposed in front of him with its hand up in the air, the jaw gaping, full of soil, and the ribs were broken. There was soil in the empty sockets of the eyes, tufts of hair lay across the forehead and the skin had not yet completely rotted from the face.

On top of it lay another tiny skeleton, curled up in the foetal position. The archaeologists had carefully brushed the dirt away from it. The arms and thighbones were the size of pencils and the cranium was the size of a tennis ball. It was lying below the ribcage of the large skeleton with its head pointing downwards.

"Could it be anyone else?" Sigurdur Óli asked. "Isn't that the fiancée? She was pregnant. What was her name again?"

"Sólveig," Elínborg said. "Was her pregnancy that far advanced?" she said as if to herself, staring down at the skeletons.

"Do they call it a baby or a foetus at this stage?" Erlendur asked.

"I don't have a clue," Sigurdur Óli said.

"Nor do I," Erlendur said. "We need an expert. Can we take the skeletons as they are to send to the morgue on Barónsstígur?" he asked Skarphédinn.

"What do you mean, as they are?"

"One on top of the other."

"We still have to unearth the large skeleton. If we clear a little more soil away from it, with little sweeps and brushes, then go under it, carefully, we ought to be able to lift the whole lot, yes. I think that should work. You don't want the pathologist to look at them here? In this position?"

"No, I want them indoors," Erlendur said. "We need to examine all this under optimum conditions."

By dinner time, the skeletons were removed intact from the ground. Erlendur, Sigurdur Óli and Elínborg watched the bones being lifted out. The archaeologists handled the task with great professionalism and Erlendur had no regrets about having called them in. Skarphédinn managed the operation with the same efficiency he had shown during the excavation. He told Erlendur that they had taken quite a liking to the skeleton, which they called the "Millennium Man" in Erlendur's honour, and that they would miss it. But their job was not finished. Having developed an interest in criminology in the process, Skarphédinn intended to go on combing the soil with his team for clues about the incident on the hill all those years ago. He had taken photographs and videos of every stage of the excavation, and said that it could make an interesting lecture for the university, especially if Erlendur ever found out how the bones had got there in the first place, he added, with a smile that exposed his fangs.

The skeletons were taken to the morgue on Barónsstígur. The pathologist was on holiday with his family in Spain and would not be back for at least a week, he had told Erlendur over the phone that same afternoon, basking in the sun at a barbecue, and tipsy to boot, the detective thought. Once the bones had been exhumed and loaded into a police van, the medical officer supervised the operation and made sure they were stored in the proper place in the morgue.

As Erlendur had insisted, instead of being separated the skeletons were transported together. To keep their relative positions as intact as possible the archaeologists had left a lot of dirt between them. So it was quite a heap lying on the table in front of Erlendur and the district medical officer when they stood together bathed in the bright fluorescent light of the autopsy room. The skeletons were wrapped in a large white blanket that the medical officer pulled back, and the two men stood contemplating the bones.

"What we probably need most is to date both skeletons," Erlendur said and looked at the medical officer.

"Yes, dating," the medical officer said thoughtfully. "You know that there's really precious little difference between a male and female skeleton except for the pelvis, which we can't see clearly enough for the little skeleton and the layer of dirt between them. All 206 bones seem to be in place on the big one. The ribs are broken, as we knew. It's fairly large, quite a tall woman. That's my first impression, but actually I'd prefer not to have anything to do with it. Are you in a hurry? Can't you wait for a week? I'm no specialist in autopsies or dating of bodies. I might miss all kinds of details that a qualified pathologist would notice, weigh up, intuit. If you want a proper job done, you should wait. Is there any rush? Can't it wait?" he repeated.

Erlendur noticed beads of sweat on the medical officer's forehead and recalled someone saying he always tried to avoid too much responsibility.

"Either way," Erlendur said. "There's no rush. I don't think so anyway. Unless the excavation throws up something that we don't know about, some tragedy."

"You mean someone who's kept an eye on the excavation knows what's been going on and sets off a chain of events?"

"We'll see," Erlendur said. "Let's wait for the pathologist. It's not a question of life or death. But see what you can do for us all the same. Take a look in your own good time. You might be able to remove the little skeleton without damaging any evidence."

The district medical officer nodded as if uncertain about his next move.

"I'll see what I can do," he said.

Erlendur decided to talk to Benjamín Knudsen's niece immediately instead of waiting until the next morning, and he went to see her with Sigurdur Óli that evening. Elsa answered the door and invited them into her sitting room. They all sat down. She looked more tired to Erlendur and he feared her reaction to the discovery of two skeletons; he imagined it must be a strain for her to have this old business dragged out again after so many years and find her uncle implicated in a murder.

He told her what the archaeologists had unearthed on the hill: it was probably Benjamín's fiancée. Elsa looked at each detective in turn while Erlendur was finishing his account, and she was unable to suppress her disbelief.

"I don't believe you," she cried. "Are you saying that Benjamín murdered his fiancée?"

"There's a probability . . ."

"And buried her on the hill by their chalet? I don't believe it. I just don't understand where you're taking all this. There must be some other explanation. There simply has to be. Benjamín was no murderer, I can tell you that. You've been free to roam around this house and rummage in the cellar as you please, but this is going too far. Do you think I would have let you go through the cellar if I, if the family, had anything to hide? No, this is going too far. You ought to leave," she said and stood up. "Now!"

"It's not as if you're involved," Sigurdur Óli said. He and Erlendur sat tight. "It's not as if you knew something and concealed it from us. Or . . . ?"

"What are you implying?" Elsa said. "That I knew something? Are you accusing me of complicity? Are you going to arrest me? Do you

249

want to put me in prison? What a way to conduct yourselves!" She stared at Erlendur.

"Calm down," Erlendur said. "We found a skeleton of a baby with the adult skeleton. It's been disclosed that Benjamín's fiancée was pregnant. The natural conclusion is that it's her. Don't you think so? We're not implying anything. We're just trying to solve the case. You've been exceptionally helpful and we appreciate that. Not everyone would have done all you have. However, the fact remains that your uncle Benjamín is the main suspect now that we've recovered the bones."

Elsa glared down at Erlendur as if he was an intruder in her house. Then she seemed to soften a little. She looked at Sigurdur Óli, back at Erlendur, and sat down again.

"It's a misunderstanding," she said. "And you'd realise that if you'd known Benjamín the way I did. He wouldn't have hurt a fly. Never."

"He found out his fiancée was pregnant," Sigurdur Óli said. "They were going to be married. He was obviously madly in love with her. His future revolved around his love, the family he was going to start, his business, his position in society. He cracked up. Maybe he went too far. Her body was never recovered. She was supposed to have thrown herself into the sea. She disappeared. Maybe we've found her."

"You told Sigurdur Óli that Benjamín didn't know who got his fiancée pregnant," Erlendur said guardedly. He wondered whether they may have jumped the gun and he cursed the pathologist in Spain. Perhaps they should have saved this visit for later. Waited for confirmation.

"That's right," Elsa said. "He didn't know."

"We've heard that Sólveig's mother went to see him later and told

250

him the story. When everything had blown over. After Sólveig went missing."

Elsa's expression changed to one of surprise.

"I didn't know that," she said. "When was that?"

"Later," Erlendur said. "I don't know exactly. Sólveig kept quiet about the father of the child. For some reason, she kept quiet. Didn't tell Benjamín what happened. Broke off their engagement and wouldn't say who the father was. Possibly to protect her family. Her own father's good name."

"What do you mean, her father's good name?"

"His nephew raped Sólveig when she was visiting his family in Fljót."

Elsa slumped into her seat and instinctively put her hand to her mouth in shock.

"I can't believe it," she sighed.

At the same time, at the other end of the city, Elínborg was telling Bára what had been found in the grave and that the most likely hypothesis was that it was the body of Sólveig, Benjamín's fiancée. That Benjamín had probably buried her there. Elínborg stressed that all the police had to go on was that he was the last person to see her alive and a child had been found with the skeleton on the hill. All further analysis of the bones was still pending.

Bára listened to Elínborg's account without blinking. As usual, she was alone in her huge house, surrounded by wealth, and showed no reaction.

"Our father wanted her to have an abortion," she said. "Our mother wanted to take her to the countryside, let her give the baby away and come back as if nothing had happened, then marry Benjamín. My parents talked it over for ages, then called Sólveig in to see them."

Bára stood up.

"Mother told me this later."

She went over to an imposing oak sideboard, opened a drawer and took out a small white handkerchief which she dabbed against her nose.

"They presented the two options to her. The third option was never discussed. Namely, having the baby and making it part of our family. Sólveig tried to persuade them, but they refused to hear a word of it. Didn't want to know about it. Wanted to kill the baby or give it away. No alternatives."

"And Sólveig?"

"I don't know," Bára said. "The poor girl, I don't know. She wanted the child, she wouldn't think of doing anything else. She was just a child herself. She was no more than a child."

Erlendur looked at Elsa.

"Could Benjamín have interpreted it as an act of betrayal?" he asked. "If Sólveig refused to name the father of the child?"

"No-one knows what passed between them at their last meeting," Elsa said. "Benjamín told my mother the main points, but it's impossible to know whether he mentioned every important detail. Was she really raped? My Lord!"

Elsa looked at Erlendur and Sigurdur Óli in turn.

"Benjamín may well have taken it as betrayal," she said in a low voice.

"Sorry, what did you say?" Erlendur asked her.

"Benjamín may well have thought she betrayed him," Elsa repeated. "But that doesn't mean he murdered her and buried her body on the hill."

"Because she kept quiet," Erlendur said.

"Yes, because she kept quiet," Elsa said. "Refused to name the father. He didn't know about the rape. I think that's quite certain."

"Could he have had an accomplice?" Erlendur asked. "Maybe got someone to do the job for him?"

"I don't follow."

"He rented his chalet in Grafarholt to a wife-beater and a thief. That tells us nothing in itself, but it's a fact all the same."

"I don't know what you're talking about. Wife-beater?"

"No, that's probably plenty for now. Maybe we're jumping to conclusions, Elsa. It's probably best to wait for the pathologist's report. Please excuse us if we ..."

"No, by no means, no, thank you for keeping me informed. I appreciate that."

"We'll let you know how the case proceeds," Sigurdur Óli said.

"And you have the lock of hair," Elsa said. "For identification."

Elínborg stood up. It had been a long day and she wanted to go home. She thanked Bára and apologised for disturbing her so late in the evening. Bára told her not to worry. She followed Elínborg to the door and closed it behind her. A moment later the bell rang and Bára opened it again.

"Was she tall?" Elínborg asked.

"Who?" Bára said.

"Your sister," Elínborg said. "Was she unusually tall, average height or short? What kind of build did she have?"

"No, she wasn't tall," Bára said with a hint of a smile. "Far from it. She was strikingly short. Exceptionally petite. A wisp of a thing, our mother used to say. And it was funny seeing her and Benjamín walking along holding hands, because he was so tall that he towered over her."

The district medical officer phoned Erlendur, who was sitting by his daughter's bedside at the hospital just before midnight.

"I'm at the morgue," the medical officer said, "and I've separated the skeletons. I hope I haven't damaged anything. I'm no pathologist. There's earth all over the tables and the floor, a filthy mess really."

"And?" Erlendur said.

"Yes, sorry, well, we have the skeleton of the foetus, which was at least seven months old."

"Yes," Erlendur said impatiently.

"And there's nothing odd about that. Except . . ."

"Go on."

"It could well have been already born when it died. Or maybe stillborn. That's impossible to tell. But it's not the mother lying underneath it."

"Hang on . . . What makes you say that?"

"It can't be the mother lying under the child or buried with it, however you want to put it."

"Not the mother? What do you mean? Who is it then?"

"There's no doubt," the medical officer said. "You can tell from the pelvis."

"The pelvis?"

"The adult skeleton is a male. It was a man who was buried under the baby."

27

The winter on the hill was long and tough.

The children's mother kept on working at the Gufunes dairy and the boys took the school bus every morning. Grímur went back to delivering coal. After the racket was discovered, the army did not want to give him his old job again. The depot was closed and the barracks were moved en bloc down to Hálogaland. Only the fencing and fence posts remained, and the concreted yard that had been in front of the barracks. The cannon was removed from the bunker. People said the war was nearing its end. The Germans were retreating in Russia and a major counter-offensive was said to be pending on the western front.

Grímur more or less ignored the children's mother that winter. Hardly uttered a word, except to hurl abuse at her. They no longer shared a bed. The mother slept in Símon's room, while Grímur wanted Tómas to stay in his. Everyone except Tómas noticed how her stomach slowly swelled during the winter until it protruded like a bitter-sweet memory of the events of the summer, and a terrifying reminder of what would happen if Grímur stuck to his threats.

She played down her condition as best she could. Grímur threatened her regularly. Said he would not let her keep the baby. He would kill it at birth. Said it would be a retard like Mikkelína and the best thing would be to kill it straight away. "Yank-fucker," he said. But he did not physically assault her that winter. He kept a low profile, sneaking silently around her like a beast preparing to pounce on its prey.

She tried talking about a divorce, but Grímur laughed at her. She did not discuss her condition with the people at the dairy and concealed the fact that she was pregnant. Perhaps, right to the end, she thought that Grímur would recant, that his threats were empty, that when it came to the crunch he would not carry out his threats, that he would be like a father to the child in spite of everything.

In the end she resorted to desperate measures. Not to take vengeance on Grímur, although she had ample reason, but to protect herself and the child she was about to bear.

Mikkelína strongly sensed a growing tension between her mother and Grímur during that tough winter and also noticed a change in Símon that she found no less disturbing. He had always been fond of his mother, but now he hardly left her side from the time he came home from school and she finished work. He was more nervous after Grímur came back from prison on that cold autumn morning. As far as he could, he avoided his father and his anxiety about his mother haunted him more with each day that went by. Mikkelína heard him talking to himself sometimes and occasionally it sounded as if he was talking to someone she could not see who could not possibly be in their house: an imaginary person. Sometimes she heard him say out loud what he had to do to protect their mother and the child she would bear by his friend Dave. How it fell to him to guard her against Grímur. How the baby's life depended on him. No-one else was at hand. His friend Dave would never return.

Símon took Grímur's threats very seriously. He firmly believed that he would not allow the baby to live. That Grímur would take it and they would never see it. Carry it off up the mountain and come back without it.

Tómas was silent as ever, but Mikkelína sensed a change in him as the winter wore on. Grímur allowed Tómas to spend the night in his room after he forbade the children's mother to sleep in the double bed and forced her to sleep in Tómas' bed, which was too small for her and uncomfortable. Mikkelína did not know what Grímur said to Tómas, but soon Tómas adopted a very different attitude towards her. He would not have anything to do with her and distanced himself from Símon as well, despite how close they had always been. Their mother tried to talk to Tómas, but he always backed away from her, angry, silent and helpless.

"Símon's turning a bit funny," Mikkelína heard Grímur say to Tómas once. "He's going funny like your mother. Keep a watch out for him. Make sure you don't get like him. Because then you'll turn funny too."

Once Mikkelína heard her mother talking to Grímur about the baby, the only time he allowed her to speak her mind, as far as she knew. Her mother's stomach was bulging by then and he prohibited her to work at the dairy any longer.

"You give up your job and say you have to look after your family," Mikkelína heard him order her.

"But you can say it's yours," her mother said.

Grímur laughed at her.

"You can."

"Shut up."

Mikkelína noticed that Símon was eavesdropping as well.

"You could easily say it's your child," their mother said in a soothing voice.

"Don't try that," Grímur said.

"No-one needs to know anything. No-one need find out."

"It's too late to try to put things right now. You should have thought of that when you were out on the moor with that fucking Yank."

"Or I could have it adopted," she said cautiously. "I'm not the first one this has happened to."

"Sure you're not," Grímur said. "Half the bloody city's been screwing them. But don't think that makes you any better for it."

"You'll never need to see it. I'll give it away as soon as it's born and you won't ever need to see it."

"Everyone knows my wife shags Yanks," Grímur says. "They all know you've been playing the field."

"No-one knows," she said. "No-one. There was no-one who knew about me and Dave."

"How do you think I knew about it, you twat? Because you told me? Don't you think that kind of story gets around?"

"Yes, but no-one knows he's the father. No-one knows."

"Shut up," Grímur said. "Shut up or . . ."

They all waited to see what that long winter would bring and what was in some terrible way inevitable.

It began when Grímur slowly began to fall ill.

*

Mikkelína stared at Erlendur.

"She started to poison him that winter."

"Poison?" Erlendur said.

"She didn't know what she was doing."

"How did she poison him?"

"Do you remember the Dúkskot case in Reykjavík?"

"When a young woman killed her brother with rat poison? Yes, it was some time around the beginning of the last century."

"Mum didn't intend to kill him with it. She only wanted to make him ill. So she could have the baby and get it out of his way before he found out the baby was gone. The woman from Dúkskot fed her brother rat poison. Put big doses in his curds, he even saw her do it but didn't know what it was, and he managed to tell someone because he didn't die until several days later. She gave him schnapps with his curds to take the taste away. At the inquest they found phosphorus in his body, which has a slow toxic effect. Our mother knew that story, it was a famous Reykjavík murder. She got hold of rat poison at the Gufunes dairy. Stole small doses which she put in his food. She used very little at a time so that he wouldn't taste it or suspect anything. Instead of keeping the poison at home she brought back what she needed each time, but when she gave up her job at the dairy she took a large dose home and hid it. She had no idea what effect it would have on him or whether such small doses would even work at all, but after a while the effects seemed to come on. He got weaker, was often ill or tired, vomited. Couldn't make it to work. Lay in bed suffering."

"Did he never suspect anything?" Erlendur asked.

"Not until it was too late," Mikkelína said. "He had no faith in doctors. And of course she didn't encourage him to go for a check-up."

"What about when he said they would take care of Dave? Did he ever mention that again?"

"No, never," Mikkelína said. "He was just bluffing really. Saying things to scare her. He knew that she loved Dave."

Erlendur and Elínborg were in Mikkelína's sitting room, listening to her story. They had told her that it was a male skeleton underneath the baby in the grave in Grafarholt. Mikkelína shook her head; she could have told them that before had they not hurried away without saying why.

She wanted to know about the baby skeleton and when Erlendur asked whether she wanted to see it, she said no.

"But I'd like to know when you don't need it any more," she said. "It's about time she was laid to rest in hallowed ground."

"She?" Elínborg said.

"Yes. She," Mikkelína said.

Sigurdur Óli told Elsa what the medical officer had discovered: the body in the grave could not be her uncle Benjamín's fiancée. Elínborg phoned Sólveig's sister, Bára, to tell her the same news.

While Erlendur was setting off with Elínborg to see Mikkelína, Ed called on his mobile to let him know that he still had not managed to find out what became of Dave Welch; he did not know whether he was posted away from Iceland, or even when that might have been. He said he would go on searching.

Earlier that morning Erlendur had gone to intensive care to visit his daughter. Her condition was unchanged and Erlendur sat beside her for a good while, and resumed his tale about his brother who had frozen to death on the moors above Eskifjördur when Erlendur was ten. They were rounding up sheep with their father when the storm broke. The brothers lost sight of their father and soon afterwards of each other. Their father made it back to the farm, exhausted. Search parties were mounted.

"They found me by sheer chance," Erlendur said. "I don't know why. I had the presence of mind to dig a shelter for myself in a snowdrift. I was more dead than alive when they poked at the snow and the stick happened to touch my shoulder. We moved away. Couldn't live there any more, knowing about him up on the moor. Tried to start a new life, in Reykjavík . . . In vain."

At that moment a doctor looked in. He and Erlendur greeted each other and briefly discussed Eva Lind's condition. Unchanged, the doctor said. No hint of a recovery or that she was regaining consciousness. They fell silent. Said goodbye. The doctor turned at the door.

"Don't expect any miracles," he said, and noticed a cold smile on Erlendur's face.

Now Erlendur was sitting opposite Mikkelína, thinking about his daughter in her hospital bed and his brother lying in the snow. Mikkelína's words trickled into his mind.

"My mother wasn't a murderer," she said.

Erlendur looked at her.

"She wasn't a murderer," Mikkelína repeated. "She thought she could save the baby. She feared for her child."

She darted a glance at Elínborg.

"After all, he didn't die," she said. "He didn't die from the poison."

"But you said he didn't suspect anything until it was too late," Elínborg said.

"Yes," Mikkelína said. "It was too late by then."

*

The night that it happened, Grímur seemed more subdued after lying in bed all day racked with pain.

Their mother felt pains in her stomach and towards evening she had gone into labour with very rapid contractions. She knew it was too soon. The baby would be premature. She had the boys bring the mattresses from the beds in their room and from Mikkelína's divan in the kitchen, spread them out on the kitchen floor, and around dinner time she lay down on them.

She told Símon and Mikkelína to have clean sheets and hot water ready to wash the baby. After having three children, she knew the procedures.

It was still winter and dark, but the weather had unexpectedly turned warmer and it had rained during the day; spring would soon arrive. Their mother had been outdoors that day clearing the beds around the redcurrant bushes and pruning dead branches. She said the berries would be good when she made jam that autumn. Símon did not let her out of his sight and went to the bushes with her. She tried to calm him down by saying that everything would be all right.

"Nothing will be all right," Símon said, and repeated it: "Nothing will be all right. You mustn't have that baby. You mustn't. That's what he says, and he'll kill it. He says so. When's the baby due?"

"Don't you worry," his mother said. "When the baby's born I'll take it to town and he'll never see it. He's ill and helpless. He lies in bed all day and can't do anything."

"But when's the baby due?"

"It could be at any time," his mother said soothingly. "Maybe sometime soon, then it's over and done with. Don't be afraid, Símon. You must be strong. For my sake, Símon."

"Why don't you go to hospital? Why don't you leave here to have the baby?"

"He won't let me," she said. "He'd fetch me and order me to give birth at home. He doesn't want anyone to find out. We'll say we found it. Entrust it to the care of good people. That's the way he wants it. Everything will be all right."

"But he says he'll kill it."

"He won't do that."

"I'm so scared," Símon said. "Why does it have to be like this? I don't know what to do. I don't know what to do," he repeated, and she could tell he was plagued by anxiety.

Now he stood looking down at his mother, who was lying on the mattresses in the kitchen. Apart from the double bedroom, that was the only place in the house large enough, and she began to strain in absolute silence. Tómas was in Grímur's room. Símon had crept to the door and closed it.

Mikkelína lay by the side of her mother, who tried to make no noise at all. The door to the double bedroom opened, Tómas came out into the passage and went to the kitchen. Grímur was sitting on the edge of the bed, moaning. He had sent Tómas to the kitchen to fetch a bowl of porridge which he had not touched. Told him to help himself to it as well.

When Tómas walked past his mother, Símon and Mikkelína, he noticed that the baby's head had appeared. Their mother pushed with all her might until the shoulders emerged as well.

Tómas took the bowl of porridge and a spoon, and suddenly his mother saw out of the corner of her eye that he was about to take a mouthful.

"Tómas! For God's sake don't touch that porridge!" she shouted in desperation.

A deathly silence descended upon the house and the children stared at their mother, who was sitting with the newborn baby in her arms and staring at Tómas, and he was so surprised that he dropped the bowl to the floor where it smashed to pieces.

The bed creaked.

Grímur came out into the passage and into the kitchen. He looked down at their mother and the newborn baby in her arms, a look of disgust on his face. He looked over to Tómas, then at the porridge on the floor.

"Can it be?" Grímur said in a low, astonished voice, as if he had suddenly found the answer to a riddle that had long been puzzling him. He looked back down at the children's mother.

"Are you poisoning me?" he shouted.

The mother looked up at Grímur. Mikkelína and Símon did not

dare look up. Tómas stood motionless over the porridge that had splashed across the floor.

"Didn't I fucking suspect as much! All that lethargy. That pain. Sickness . . ."

Grímur looked around the kitchen. Then he jumped at the cupboards and jerked open the drawers. He went berserk. He swept the contents of the cupboards onto the floor. Picked up an old bag of cornmeal and hurled it at the wall. When it burst, he heard a glass jar drop out of it.

"Is this it?" he shouted, picking up the jar. "How long have you been doing this?" he hissed.

The children's mother stared into his eyes. A candle was burning on the floor beside her. While he was searching for the poison she had hurriedly picked up a large pair of scissors that she had kept by her side to heat in the flame, then cut the umbilical cord and knotted it with shaking hands.

"Answer me!" Grímur screamed.

She did not need to answer. He could tell from her eyes. Her expression. Her obstinacy. How she had always, deep down inside, defied him, unflinching, no matter how often he thrashed her, he saw it in her silent dissent, the challenge glaring back at him with the soldier's bloodstained bastard in her arms.

Saw it in the baby she hugged to her breast.

"Leave Mum alone," Símon said in a low voice.

"Give it to me!" Grímur screamed. "Give me the baby, you fucking serpent!"

"Leave Mum alone," Símon said, more loudly.

"Give it here!" Grímur screamed, "or I'll kill you both. I'll kill you all! Kill you! All!"

He foamed at the mouth with rage.

"You fucking whore! Are you trying to kill me? Do you reckon you can kill me?"

"Stop it!" Símon shouted.

The children's mother clutched the baby tight with one arm, and groped for the scissors with the other, but she could not find them. She glanced away from Grímur and looked around for them in a frenzy, but they were gone.

*

Erlendur looked at Mikkelína.

"Who took the scissors?" he asked.

Mikkelína was standing by the window now. Erlendur and Elínborg exchanged glances. They were both thinking the same thing.

"Are you the only one left to tell what happened?" Erlendur asked.

"Yes," Mikkelína said. "There's no-one else."

"Who took the scissors?" Elínborg asked.

28

"Do you want to meet Símon?" Mikkelína asked. Her eyes were moist with tears.

"Símon?" Erlendur said, not knowing what she meant. Then he remembered. The man who had collected her from the hill. "You mean your son?"

"No, not my son, my brother," Mikkelína said. "My brother Símon."

"Is he alive?"

"Yes, he's alive."

"Then we have to talk to him," Erlendur said.

"You won't get much out of him," Mikkelína smiled. "But let's go and see him anyway. He enjoys visits."

"Aren't you going to finish your story?" Elínborg asked. "What kind of a beast was that man? I don't believe it. Someone behaving that way."

Erlendur looked towards her.

"I'll tell you on the way," Mikkelína said. "Let's go and see Símon."

*

"Símon!" their mother shouted.

266

"Leave Mum alone," Símon screamed in a quavering voice, and before they knew it he had plunged the scissors into Grímur's chest.

Símon pulled back his hand and saw that the scissors had gone in up to the handle. He looked in disbelief at his son, as if he did not fully realise what had happened. He looked down at the scissors, but seemed incapable of moving. He looked again at Símon.

"Are you killing me?" Grímur groaned and fell to his knees. Blood pumped out from the scissor-wound onto the floor, and slowly he slumped backwards and slammed against the wall.

Their mother clutched the baby in silent terror. Mikkelína lay motionless by her side. Tómas was still standing where he had dropped the porridge. Símon began shivering, standing beside his mother. Grímur did not move.

Everything went silent.

Until their mother let out a piercing, anguished howl.

*

Mikkelína paused.

"I don't know whether the baby was stillborn or whether Mum squeezed it so hard that it suffocated in her arms. It was quite premature. She was expecting the baby in the spring, but it was still late winter when it was born. We never heard it make a sound. Mum didn't clear its throat and she held it with its face buried in her clothes, for fear of him. For fear that he would take it from her."

At Mikkelína's instruction, Erlendur pulled over near a plain-looking detached house.

"Would he have died that spring?" Erlendur asked. "Her husband? Was she counting on that?"

"I don't think so," Mikkelína said. "She'd been poisoning him for three months. It wasn't enough."

Erlendur stopped in the drive and switched off the engine.

"Have you heard of hebephrenia?" she asked, opening the car door.

*

Their mother stared at the dead baby in her arms, rocked it frantically back and forth and sobbed and cried out.

Seemingly impervious to her, Símon stared at his father's body as if he could not believe what he saw. A puddle of blood was beginning to form under him. Símon was shaking like a leaf.

Mikkelína tried to console her mother, but it was impossible. Tómas walked past them into the bedroom and closed the door without saying a word. Without any change of expression.

A good while passed.

Eventually Mikkelína managed to calm her mother. When she came to her senses and stopped crying, she took a good look around. She saw Grímur lying in his own blood, saw Símon trembling beside her, saw the look of anguish on Mikkelína's face. Then she started to wash her baby in the hot water that Símon had brought her, cleaning it meticulously with slow, careful movements. She seemed to know what to do without thinking about the details. She put the baby down, stood up and hugged Símon, who was rooted to the spot, and he stopped trembling and broke instead into heavy sobs. She led him to a chair and made him sit down, facing away from the body. Then went over to Grímur, pulled the scissors out of the wound and threw them in the sink.

Then she sat down on a chair, exhausted after the birth.

She talked to Símon about what they needed to do and she gave instructions to Mikkelína too. They rolled Grímur onto a blanket and pulled his body to the front door. She went outside with Símon and they walked a good way from the house, where he started to dig a hole. The rain, which had stopped during the day, began again —

cold, heavy winter rain. The ground was only partially frozen. Símon loosened the soil with a pickaxe, and after he had dug for two hours, they fetched the body and lugged it to the grave. They dragged the blanket over the hole, the body fell in and they tugged the blanket back up from under it. The corpse lodged in the grave with the left hand sticking up in the air, but neither Símon nor his mother could bring themselves to move it.

Their mother plodded back to the house and fetched the baby, carried it out into the cold rain and laid it down with Grímur's body.

She was about to make the sign of the cross over the grave, but stopped.

"He doesn't exist," she said.

Then she started shovelling earth over the bodies. Símon stood by the grave watching the wet, dark soil slam down onto the corpses and saw how they gradually disappeared beneath it. Mikkelína had begun to tidy up in the kitchen. Tómas was nowhere to be seen.

A thick layer of mud was in the grave when Símon suddenly had the impression that Grímur twitched. With a shudder he looked at his mother, who had not noticed anything, then he stared down into the grave and to his horror he saw the face, half-covered with dirt, move.

The eyes opened.

Símon froze.

Grímur stared up at him from the grave.

Símon let out a mighty scream and his mother stopped shovelling. She looked at Símon, then down into the grave, and saw that Grímur was still alive. She stood on the edge of the grave. As the rain beat down on them it cleared the mud from Grímur's face. For a moment they looked each other in the eye, then Grímur's lips moved.

"Please!"

His eyes closed again.

She looked at Símon. Down into the grave. Back at Símon. Then took the shovel and went on filling the hole as if nothing had happened. Grímur disappeared from sight, buried beneath the soil.

"Mum," Símon wailed.

"Go to the house, Símon," she said. "It's over. Go to the house and help Mikkelína. Please, Símon. Go to the house."

Símon looked at his mother, who was bent over, holding the shovel, drenched by the cold rain, as she finished filling the hole. Then he walked away without saying another word.

*

"Tómas possibly thought that it was all his fault," Mikkelína said. "He never mentioned it and refused to talk to us. Went completely into his shell. When Mum shouted and he dropped the bowl on the floor, it set off a sequence of events that changed our lives and led to his father's death."

They were in a tidy sitting room waiting for Símon. He had gone out for a stroll around the neighbourhood, they were told, but would be back any minute.

"Really nice people here," Mikkelína said. "No-one could treat him better."

"Did nobody ever miss Grímur, or . . . ?" Elínborg said.

"Mum cleaned the house from top to bottom and four days later she reported that her husband had set off on foot over Hellisheidi moor for Selfoss, but that she had not heard from him since. No-one knew she had been pregnant, or at least she was never asked about it. Search parties were sent out onto the moor, but of course his body was never found."

"What business was he supposed to have in Selfoss?"

"Mum never needed to go into that," Mikkelína said. "She was never asked for an explanation of his travels. He was an ex-convict. A thief. What did they care about what he was doing in Selfoss? He didn't matter to them. Not in the least. There was plenty else to think about. The day that Mum reported him missing, some American soldiers shot an Icelander dead."

Mikkelína half-smiled.

"Several days went by. They turned into weeks. He never showed up. Written off. Lost. Just your ordinary Icelandic missing person." She sighed.

"It was Símon that Mum wept for the most."

*

When it was all over, the house seemed eerily silent.

Their mother sat at the kitchen table, still soaking from the downpour, staring into space with her dirty hands on the table and paying no attention to her children. Mikkelína sat beside her, stroking her hands. Tómas was still in the bedroom and did not come out. Símon stood in the kitchen and looked out at the rain, tears running down his cheeks. He looked at his mother and Mikkelína and back out of the window where the outlines of the redcurrant bushes could be seen. Then he went out.

He was wet, cold and shivering from the rain when he walked over to the bushes, stopped by them and stroked the bare branches. He looked up into the sky, his face towards the rain. The sky was black and rolls of thunder rumbled in the distance.

"I know," Símon said. "There was nothing else to be done." He paused and bowed his head, the rain pounding down on him. "It's been so hard. It's been so hard and so bad for so long. I don't know why he was like that. I don't know why I had to kill him."

"Who are you talking to, Símon?" his mother asked. She had followed him outside, and she put her arm around him.

"I'm a murderer," Símon said. "I killed him."

"Not in my eyes, Símon. You can never be a murderer in my eyes. Any more than I am. Maybe it was a fate he brought upon himself. The worst thing that can happen is if you suffer because of what he was like, now that he's dead."

"I killed him, Mum."

"Because there was nothing else you could do. You must understand that, Símon."

"But I feel so terrible."

"I know, Símon. I know."

"I don't feel well. I never have, Mum."

She looked at the bushes.

"There'll be berries on the bushes in the autumn and everything will be okay then. You hear that, Símon. Everything will be okay then."

29

They looked over to the front door of the home when it opened and a man came in, aged about 70, stooping, with thin white hair and a friendly, smiling face, wearing a smart thick pullover and grey trousers. One of the helpers with him was told that the resident had visitors. Símon was pointed in the direction of the sitting room.

Erlendur and Elínborg stood up. Mikkelína walked over to the man and hugged him, and he smiled at her, his face beaming like a child's.

"Mikkelína," the man said in an astonishingly youthful voice.

"Hello, Símon," she said. "I've brought some people with me who wanted to meet you. This is Elínborg and this man's name is Erlendur."

"My name's Símon," the man said, shaking them by the hand. "Mikkelína's my sister."

Erlendur and Elínborg nodded.

"Símon is very happy," Mikkelína said. "Even if the rest of us never have been, Símon is happy and that's all that matters."

Símon sat down with them, took hold of Mikkelína's hand, smiled at her and stroked her face, and he smiled at Erlendur and Elínborg too.

"Who are these people?" he asked.

"They're my friends," Mikkelína said.

"Do you feel good here?" Erlendur asked.

"What's your name?" Símon asked.

"My name's Erlendur."

Símon smiled.

"I'm Mikkelína's brother."

Mikkelína stroked his arm.

"They're detectives, Símon."

Símon looked at Erlendur and Elínborg in turn.

"They know what happened," Mikkelína said.

"Mum's dead," Símon said.

"Yes, Mum's dead," Mikkelína said.

"You do the talking," Símon said imploringly. "You talk to them." He looked at his sister and avoided Erlendur and Elínborg.

"All right, Símon," Mikkelína said. "I'll come and see you afterwards."

Símon smiled and stood up, went into the hallway and shuffled away down a passage.

"Hebephrenia," Mikkelína said.

"Hebephrenia?" Erlendur said.

"We didn't know what it was," Mikkelína said. "Somehow he just stopped growing up. He was the same good, kind boy, but his emotions didn't mature with his body. Hebephrenia is a variant of schizophrenia. Símon's like Peter Pan. Sometimes it's connected with puberty. Perhaps he was already ill. He had always been sensitive and when those terrible incidents took place he seemed to lose his grip. He'd always lived in fear and felt the burden of responsibility. He thought it was up to him to protect our mother, simply because there was no-one else who could. He was the biggest and strongest of us, even if he turned out to be the smallest and weakest."

"And he's been in institutions since his youth?" Elínborg asked.

"No, he lived with my mother and me until she died. She died, what, 26 years ago. People like Símon are very manageable patients, usually gentle and easy to be with, but they need a lot of steady care and Mum provided him with that for as long as she lived. He worked for the council when he could. As a dustman or picking up litter with a stick. Walked the length and breadth of Reykjavík counting the pieces of rubbish that he put in his bag."

They sat in silence for a while.

"David Welch never got in contact again?" Elínborg asked eventually.

Mikkelína looked at her.

"Mum waited for him until her dying day," she said. "He never came back."

She paused for a while.

"She phoned him from the dairy that morning when my stepfather came back," she said eventually. "And she talked to him."

"But," Erlendur said, "why didn't he go over to the hill?"

Mikkelína smiled.

"They had said goodbye to each other," she said. "He was going to the continent. His ship was sailing that morning and she didn't phone him to tell him about the danger, but to say goodbye to him and tell him everything was all right. He said he'd come back. Probably he was killed in action. She never heard any news of him, but when he didn't come back after the war..."

"But why..."

"She thought Grímur would kill him. That's why she went back to the hill by herself. Didn't want him to help her. It was her business to sort out."

"He must have known that your stepfather was due for release, and word got around about Dave and your mother," Erlendur said. "Your stepfather knew about it, he'd heard something."

"They had no way of telling how he knew. It was a very secret romance. We don't know how my stepfather found out."

"And the child ...?"

"They didn't know she was pregnant."

Erlendur and Elínborg remained silent for some time while they pondered Mikkelína's words.

"And Tómas?" Erlendur asked. "What happened to him?"

"Tómas is dead now. He only lived to be 52. Divorced twice. Had three children, boys. I don't have any contact with them."

"Why not?" Erlendur asked.

"He was like his father."

"How?"

"He had a miserable life."

"Excuse me?"

"It made him like his father."

"You mean ...?" Elínborg gave Mikkelína a searching look.

"Violent. Beat his wife. Beat his children. Drank."

"His relationship with your stepfather? Was it ...?"

"We don't know," Mikkelína said. "I don't think so. I hope not. I try not to think about it."

"What did your stepfather mean by what he said from the grave? 'Please!' Was he asking her to help him? Was he asking for mercy?"

"We discussed that a lot, Mum and I, and she had an explanation that satisfied her and satisfied me."

"What was that?"

"Grímur knew who he was."

"I don't follow," Erlendur said.

"Grímur knew who he was, and I think he knew, deep down inside, the reason he was like that, although he never mentioned it. We know he'd had a tough childhood. He was a little boy once and

276

he must have had some link with that boy, some part of his soul that called out to him. Even when he was at his worst and his rage knew no bounds, that little boy shouted at him to stop."

"Your mother was an incredibly brave woman," Elínborg said.

"May I talk to him?" Erlendur asked after a short silence.

"You mean Símon?" Mikkelína said.

"Is it okay? If I go in and see him? Alone?"

"He's never talked about those incidents. Not in all this time. Mum thought it was best to act as if none of it had ever happened. After she died I tried to get Símon to open himself up, but I could tell at once that it was hopeless. It's as if he only has memories from afterwards. Like everything else has vanished. But he will say the occasional sentence if I press him. Otherwise he's totally closed. He belongs to a different, more peaceful world that he's created for himself."

"Do you mind?" Erlendur said.

"It's fine as far as I'm concerned," Mikkelína said.

Erlendur stood up, went into the hallway and down the corridor. Most of the doors to the rooms were open. He saw Símon sitting on the edge of his bed, looking out of the window. Erlendur knocked on the door and Símon looked round.

"May I join you?" Erlendur said, waiting for permission to enter.

Símon looked at him, nodded, turned back to the window and went on looking out.

Although there was a chair at the desk, Erlendur sat down on the bed beside Símon. Some photographs were on the desk. Erlendur recognised Mikkelína and thought that an elderly woman in one of them could have been their mother. He reached out and picked it up. The woman was sitting at a table in the kitchen, in a thin nylon dressing gown with a coloured pattern on it, which many women of her age wore at that time, and she smiled a tight, enigmatic smile at the camera. Símon was sitting beside her, laughing. Erlendur thought it might have been taken in Mikkelína's kitchen.

"Is that your mother?" he asked Símon.

Símon looked at the photograph.

"Yes. That's Mum. She's dead."

"I know."

Símon looked out of the window again and Erlendur put the photograph back on the desk. They sat in silence for a while.

"What are you looking at?" Erlendur asked.

"Mum told me everything was all right," Símon said, still looking out of the window.

"It is all right," Erlendur said.

"Are you going to take me away?"

"No, I'm not going to take you anywhere. I just wanted to meet you."

"Perhaps we could be friends."

"Definitely," Erlendur said.

They sat in silence and now both of them looked out of the window.

"Did you have a good father?" Símon suddenly asked.

"Yes," Erlendur said. "He was a good man."

They fell silent.

"Will you tell me about him?" Símon said eventually.

"Yes, some time I will tell you about him," Erlendur said. "He . . ."
Erlendur paused.

"What?"

"He lost his son."

They stared out of the window.

"There's just one thing I want to know," Erlendur said.

"What's that?" Símon said.

"What was her name?"

"Who?"

"Your mother."

"Why do you want to know?"

"Mikkelína has told me about her, but never what her name was."

"Her name was Margrét."

"Margrét."

At that moment Mikkelína appeared in the doorway and when Simon saw her he stood up and went to her.

"Did you bring me any berries?" he asked. "Did you bring any redcurrants?"

"I'll bring some berries in the autumn," Mikkelína said. "This autumn. I'll bring you some berries then."

30

At that very moment a small tear began to form in one of Eva Lind's eyes as she lay motinless in the gloom of intensive care. It grew into a large drop that ran slowly out of the corner of her eye, down her face, under her oxygen mask and across her lips.

A few minutes later she opened her eyes.

Read on for an excerpt from
the next Inspector Erlendur thriller

VOICES

Now Available

1

Elínborg was waiting for them at the hotel.

A large Christmas tree stood in the lobby and there were decorations, fir branches and glittering baubles all around. "Silent night, holy night," over an invisible sound system. A large shuttle coach stood in front of the hotel and a group approached the reception desk. Tourists who were planning to spend Christmas and the New Year in Iceland because it seemed to them like an adventurous and exciting country. Although they had only just landed, many had apparently already bought traditional Icelandic sweaters, and they checked into the exotic land of winter. Erlendur brushed the sleet off his raincoat. Sigurdur Óli looked around the lobby and caught sight of Elínborg by the lifts. He tugged at Erlendur and they walked over to her. She had examined the scene. The first police officers to arrive there had made sure that it would remain untouched.

The hotel manager had asked them not to cause a fracas. Used that phrase when he rang. This was a hotel and hotels thrive on their reputations, and he asked them to take that into account. So there were no sirens outside, nor uniformed policemen bursting in through the lobby. The manager said that at all costs they should avoid arousing fear among the guests.

Iceland mustn't be too exciting, too much of an adventure.

Now he was standing next to Elínborg and greeted Erlendur and

Sigurdur Óli with a handshake. He was so fat that his suit hardly encompassed his body. His jacket was done up across the stomach by one button that was on the verge of giving up. The top of his trousers was hidden beneath a huge paunch that bulged out of his jacket and the man sweated so furiously that he could never put away the large white handkerchief with which he mopped his forehead and the back of his neck at regular intervals. The white collar of his shirt was soaked in perspiration. Erlendur shook his clammy hand.

"Thank you," the hotel manager said, puffing like a grampus. In his twenty years of managing the hotel he had never encountered anything like this.

"In the middle of the Christmas rush," he groaned. "I can't understand how this could happen! How could it happen?" he repeated, leaving them in no doubt as to how totally perplexed he was.

"Is he up or down?" Erlendur asked.

"Up or down?" the fat manager puffed. "Do you mean whether he's gone to heaven?"

"Yes," Erlendur said. "That's exactly what we need to know . . ."

"Shall we take the lift upstairs?" Sigurdur Óli asked.

"No," the manager said, casting an irritated look at Erlendur. "He's down here in the basement. He's got a little room there. We didn't want to chuck him out. And then you get this for your troubles."

"Why would you have wanted to chuck him out?" Erlendur asked.

The hotel manager looked at him but did not reply.

They walked slowly down the stairs beside the lift. The manager went first. Going down the stairs was a strain for him and Erlendur wondered how he would get back up.

Apart from Erlendur, they had agreed to show a certain amount of consideration, to try to approach the hotel as discreetly as possible. Three police cars were parked at the back, with an ambulance. Police officers and paramedics had gone in through the back door. The district medical officer was on his way. He would certify the death and call out a van to transport the body.

They walked down a long corridor with the panting manager leading the way. Plainclothes policemen greeted them. The corridor grew darker the further they walked, because the light bulbs on the ceiling had blown and no one had bothered to change them. Eventually, in the darkness, they reached the door, which opened onto a little room. It was more like a storage space than a dwelling, but there was a narrow bed inside, a small desk and a tattered mat on the dirty tiled floor. There was a little window up near the ceiling.

The man was sitting on the bed, leaning against the wall. He was wearing a bright red Santa suit and still had the Santa cap on his head, but it had slipped down over his eyes. A large artificial Santa beard hid his face. He had undone the thick belt around his waist and unbuttoned his jacket. Beneath it he was wearing only a white vest. There was a fatal wound to his heart. Although there were other wounds on the body, the stabbing through the heart had finished him off. His hands had slash marks on them, as if he had tried to fight off the assailant. His trousers were down round his ankles. A condom hung from his penis.

"Rudolph the red-nosed reindeer," Sigurdur Óli warbled, looking down at the body.

Elínborg hushed him.

In the room was a small wardrobe and the door was open. It contained folded trousers and sweaters, ironed shirts, underwear and socks. A uniform hung on a coat hanger, navy blue with golden epaulettes and shiny brass buttons. A pair of smartly polished black leather shoes stood beside the cupboard.

Newspapers and magazines were strewn over the floor. Beside the bed was a small table and lamp. On the table was a single book: *A History of the Vienna Boys' Choir*.

"Did he live here, this man?" Erlendur asked as he surveyed the scene. He and Elínborg had entered the room. Sigurdur Óli and the hotel manager were standing outside. It was too small for them all inside.

"We let him stay here," the manager said awkwardly, mopping the sweat from his brow. "He's been working for us for donkey's years. Since before my time. As a doorman."

"Was the door open when he was found?" Sigurdur Óli asked, trying to be formal, as if to compensate for his little ditty.

"I asked her to wait for you," the manager said. "The girl who found him. She's in the staff coffee room. Gave her quite a shock, poor thing, as you can imagine." The manager avoided looking into the room.

Erlendur walked up to the body and peered at the wound to the heart. He had no idea what kind of blade had killed the man. He looked up. Above the bed was an old, faded poster for a Shirley Temple film, sellotaped at the corners. Erlendur didn't know the film. It was called *The Little Princess*. The poster was the only decoration in the room.

"Who's that?" Sigurdur Óli asked from the doorway as he looked at the poster.

"It says on it," Erlendur said. "Shirley Temple."

"Who's that then? Is she dead?"

"Who's Shirley Temple?" Elínborg was astonished at Sigurdur Óli's ignorance. "Don't you know who she was? Didn't you study in America?"

"Was she a Hollywood star?" Sigurdur Óli asked, still looking at the poster.

"She was a child star," Erlendur said curtly. "So she's dead in a sense anyway."

"Eh?" Sigurdur Óli said, failing to grasp the remark.

"A child star," Elínborg said. "I think she's still alive. I don't remember. I think she's something with the United Nations."

It dawned on Erlendur that there were no other personal effects in the room. He looked around but could see no bookshelf, CDs or computer, no radio or television. Only a desk, chair, wardrobe and bed with a scruffy pillow and dirty duvet cover. The little room reminded him of a prison cell.

He went out into the corridor and peered into the darkness at the far end, and could make out a faint smell of burning, as if someone had been playing with matches there or possibly lighting their way.

"What's down there?" he asked the manager.

"Nothing," he replied and looked up at the ceiling. "Just the end of the corridor. A couple of bulbs have gone. I'll have that fixed."

"How long had he lived here, this man?" Erlendur asked as he went back into the room.

"I don't know, since before my time."

"So he was here when you became the manager?"

"Yes."

"Are you telling me he lived in this hole for twenty years?"

"Yes."

Elínborg looked at the condom.

"At least he practised safe sex," she said.

"Not safe enough," Sigurdur Óli said.

At that point the district medical officer arrived, accompanied by a member of the hotel staff who then went back along the corridor. The medical officer was very fat too, although nowhere near a match for the hotel manager. When he squeezed into the room, Elínborg darted back out for air.

"Hello, Erlendur," the medical officer said.

"What does it look like?" Erlendur asked.

"Heart attack, but I need a better look," replied the medical officer, who was known for his appalling sense of humour.

Erlendur looked out at Sigurdur Óli and Elínborg, who were grinning from ear to ear.

"Do you know when it happened?" Erlendur asked.

"Can't be very long ago. Some time during the last two hours. He's hardly begun to go cold. Have you located his reindeer?"

Erlendur groaned.

The medical officer lifted his hand from the body.

"I'll sign the certificate," he said. "You send it to the mortuary and they'll open him up there. They say that orgasm is a kind of moment of death," he added, looking down at the body. "So he had a double."

"A double?" Erlendur didn't understand him.

"Orgasm, I mean," the medical officer said. "You'll take photographs, won't you?"

"Yes," Erlendur said.

"They'll look nice in his family album."

"He doesn't appear to have any family," Erlendur said and looked around the room again. "So you're done for the time being?" he asked, eager to put an end to the wisecracks.

The district medical officer nodded, squeezed back out of the room and went down the corridor.

"Won't we have to close down the hotel?" Elínborg asked, and noticed the manager gasp at her question. "Stop all traffic in and out. Question everyone staying here and all the staff? Close the airports. Stop ships leaving port . . ."

"For God's sake," the manager groaned, squeezing his handkerchief with an imploring look at Erlendur. "It's only the doorman!"

Mary and Joseph would never have been given a room here, Erlendur thought to himself.

"This . . . this . . . filth has nothing to do with my guests," the manager spluttered with indignation. "They're tourists, almost all of them, and regional people, businessmen and the like. No one who has anything to do with the doorman. No one. This is one of the largest hotels in Reykjavík. It's packed over the holidays. You can't just close it down! You just can't!"

290

"We could, but we won't," Erlendur said, trying to calm the manager down. "We'll need to question some of the guests and most of the staff, I expect."

"Thank God," the manager sighed, regaining his composure.

"What was the man's name?"

"Gudlaugur," the manager said. "I think he's around fifty. And you're right about his family, I don't think he has any."

"Who visited him?"

"I haven't got a clue," the manager puffed.

"Has anything unusual happened at the hotel involving this man?"

"No."

"Theft?"

"No. Nothing's happened."

"Complaints?"

"No."

"He hasn't become embroiled in anything that could explain this?"

"Not as far as I know."

"Was he involved in any conflicts with anyone at this hotel?"

"Not that I know of."

"Outside the hotel?"

"Not that I know of but I don't know him very well. Didn't," the manager corrected himself.

"Not after twenty years?"

"No, not really. He wasn't very sociable, I don't think. Kept himself to himself as much as he could."

"Do you think a hotel is the right place for a man like him?"

"Me? I don't know . . . He was always very polite and there were never really any complaints about him."

"Never really?"

"No, there were never any complaints about him. He wasn't a bad worker really."

"Where's the staff coffee room?" Erlendur asked.

"I'll show you." The hotel manager mopped his brow, relieved that they would not close the hotel.

"Did he have guests?" Erlendur asked.

"What?" the manager said.

"Guests," Erlendur repeated. "It looks like someone who knew him was here, don't you think?"

The manager looked at the body and his eyes dwelled on the condom.

"I don't know anything about his girlfriends," he said. "Nothing at all."

"You don't know very much about this man," Erlendur said.

"He's a doorman here," the manager said, and felt that Erlendur should accept that by way of explanation.

They left the room. The forensics team went in with their equipment and more officers followed them. It was difficult for them all to squeeze their way past the manager. Erlendur asked them to examine the corridor carefully and the dark alcove further down. Sigurdur Óli and Elínborg stood inside the little room observing the body.

"I wouldn't like to be found like that," Sigurdur Óli said.

"It's no concern of his any more," Elínborg said.

"No, probably not," Sigurdur Óli said.

"Is there anything in it?" Elínborg asked as she took out a little bag of salted peanuts. She was always nibbling at things. Sigurdur Óli thought it was because of nerves.

"In it?" Sigurdur Óli said.

She nodded in the direction of the body. After staring at her for a moment, Sigurdur Óli realised what she meant. He hesitated, then knelt down by the body and stared at the condom.

"No," he said. "It's empty."

"So she killed him before his orgasm," Elínborg said. "The doctor thought—

"She?" Sigurdur Óli said.

"Yes, isn't that obvious?" Elínborg said, emptying a handful of peanuts into her mouth. She offered some to Sigurdur Óli, who declined. "Isn't there something tarty about it? He's had a woman in here," she said. "Hasn't he?"

"That's the simplest theory," Sigurdur Óli said, standing up.

"You don't think so?" Elínborg said.

"I don't know. I don't have the faintest idea."

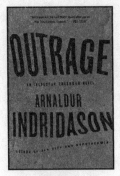
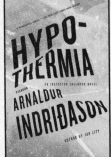
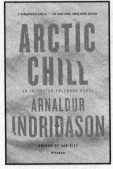
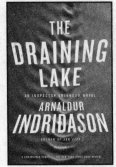
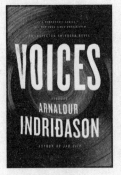
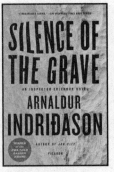
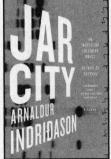
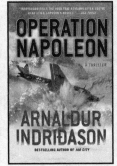